THE PILGRIM'S REVENGE

THE PILGRIM'S REVENGE

Julian Mitchell

Matador
9 Priory Business Park,
Wistow Road, Kibworth Beauchamp,
Leicestershire. LE8 0RX
Tel: 0116 279 2299
Email: books@troubador.co.uk
Web: www.troubador.co.uk/matador
Twitter: @matadorbooks

ISBN 978 1800465 718

British Library Cataloguing in Publication Data.
A catalogue record for this book is available from the British Library.

Printed and bound in Great Britain by 4edge Limited
Typeset in 11pt Century Gothic by Troubador Publishing Ltd, Leicester, UK

Matador is an imprint of Troubador Publishing Ltd

My thanks to all the people who
read my first two novels.

PART ONE

ONE

Desperate people do desperate things; the desperation of these people was palpable. Why else would each pay €10,000 to be transported in the back of a virtually airless lorry to an isolated cove on the French coast in the late evening, with no food, no belongings, no sanitation and precious little water? Nevertheless, halfway through the next stage of their transportation, most would have willingly swapped it for the relative comfort of the lorry.

On a cold Monday evening in the first week of October 2020 the rigid inflatable boat rose out of the angry sea before dropping back into the trough that was sandwiched between the enormous crests of the huge waves. Although it was called 'rigid', the polyurethane sides of the boat twisted, momentarily being distorted by the power of the sea. The craft would surely have sunk from the wash of the towering wall of water, but the fare-paying passengers were crammed so closely together that only a small amount came into the boat. This was somewhat reassuring for them, but only increased their physical discomfort and mental anguish.

They were not refugees as they had not been forced to flee their country due to armed conflict or persecution. These people were economic migrants as they were seeking to make improvements to their lives and relieve the poverty of their families back home. Sadly, they were destined to be treated as cheap slave labour at a factory in Birmingham. As soon as they set foot in England they would be classed as illegal immigrants.

On their journey to the coast, ventilation in the lorry was provided by a vent, no bigger than an A4-size sheet of paper, with a grille partially blocked by cobwebs and road debris. When it was moving, air was forced through the grimy slats of the vent; when stationary, the container quickly developed a putrid atmosphere as the carbon dioxide breathed out by seventeen people overwhelmed the oxygen in the increasingly lifeless air. They were not to know that over a fairly short period, concentration levels above 10% of the noxious gas could cause nausea and vomiting; in extreme circumstances, coma and death. Even if they had known, however, they would still have made the journey.

The two menacing traffickers in the lorry, both carrying pistols, knew that life could be sustained in that harsh environment, but only just. Concealment was paramount to them and they were not about to be compromised by stopping for a welfare check. They had made this perilous transfer many times before with their lucrative human cargo and so far such deprivation had only taken the life of one migrant: an asthmatic man.

The people who had been herded into the lorry were thrown from side to side as the driver took the bends at reckless speeds without a scrap of thought for those in the back. The track from the main road led to a car park on the promontory of Anse Saint-Martin from where, on a clear day, the Channel Islands could be seen to the west. This was not a clear day; in fact it was a dark, black night. The car park, which during the day was well used, was now deserted save for a battered Nissan 4x4 with an empty boat trailer attached. Two other traffickers had arrived ahead of the lorry and manhandled the RIB to the water's edge.

The lorry suddenly came to a shuddering halt, throwing most of the migrants forward and piling them in a heap at the front. They were uncomplaining – not that it would have done them any good – sensing the final leg of their journey to a better life was about to begin. The huge doors were swung open, the blackness of the container matching the blackness of the night.

'*Allez! Allez! Vite! Vite!*' shouted the lead trafficker as he pulled himself up into the back of the lorry – covering his face with his handkerchief to overcome the smell of stale air and sweating bodies – and immediately began urging the people to get out. He was well aware that the transfer was the time when he and his three partners in crime were at their most vulnerable to detection. The sharpness and urgency in his voice overcame any need for translation. The weary travellers crawled out, each tumbling to the wet tarmac, partly from exhaustion and partly due to the darkness masking the depth of the drop. The slowest was helped along by the sole of a boot thrust from behind by the cold-hearted trafficker.

Most were dressed in clothes more suited to the warmer climes of their native country. Initially, the fresh sea breeze was a blessed relief before the cold night air turned sweating to shivering. The brightly coloured orange lifejackets they were ordered to put on were of little help in combatting the chill, but optimism sustained them; all their discomfort would be worth it in the end.

The beam from a torch app on the mobile held by one of the armed men guided the dishevelled group across the car park and onto the shingle that marked the edge of the beach. In the torchlight they could just see the outline of a rigid inflatable boat. This RIB was designed to hold a dozen people; tonight it would have to hold seventeen for the potentially dangerous three-hour voyage to a better life.

One by one they climbed in. The third migrant stumbled on a folded tarpaulin discarded in the bottom of the vessel. This had not been put there in any act of consideration by the traffickers, it had simply been left in the boat when it was bought from a disreputable seller, having previously been stolen from close to the ferry terminal in Cherbourg. The enterprising migrant opened it up with some difficulty as it was bulky. He passed a corner of the heavy-duty waterproof cloth, which had a length of thick rope attached to each corner, to the person sitting in the front of the boat. Others could just make out the canvas as the men now sitting halfway along the RIB grabbed another corner. It now formed a welcome improvised tent over most of the people.

They were wedged so tightly together that movement below their waists was virtually impossible; this close proximity would prove to be a lifesaver for most, but not all. The last but one to board had no room left to sit down inside the vessel and could only place his feet in the bottom of the boat; he sat precariously balanced on the edge. The last available space was next to the outboard motor and was reserved for the migrant who had agreed to steer the boat to its destination on the South Devon coast. His fare had been reduced by €1,000, for which he was grateful, but he would have done it without an incentive: after all, the other migrants' freedom was his freedom too.

As the newly appointed "captain", he had been instructed on how to use the satellite navigation aid before he boarded the lorry in Cherbourg. The traffickers used a satphone as they knew conventional navigation provided by a standard mobile phone, and linked to a network, would not have worked on a sea crossing. They were aware the same satphones were used by explorers on expeditions into remote areas where a terrestrial cellular service is unavailable. The callous men would have been content to launch the RIB without any navigational aid on board. However, this additional expense was deemed justifiable in view of the vast sums of money they earned from these trips. Nevertheless, they were indifferent to the plight of the migrants. Their role finished when all were loaded ready for the crossing and the RIB had been pushed out to sea.

The destination of this voyage was not any random spot on the south coast of England; instead the destination was very specific and the handheld device gave a tolerance rating of plus or minus fifty metres. As well as receiving instructions on the use of the satellite phone, the "captain" had also been shown the rudiments of operating the outboard motor; paramount among them was using the tiller to steer.

As he slid into his cramped position at the back of the boat, with barely enough space to operate the tiller, the phone was thrust into his hand by one of the traffickers while the other started the motor. This was no state-of-the-art outboard with push-button start. This was a two-stroke engine that needed coaxing to life. After three pulls of the starter cord, it burst into life. The boat had sufficient depth of water under it to float.

Four traffickers, two either side at the stern of the RIB and up to their knees in the chill water, heaved it forward. There was no 'bon voyage' salutation. The engine spluttered with greater urgency. The boat had barely chugged into deeper water before the traffickers were already heading back to Cherbourg.

The "captain", who was already shivering and whose hands were turning blue with cold, pulled the sleeve of his acrylic jumper over his freezing tiller hand, but it gave him little respite. In his other, he held the mobile whose destination was set for Slapton

Sands on the South Devon coast. The wind became stronger away from the protection of the shore and the calmness of the water gave way to a rougher sea. The frightened passengers huddled together, bowed their heads and prayed.

The sea swell gradually increased as the small craft entered the English Channel. Their journey was made all the more treacherous due to their fear that they might encounter passing ships. At its narrowest point between the coasts of France and England – where the Strait of Dover separates it from the North Sea – the Channel is recognised as one of the busiest shipping routes in the world. The leviathan tankers, some over 200 metres in length, dwarf other vessels. The sea code of 'power gives way to sail' is all well and good in theory, but the manoeuvrability of a giant tanker is limited, to say the least, and that is always assuming any small craft is shown up on the ship's radar. Undaunted, they motored remorselessly on. Most of those on board had no understanding of the distance they had to travel. Some were already occasionally lifting their heads, staring into the distance, hoping to see twinkling lights that would have signalled the coast of England outlined on the black horizon. Far from ending, however, their treacherous journey was only just beginning.

All of a sudden on the port side a gigantic ship loomed out of the gloom. The inexperienced refugee at the helm jerked the outboard's tiller sharply to starboard to avoid a collision that would surely have killed all on board. The quick change of course succeeded in avoiding what would have been a catastrophic impact, but the man who had been forced to sit on the edge of the RIB was not so lucky.

The unexpected change of direction flung him into the sea and he was eagerly devoured by the black, restless water. He resurfaced unseen by the other passengers as all they heard was an anguished cry for help in his native tongue before silence. His only hope of survival was rescue as he could only survive for a matter of minutes before hypothermia claimed his life. The RIB circled back, but even though the man had been wearing a bright orange fluorescent life jacket, there was still no sign of him in the vast sea. The 'captain' peered in vain for the unfortunate man before regaining his course, knowing any further attempt at a rescue was futile and risked the lives of all on board as the boat was buffeted around when it turned side-on against the waves. The tanker that had caused the near miss ploughed on, oblivious to the drama left in its wake.

The wind and sea spray were relentless. An extra-powerful gust forced its way under the tarpaulin, tentatively anchored by a migrant at each corner. The man at the front, who was tightly gripping the rope attached to his corner, was partly lifted from his sitting position as the canvas billowed in the squall. Despite being wedged in, the power of the wind was not to be denied. Two things prevented him being unceremoniously ripped out of the RIB: letting go of the rope and the person next to him grabbing him around the waist. The tarpaulin was whipped away as if it were a tissue, tearing it from the hands of the other anchors. Everyone in the boat was now exposed to the ferocity of the elements.

Over halfway across, the sea swell increased inexorably and some began to suffer from seasickness from which, for most, there would be no reprieve until they were back on land. Those migrants in the back of the boat whose heads were raised above the others were in danger of either having their faces lacerated by the wind and sea spray or becoming momentarily covered in vomit – surprising though that was considering the paltry amount of food they had eaten – before the spray lashed it from their face.

The determined "captain" on the tiller kept wiping his eyes so he could see the screen of the device he was clutching. He was constantly looking both ways, ever mindful that more massive tankers could be lurking in the darkness. He had lost the feeling in both of his hands, but despite his personal anguish his determination was undiminished. The rhythmic monotony of wave after wave seemed to dull his senses somewhat as he almost subconsciously made adjustments to the course of the RIB.

He knew they were getting close to their destination, but did not inform the other passengers as he still had to negotiate the landing. As it was, they might not have been able to hear over the noise from the outboard motor and the fierce wind that would have whisked his words away as soon as they had left his mouth. If the passengers had looked, they would have seen lights twinkling sporadically in the distance. He had been told to head for the part of the shore showing two bright red LED lights about two metres apart.

In the meantime, the traffickers, on the English side of the Channel, had arrived in the car park at Slapton Sands, ten minutes before the RIB was due to come ashore. They knew that a large commercial vehicle parked near the beach would arouse suspicion, so were keen to limit the time of their stay. The white 7.5 tonne vehicle was an Iveco Box Body large van and it was easy to understand how it got its name: it was a metal box welded to a chassis.

They had no appreciation of the historical significance of their location where, in April 1944, Slapton Sands was used as a rehearsal for the planned D-Day invasion of Normandy. The RIB was heading for that South Devon stretch of beach where many American and British soldiers lost their lives, due partly to so-called 'friendly fire' and partly to lurking German E-boats offshore. A granite monument had been presented by the United States Army and erected adjacent to the car park where they were now parked. Seventy-seven years later, it was sacrilegious that the same stretch of coast was being used for illegal purposes. This symbolic obelisk to freedom was now the destination for the migrants, who would soon become modern-day slaves. The irony was lost on the traffickers.

The van was facing away from the sea allowing its rear fog lights to send a piercing red glow seaward. Its front sidelights were temporarily and discreetly covered with black masking tape so as not to alert any late-night passing motorist.

The tiller man "captain" soon picked out the two bright red lights and headed in their direction, the sea calming a little as the boat approached the beach, the high tide allowing it to get close into the shore. Two traffickers waded knee-deep into the water and pulled the RIB up and onto the shingle. They offered no help to the exhausted passengers onto the small stones; they were left to climb out and crawl or stumble towards the large van indicated by the two men with a flicked arm gesture. The small boat and the lifejackets were abandoned on the beach. The people – now officially illegal immigrants – were unceremoniously ushered into the back of the van, which contained a dozen shrink-wrapped small water bottles to sustain them on their journey north, which they would have to share. As soon as the last dishevelled immigrant was loaded, the rear doors were slammed shut.

The traffickers cursed as the headlights of a car could be seen in the far distance heading for Torcross along the coast road. It would pass by where they were parked in a matter of minutes. The driver panicked and overlooked switching off the van's lights to avoid detection, although the front sidelights were still blacked out. He crouched down in his cab in the mistaken belief that if he could not see the car, the car driver could not see him.

As it approached, the car slowed and cruised by before resuming its previous speed and continuing along the road and out of sight. Both traffickers were partly reassured that they had not been conspicuous in the dark, although they could have done without the unwelcome intrusion.

It had required two men to load the immigrants, but only one to drive the van north to a rendezvous in Birmingham. As planned, the driver and lead trafficker, Blink Davis – so called as he suffered from a tic that manifested itself by excessive movement of his eyelids – would drop off his mate in a car park at Taunton Deane services on the M5 from where he had collected him earlier. He had drugs business to attend to in the city as part of a County Lines gang. However, the rendezvous was not scheduled until later and the drop-off would have to wait. Davis did not want to chance being randomly stopped by the police as one of the few vehicles on the road at that time of night. He had already planned to stop off until first light in an isolated lorry park in Newton Abbot before joining the main road out of Devon that led to the M5.

Before they left, the masking tape was removed from the sidelights. They were not about to waste time recovering the lifejackets and RIB; the money they were being paid for the transportation of their human cargo more than covered their cost. They smugly exited the car park and thought that they had left no incriminating evidence behind to help the authorities track their nocturnal escapade. They were wrong.

TWO

The deadly virus that had arrived unannounced over a year earlier still lingered menacingly. The wearing of face masks was still required in certain environments and long-practised social distancing was now a subliminal act for most people, save for those who were in denial or just bloody-minded.

Lockdown in the spring of 2020 had led to a massive drop in crime rates giving the police a welcome break from apprehending the wrongdoers. Predictably, as restrictions were eased, they were active again.

Detective Inspector Richard King and his team of detectives had never been idle during this respite as there were always cold cases to pursue. The team of four – including the inspector – had successfully worked together on several cases over the previous two years. As often happened after a period of relative calm in policing terms, several investigations were about to require their attention at the same time.

The inspector was in the twilight of a very successful career as a detective. He had reached his career grade in his mid-forties, but he was content to stay at that rank despite successive bosses urging him to apply for promotion. Sitting behind a desk all day was not for Richard King. Administrative work and attending policy meetings were anathema to him. Many criminals have since rued the day he decided to remain a hands-on copper.

He was always smartly dressed at work, preferring a jacket and tie to a suit, with a demeanour to match his clothes: unruffled. He was average height and build, with a full head of hair, and was always clean-shaven. Not for him the modern stubble many younger men had adopted, which to King was less a fashion statement and more a could-not-be-bothered-to-shave statement. His social and interpersonal skills were well honed; nevertheless, he was happiest in his own company, reading his newspaper over a pint of beer in his local pub, his rugged good looks occasionally attracting the attention of younger women. However, since the death of his wife, he had lived alone and liked it that way. He was flattered by the attention, but was not yet ready for another emotional attachment.

He had one particular personal liking: he was partial to sherbet lemons. When wrestling with difficult cases, he would often suck one of the fizzy sweets as they seemed to help his thought processes. Many a time the turning point in cases could be traced back to a contemplative sweet-sucking moment as King, uninterrupted by his detective colleagues – who knew when to let their boss have thinking time – decided on a course of action that would eventually prove to be the defining moment in any investigation.

His sergeant, Lucy Harris, had worked with the inspector for over two years. She spent part of her off-duty time mountain bike riding and running across the wilds of Dartmoor. She had become fascinated by the moor ever since her involvement in an investigation over a missing woman. Her short-cropped blond hair, slender body and evident lively personality were an attractive combination, but she seldom dated as exercise and work dominated her life.

As often happened in a boss/subordinate relationship, a certain mutual fondness can develop; occasionally that affection goes deeper. Undoubtedly, their association fell into this category. Both were unattached; King's wife had died fairly recently from a brain tumour and Harris's career ambition and drive had frightened off many would-be suitors. As her feelings for him had strengthened, she had considered asking for a transfer, such was her frustration at working with her boss so closely on a daily basis, without any possibility of a personal, and potentially romantic, relationship developing. They had enjoyed an occasional meal together, with those occasions ending with no more than a hug, which she felt was more in mutual appreciation than growing affection.

For King's part, the memory of his wife prevented him acting on his instinct; the scars left by his loss were gradually healing and he was slowly beginning to feel ready to move on. Lucy Harris had come to terms with her feelings and was now patiently waiting for his grieving to pass. King was just the right side of fifty and Harris just the wrong side of thirty.

The detective constables in the team relished working with their inspector. Without doubt, he was a mentor to both Sam Dyson and Alexander Hammond. DC Dyson was growing in confidence thanks to her latent ability and eagerness to learn, sometimes from her own mistakes. Her diminutive stature belied a fierce determination and tenacity when investigating crimes.

King was an astute manager who got the best from his staff by giving encouragement, utilising their knowledge and developing their skills. He tactfully identified where Dyson could improve, couching his advice in constructive terms. For all her strengths, she was very self-critical, occasionally becoming demoralised when she did not meet the high standards she had set herself. As she gained experience and her confidence grew, these bouts of self-doubt diminished.

Alex Hammond's grandfather had come to England from Jamaica on the Empire Windrush ship in the late 1940s to help rebuild post-war Britain. His father had joined the Metropolitan Police and Alex had decided to follow in his footsteps. However, he preferred policing in the provinces to London and had joined Exeter Police as a detective after attending the university in that city. He was a mild-mannered individual, but when needed could use his well above average height and muscular body effectively when villains declined to go quietly!

Often the target of racial abuse from drunks when out on late-night investigations, he had learned to control his anger, instead feeling pity bordering on contempt for those individuals who displayed such ignorance for attacking the colour of his skin.

Hammond and Dyson often went for a drink after work if their finishing times coincided. They were the 'Little and Large' of the force. He was nearly 200 centimetres tall and she was a diminutive 160, when wearing shoes. Although they were both unattached, theirs was a purely platonic relationship... for now.

In overall charge of King and one other inspector was Detective Chief Inspector Steve Burrows. He had been appointed after the death in service of the previous officer in overall charge, Superintendent Roberts. He was not a tough act to follow as he had been rather arrogant and brusque. DCI Burrows was far more to Inspector King's liking as he took a genuine interest in investigations without interfering. A mutual respect had soon been established between the two detectives. He trusted King and had no qualms about allocating complicated investigations to him.

The other inspector was Jim Best. He did not quite possess King's flair for crime solving – not many did – but Best was dependable and always willing to help others when work pressures increased.

*

On this particular morning, all of King's team were in Plymouth Central Police Station working independently on various administrative tasks, some of which

involved the preparation of reports on recent arrests for consideration by the Crown Prosecution Service.

Police jurisdictions – areas they were responsible for – sometimes became blurred around the edges if one force was overburdened. King's DCI had asked him to deal with an apparent illegal immigrant investigation as a favour to a DCI in a neighbouring district whose detectives were extremely busy.

The inspector welcomed the task given to him as his team were not exactly inundated with recent crimes to investigate. The police had received a report of a rigid inflatable boat and life jackets found abandoned on Slapton Sands indicating that illegal immigrants had entered the country. Immigration Enforcement, as part of the Home Office, had been informed. Its role was mainly visiting residential and business premises in search of people who had entered the UK illegally. As the abandoned RIB suggested unlawful entry, police involvement was required. The location was outside their usual jurisdiction, but crime was crime.

A murder investigation was usually the only time that warranted the whole team attending a potential scene of a crime, but Inspector King decided they could do with some sea air as they had been cooped up in the station for too long. Soon they were heading for Torcross to the site of the abandoned RIB. They travelled in pairs in separate cars, King and Harris in one and the DCs in the other.

All wore face coverings when in a car as that was now police policy due to Covid 19 infections rising across the country, even though the South West had fortunately largely escaped the worst of the devastating disease.

*

As they arrived in the car park at Slapton Sands, the RIB and abandoned life jackets were clearly visible, having been deposited around the time of the previous evening's high tide. All the detectives understood why the traffickers would pick a time when the tide was high as it made their task easier.

'Sir, I've checked and high tide last night was about one o'clock,' DC Dyson informed the others. King responded: 'Thanks, Sam. It's reasonable to assume the boat would approach the shore just before or just after the high tide. So, a working hypothesis would be arrival between half past midnight and half past one.'

The four detectives were briefed by a uniformed sergeant who told them that two members of the public had come forward, one a late-night dog walker from Torcross. He had spoken with the sergeant that morning soon after the police cars had arrived at the scene. The walker was able to report that the landing had not taken place before midnight as he had walked as far as the memorial the night before and the RIB was not there then.

The sergeant said that the other witness was a passing motorist who lived about a mile further on from where the incident had occurred. Apparently, she had phoned the police after seeing several police cars pass her house that morning. She thought it could possibly be in connection with the van she had seen illegally parked the previous night when she passed on her way home from working at a supermarket in Dartmouth.

Turning back to the uniformed sergeant, King asked: 'So, the dog walker can confirm when the RIB wasn't here; can the other eyewitness confirm when it was?'

'She lives just down the road, sir, and last night was driving home after her overtime shift at the supermarket. She passed here about 1.15 a.m. and saw a lorry in this car park. She initially thought it might be parked overnight, which she knows is not allowed, that's why she slowed down to have a good look. She noticed a red glow on the shingle behind the lorry, but no lights on at the front, which she thought was odd.'

'Thank you, sergeant. Please give her name and address to one of the detectives.' Hammond stepped forward and was given a page from the sergeant's notebook. King continued: 'Right, let's have a look around the RIB and surrounding beach and see if we can...' He was interrupted by Sergeant Harris taking a call on her police mobile. King sensed the team were about to get involved in another investigation. Harris listened for a few moments and thanked the caller.

'Sir, a report has come in of an apparent suicide in Plymbridge Woods. Our uniform colleagues are attending, but are suspicious that it may not be as straightforward as it seems and would like us to take a look.'

'Okay, Lucy. Sam and Alex, you have a look around here and see if you can find any evidence to identify the illegals or, better still, the traffickers. Then as soon as you can, visit the eyewitness who lives along the road; Alex has her address. See if she can give us more information on what she actually saw last night. We'll see you back at the station later. Lucy and I will take a look at what's happened in Plymbridge Woods.'

As they walked to their car, King asked his sergeant for the keys: 'Whenever I hear the word "suspicious" used, I always find it useful to have a pathologist at the scene. Check if John Gleeson is already there would you, Lucy? If he isn't, get a message to him that I'd appreciate his attendance. I'll drive and you can make the call.'

THREE

The detectives left at Slapton Sands decided that Hammond would immediately interview the eyewitness, while Dyson would inspect the RIB and beach, particularly looking for any footprints – such as they were on the shingle – that led to the car park. There was a metre drop from the park to the beach below. Vehicles were prevented from going over the drop and onto the shingle by telegraph poles that were intermittently laid horizontally along its edge. This artificial barrier was gradually being eaten away by the sea. Erosion was limited to when storms coincided with high tides as normally the waves never threatened that far inland. The village of Torcross, which is on the same tideline, is protected from such intrusion by mounds of huge boulders topped with a concave sea wall. Even then, those defences were not always able to prevent pebbles, whipped up by the angry sea, smashing against the windows of bordering houses. The eyewitness lived in one of the houses.

Dyson could see where the human cargo had staggered from the beach through a gap between the telegraph poles, their path the previous evening having been lit by the red glow from the rear fog lights of the van. Uniformed officers began collecting the discarded lifejackets and counted sixteen in total. Dyson asked for the abandoned RIB to be left until she had inspected it, although she was not expecting to find anything significant. From a cursory look it appeared completely empty. However, on closer inspection, having gone down on her knees and leaned over the side, she could see something jammed between the rounded edge of the boat and its black, non-slip bottom. Out of habit she pulled on blue latex gloves and, leaning further over, she pulled out a satellite phone, still emitting a signal and showing the outline of the South Devon coast; a flashing red dot marked the spot exactly where Dyson was now kneeling. She then understood how the illegal immigrants had been able to arrive at the precise pick-up point.

She rang Hammond, who was now at the front door of the eyewitness, and told him what she had found. Hammond congratulated her and before ringing the doorbell, offered his advice: 'I reckon that's one for our Cyber Unit, Sam.'

After she explained the screen was showing their location by a red dot on a map, Hammond added: 'If it's showing where we are it will probably indicate where the journey began. Of course, the traffickers on the other coast will be long gone, but I'm sure our French counterparts will be interested in knowing the departure point. I recall about a month ago that an abandoned RIB was found not far from here at Whitsand Bay, so this part of the Devon and Cornwall coast seems to be becoming a favoured drop point: I wonder if the start point is always the same?'

He hung up and rang the doorbell. It was immediately answered by a woman.

'Mrs Brenda Knox? I am Detective Constable Hammond,' he said and held out his warrant card. 'I believe you reported seeing a van or lorry parked in the car park last night along by the memorial?'

'Yes, that's right, detective. It was about one fifteen and I thought it looked a bit suspicious, so when I saw the police cars pass my house this morning, I thought I'd better report it. Is it something to do with what you're investigating?'

'It might be linked, but we're keeping an open mind. How would you describe the vehicle you saw?'

'Well, it was more a large white van than a lorry. It was backed facing the sea and there was a red glow coming from the rear. I could just make out the red light cast on the shingle. Funny thing was, the sidelights at the front weren't on, but the number plate light was illuminated.'

'And could you read the plate?'

'I was only going slowly, but, I'm sorry, I didn't catch it.'

'Can you remember anything else from when you drove by?'

'I'm afraid that's about it, detective.'

'Thank you for reporting it and please let us know if anything else comes to mind.' With that Hammond turned to walk away and suddenly stopped. The eyewitness had closed her front door as Hammond turned back.

On closer inspection, he confirmed what he thought he had seen. He once again rang the doorbell.

'Mrs Knox. I'm sorry to bother you again, but is that your car parked there?' Hammond enquired pointing at a blue Mazda right outside the front of her property.

'Well, actually it's my husband's. Mine is in the local garage for a service. Why do you ask?'

'Is that the car you were driving last night?'

'Yes it was, as I was too late home to collect mine from the garage. I'll have to wait until my husband gets home to collect it.'

'Do you know it's fitted with a dash camera?'

'Oh, yes I do, but I don't bother with that. My husband fitted it in his, but I said I didn't want one in my car.'

'Where is your husband now?'

'He was picked up earlier by one of his mates, before my garage opened, and they went fishing over Dartmouth way. He left his car for me to use in case I needed to go anywhere.'

'Have you got the keys, Mrs Knox, as I'd like to view the footage from the camera?'

'I'll get them for you, but I don't think it'll be any use as I didn't switch it on when I was using it last night.' With that she went indoors and quickly returned with the keys. Hammond was aware that the dash cam was automatically switched on by the ignition. He asked DC Dyson to join him and she was there within minutes as she had finished inspecting the abandoned RIB.

It was by no means certain the camera would have captured any images peripheral to the road, but Hammond thought it was worth checking. He sat in the driver's seat and Dyson sat next to him. Mrs Knox peered in through the open driver's door. Hammond rewound the recording until it reached a point where Mrs Knox was approaching the memorial the previous night.

The image of the road was of surprisingly good quality and the large white van slowly came into view. As the eyewitness had reported, her speed had slowed as she approached. The detectives simultaneously moved their heads closer to the screen. The footage continued until the van went out of the picture, but not before they had a fleeting glimpse of its illuminated number plate. The darkness surrounding the plate seemed to enhance its image. Hammond rewound the footage, froze the frame and enlarged the part showing the plate. Dyson took out her notebook and wrote down the registration. Hammond pulled out the connecting wire and slid the device from its mounting. He stepped out of the car and shut the door.

'If you could inform your husband, Mrs Knox, that we have taken his dash cam, as the footage it contains is needed for a criminal investigation. He will get it back in due course when we have downloaded the recording.' With that he gave her a receipt and thanked her for her cooperation.

As they briskly walked back to their car, Hammond spoke: 'Okay, Sam, I suspect that the traffickers wouldn't use a traceable plate and, therefore, I doubt that the registration number actually belongs to the vehicle we saw in the footage. However, that's good enough to identify it on the road. We'd better let Inspector King know right away what we've found.'

FOUR

King drove himself and his sergeant from Slapton Sands, near Torcross, to Plymbridge Woods, the place of the suspected suicide, a journey that took nearly an hour. The woods were National Trust-owned and comprised a wooded valley eventually opening onto the Dartmoor National Park. Harris normally drove, but the inspector wanted her to arrange for the forensic pathologist to meet them at the site and also update him on the phone call she had taken at Torcross. After several miles along Devon lanes they joined the A38 heading west along the main road to Plymouth. The woods were situated on the east side of the city and the main car park was sandwiched between the River Plym and the site of an old canal.

During their journey, after checking that the pathologist would meet them there, Harris updated her boss on the information she had gleaned from the phone call she had received while at Slapton Sands.

'The name of the deceased is Daniel Freeman. His wife raised the alarm when she returned from her local supermarket shopping at about ten o'clock this morning and discovered her husband was not at their home in Efford. The call was logged as a missing person report and patrols were informed to be on the lookout for Mr Freeman.

'Apparently he suffers from dementia and his wife only leaves him alone for an hour each week to do the food shopping. She used to take him with her, but as his condition deteriorated he couldn't even push the trolley. She was distraught when she rang the emergency services and told the operator she couldn't understand how he managed to get out of the house. She always tells him not to answer the door, but such is his condition he forgets.

'He was found by a dog walker who apparently wouldn't have gone that way normally, but his dog must have sensed something and gone to explore.'

'That sounds like a very detailed emergency call, Lucy,' he commented as they arrived at Plymbridge Woods. The untarmacked car park was busy with police vehicles and an ambulance. They also recognised the car of John Gleeson, the pathologist from Forensics.

As they were about to get out of their car, Harris took another call. King patiently waited and, sensing an update on the trafficking investigation, popped a sherbet lemon into his mouth. He didn't have to wait long before Harris enlightened him.

'That was Alex Hammond, sir. They've found a satellite phone in the RIB, which they suspect was used to guide the migrants to the beach. Of even greater importance is they've got the registration of the large van that took them away from Slapton Sands. Apparently, it was dash cam footage from the car the eyewitness was driving last night. It was her husband's and she didn't even know how it worked. Hammond spotted it when he visited her and he and Dyson have viewed the images.' With that, Harris took out her notebook and wrote down the registration of the van using the phonetic alphabet. King was pleased and realised swift action was needed.

'It starts Bravo/Bravo. That's a Birmingham registration. Ask the DCs to return to the station and start checking the Automatic Number Plate Recognition system for the M5 heading north and see if the van can be tracked. Get the DCI on your phone, Lucy, and let me speak to him. He will urgently need to alert the West Midlands Police. Bearing in mind the migrants were landed over eight hours ago, we might be too late to stop them being transferred, but if our police colleagues can find the van, we might just have a chance of arresting the traffickers.'

King then updated DCI Burrows who replied: 'Good work, Richard. I'll get on to West Midlands straightaway. I'll keep you informed of any developments.' King acknowledged what the DCI had said and turned his attention once more to Plymbridge Woods.

'Right, Lucy, we can't do any more on the trafficking case for the moment, so let's get back to the suspected suicide. Any initial thoughts?'

'Well, sir, what I find hard to understand is how a man who, according to his wife, was suffering from advanced dementia, could leave his home, travel to these woods – yet another mystery in itself – and secure one end of a rope to a tree, sling it over a branch and put his head in a perfectly formed noose, which is what a PC told me when I rang him to say we were on our way. That's what aroused his suspicions that it may not be a straightforward suicide. The PC also said that when he and his colleague arrived there were quite a few cars in the car park. They stopped others entering, but when the other cars were retrieved by their owners – mainly dog walkers – there were none left behind. So, how did Mr Freeman get here?'

'Of course, he could have come by taxi, but that's unlikely given his mental state. The PC did very well, Lucy, by calling us in at an early stage and telling us about the absence of a car. Right now, as ever, I'm concerned that the scene isn't compromised by well-intentioned emergency workers whose instinct is to help people rather than preserving a crime scene intact.'

Sergeant Harris could see where the emergency personnel had gathered deeper into the woods and started to head in their direction from the main car park.

'Not that way, Lucy.' King looked around and then set off walking back up the road they had come in on with his sergeant behind him. He then left the road and began walking parallel to a woodland path – not on it. Harris wore a quizzical expression. She could not understand why her boss was moving away from the scene of the investigation. As he walked, King was scanning the ground in front of him;

he stopped by a recessed gated access as she drew alongside. The five-bar gate was set back about six paces from the road allowing a vehicle to pull in off the tarmac, with the gate then opening onto the start of the rough track. He took out a sherbet lemon from the bag he always carried. There was something about that fizzy little sweet that helped him focus his concentration. He rolled it around his mouth with his tongue several times before speaking. His sergeant knew not to interrupt.

'According to his wife, Mr Freeman left his house sometime between nine and ten o'clock this morning. The journey from his house to here would have taken no more than twenty minutes by car, so arrival was probably around nine thirty. By then there was every chance the main car park would have been busy with dog walkers. If, as we suspect, foul play is involved, it is probable that the person or persons responsible would not have used the main car park. Therefore, where would they park? Where we are standing now is a possible place as it can't be seen from where the emergency vehicles are now in the main car park.' He moved forward for a closer inspection.

'There are tyre marks here that look fairly fresh and they stop just before the five-bar gate, so someone could have parked here to avoid being seen by other people who were using the woods; whether the marks have any connection to this investigation is open to question. Nevertheless, I think it's worth our Scene of Crime Officers taking a look. Remind me to ask the SOCOs to check out the tracks.'

They then walked towards where Mr Freeman's body had been found, inspecting the ground as they went. The detectives clambered down a bank with the inspector leading the way. He could see the emergency services personnel through the trees, about fifty metres ahead. King continued to scrutinise the ground, occasionally nodding to himself. He then indicated to his sergeant she should wait where she was as he moved about five paces to his left and squatted on his haunches, rubbing his chin with his forefinger and thumb. He then returned to where Harris was standing and continued towards the hanging.

Harris, who was closely following her boss, suddenly lost her footing on a loose stone and because of the steepness of the ground knew she was about to take a fall. King, glancing back, was just in time to see her stumble towards him and braced himself. Fortunately, her momentum had not reached its peak and he was able to throw his arms around her and prevent both of them tumbling into an ignominious heap at the bottom of the bank. They held each other for possibly longer than was necessary.

'Thank you, sir,' she said sheepishly; he just nodded and smiled.

They arrived at the scene surprising some of their colleagues as they had not come down the obvious route from the car park. They lifted the POLICE DO NOT CROSS tape over their heads. Mr Freeman's lifeless body was still hanging from the noose with his neck angled to one side due to the tautness of the rope. The body was rigid as rigor mortis had 'frozen' him, but it could not prevent the lifeless corpse swaying in the gentle breeze that was filtering through the trees.

The inspector spoke to one of the Scene of Crime Officers – the so-called SOCOs – who was already busy recording data, clad in a white plastic onesie and wearing a facemask, as was normal protocol. The SOCOs were not police officers, but were specially trained in crime scene detection. Anything they found that required further analysis, for example DNA testing, would be sent to Forensics. King gestured in the direction of the path to a SOCO and told her of his entry theory, requesting her to do the necessary recording of footprints and tyre tracks. He also asked her to photograph the area surrounding the hanging body in addition to the tracks leading from the recessed access where the two detectives had entered the scene.

King sought out the uniformed officer who had alerted them to a potential crime and thanked him for his diligence. Then he spoke with Pathologist Gleeson, who was taking photographs of the body.

'Hi, John. First impressions?'

'Hello, Richard. Well, the officers who were first on the scene did the right thing in leaving the body as they found it. Clearly, he was dead and I would estimate had been for no more than a couple of hours. Evidently, as the ground falls away quite sharply, once his head was in the noose, all he had to do was let his body fall forward and his weight did the rest. The funny thing is he was wearing slippers and, although it was quite chilly this morning, he wasn't wearing a coat.

'I'll be able to tell you more when I get him back to the lab, but it gives me a starting point to see where the body was found. I'll let you inspect the area and when you've finished let me know and I'll have him removed.'

'Thanks, John. We'll have a look around and let you know if we find anything suspicious.' With that they slipped on disposable plastic overshoes and began inspecting the corpse and the surrounding ground. After ten minutes, the pathologist approached them for an update: 'Seen enough, Richard?'

'Yes, thanks, John. I've seen enough to know this man had help to carry out his demise. I'll catch up with you tomorrow morning if you've done the post-mortem by then?'

'Yes, that'll be fine. I'll let you know if not.' The corpse was then carefully taken down, placed in a body bag and removed to a waiting black van on a stretcher.

The detectives climbed back up the slope leading to the car park, her boss giving Harris a helping hand. When they reached it, he paused before getting back in their car.

'I agree with all the points you made earlier, Lucy. What about the ground surrounding the hanging?'

'Not sure what you're getting at, sir.'

'As there were no leaves on the ground, the marks were very interesting. There were holes or indentations a metre apart, about the size of a fifty pence piece, but round, not heptagonal. Suggesting what?'

'A walking stick?'

'That's my thinking. Also, in places, particularly where I think the car that brought them here was parked, the ground is soft enough to leave footprints. There were two sets of prints with one leading and the other following. Why two? One had a quite deep tread on the sole, suggesting some kind of boot rather than a shoe. The other had no tread at all with occasional slide marks. We know now that belonged to Mr Freeman as he was wearing slippers. The left foot of the one wearing boots made a slightly deeper imprint from the toe of his boot as that's what we push off with when walking. The impression of the other print from the right foot, next to the holes made by the walking stick, made a lighter impression, and the indentation was equally deep across the whole sole. Conclusion?'

'This person had some sort of injury, which meant they needed support and couldn't put their full weight on their right leg. The shallower indentation was because some of the weight was taken by the stick.'

'I think you're right, Lucy. Some sort of injury, or the lower leg is a prosthetic. I've mentioned my theory to John Gleeson and the forensic people; they'll do the necessary by way of recording the impressions.

'Why only two sets of footprints both walking the same way and none leading back to the car? That's because the person with the stick chose a different way back, possibly because the way they came was too challenging for him with his bad leg and stick. When returning, he preferred the slightly flatter ground as evidenced by the telltale tracks a few paces to the right of their entry route.

'So, Lucy, Mr Freeman was clearly not alone when he died. We can assume the other person was another man – not a woman – using a walking stick, wearing size eleven or twelve boots, possibly with a prosthetic on his right leg, probably over 190 centimetres tall, weighing around ninety kilograms and driving a 4x4 that is black in colour!'

Sergeant Harris was open-mouthed: 'Sorry, sir, you've lost me. How can you deduce all of that from what we've seen? Even the colour of his car!'

'I can't, Lucy, as most of it is purely conjecture, but I think I'm right about some things. The entry point into the woods for one, as it's the obvious place for someone who doesn't want to be seen in the main car park. I didn't see any other suitable parking that would have afforded such seclusion. Having established that, then the tyre tracks and footprints naturally follow on. From the prints I can see that he is wearing a larger than average shoe size. The average for men is a size ten, or size 44.5 in EU terms. This chap was wearing close to a size 47 so I reckon he must be over 190 centimetres tall, so six foot two or six foot three.

'Why was he using a stick? As you said, it could be an injury, but my hunch is the problem with his leg is more permanent. Don't forget the ground he walked down with Freeman. I think the stick was more for balance than to cope with an injury, but that's a pure guess.

'As for the tyre tracks, if they belong to the vehicle that brought the two of them here, they show the tyres are wider than an average saloon car. More likely a 4x4 or a rough terrain vehicle judging by the tread.

'Part of that may be true and it's all we've got to go on until we speak with Mrs Freeman. As to me guessing the colour of the car, aren't all 4x4s black?' He smiled as, for a moment, he had his sergeant believing the car colour bit of his hypothesis. As they were about to get in their car and return to the police station, King offered an overall observation.

'Seriously, we have to ask ourselves why there was no vehicle left at the scene? Also, how could Freeman secure a rope at one end then expertly form a noose, even though he probably couldn't even tie his own shoelaces? He didn't take his own life, someone took it from him. What we are dealing with here is either assisted suicide or a carefully planned premeditated murder. If it's the latter, what sort of monster would go to such lengths to murder someone already suffering from such a terrible and debilitating disease?'

FIVE

Following the call from Inspector King, DCI Burrows contacted a superintendent in the West Midlands Police headquarters based in Birmingham. He told her of the people-trafficking incident on the south coast of Devon and gave her the registration of the large white van that Burrows' detectives suspected was being used to transport illegal migrants to Birmingham. He also told her his officers were using the ANPR system to try and track the vehicle's movements and would alert the superintendent if they were successful. For her part, she would alert all the motorway police patrols to be on the lookout for the van.

*

Hammond and Dyson returned to the central police station in Plymouth and entered the registration of the van into the ANPR system. To their surprise, the van was shown on the imaging system as only passing Exeter at 6.30 a.m., over five hours after the suspected departure of the illegal immigrants from Slapton Sands, a journey which, to that point, which should have taken a little over an hour. The detectives then checked other data from cameras along the M5 heading north to Birmingham. Two hours later the van was logged as passing Gordano services in Bristol and, an hour later, passing Gloucester at 9.30 a.m. The detectives now believed that the traffickers were still on the road. They eagerly checked other cameras and were delighted the van had not been registered as passing Worcester. That placed it somewhere between Gloucester and Worcester.

King and Harris had now also returned to the station and although they wanted to interview the widow of Mr Freeman, King realised the trafficking investigation was the priority. Dyson excitedly rushed into the main office: 'Sir, we think we know approximately where the van might be. From the ANPR system we think it's north of Gloucester and south of Worcester!'

King was encouraged at this positive news: 'I know that stretch of motorway fairly well. After the services at Gloucester, which you say the van has passed, the next services south of Birmingham is Frankley. If the van isn't showing on the ANPR system that far north, it's either on the motorway or it's stopped at Strensham Services!'

King immediately contacted his DCI and told him what his detectives had found. Burrows rang the superintendent he had spoken to earlier and informed her of the new information. Before she could alert all the police patrols in the area, two of her officers, already at the services, had their suspicions and were about to investigate.

*

The Central Motorway Police Group is responsible for policing a number of motorways, including the M5. The two police officers in their big BMW car, needing a break, left the motorway about a mile north of junction 8 and glided to a halt, close to the Roadchef at Strensham Services (Northbound). They had started their shift at 8 a.m. and as it was now after 10.30 a.m., they were peckish. What had so far been an uneventful shift was about to change.

The lorry park was very busy with over seventy vehicles parked quite closely together. The usual mix of large articulated lorries was parked side by side with Scania, Iveco and Mercedes-Benz dominating the varied makes from the hauliers based in the UK and from abroad. Some drivers were taking a compulsory break after six hours' driving, others were sleeping in their in-cabin bed.

One of the drivers had used the facilities in the services and bought a takeaway coffee. He was walking back to his vehicle, parked at the far end of the lorry park as that was the closest he could get to the main building. He walked past the front of a large white van which, like his own, had been parked some way away from the other vehicles. As he walked by it, he thought he heard a tapping sound coming from the back, but initially dismissed it. He walked on a few paces, then stopped and turned back. The cab looked empty and there were no lights on any part of the van. This time he moved down the side to the back and the sound of the tapping noise increased. He could not work out what the cause could be. He shrugged, took a swig of his coffee and headed for his lorry.

The two police officers had cruised around the whole services site as they had been asked to be on the lookout for a large white van and knew its registration, which had been supplied by their colleagues in the Devon and Cornwall Police. What made the officers really focus their attention was the fact they had just been informed that where they were was a possible location for the van or it was close by on the motorway headed for Birmingham. They only had the far end of the lorry park to check, and, if they did not find the van, then they intended to head out onto the motorway. As they drove slowly in front of another echelon of lorries they were approached by a man holding a takeaway coffee. He indicated he wanted to speak to the officers.

'Can we help you, sir, as we have an emergency to deal with?'

'I'm not sure, officer. As I was walking back to my lorry parked over there, I passed that white van on the end of the row and I thought I heard a tapping sound coming from it. I went back and listened more closely and definitely heard a sound like someone was banging something on the doors at the back. It might be nothing, but I thought I'd let you know.'

Both officers looked at each other, simultaneously registering what the man had just told them.

'Thank you for reporting it, sir. We'll investigate. Please return to the main building, sir, until we've checked it out.'

With that, both officers got out of their patrol car and instead of approaching the van from the front, they initially quickly walked away from it, one to the left and one to the right, arriving at the back of the van at the same time. Glancing down towards the back bumper, the registration confirmed this was the van the police were looking for. They could not see the driver anywhere and acting on the report they had been given they just listened. They heard nothing.

They looked at each other and were about to walk to the front and look in the cab, but then stopped. They could now hear a faint knocking coming from inside. One officer silently beckoned the other to follow him away from the van and they headed back to their car.

'We've been told, Joe, not to search the van if we find it as it's suspected of being involved with people-trafficking. Let's call for backup as we know that some of these traffickers will stop at nothing to protect themselves and their "investments".'

They got back into their car and reported what they had seen and heard. They were not far away from the lorry and they started their engine in readiness to intercept the van if it attempted to leave. Within twenty minutes, two armed-response units and other police cars swept into the lorry park, without announcing their arrival. The usual fanfare of sirens was muted. Armed officers quickly took up their positions on either side of the van's cab, while other officers ushered other people away from the van. The armed officers edged closer to the vehicle with guns raised and laser red sight dots flickering over the vehicle. A head suddenly appeared from inside the cab above the dashboard, before disappearing. The driver had stopped for breakfast and, due to his late night, had nodded off.

'Armed police! Armed police! Come out with your hands in the air!' shouted an armed officer and waited for the occupant to surrender.

The driver, however, had other thoughts and had no intention of surrendering. From his prone position across the front seats in his cab, where he had been asleep, he reached across to the right side of the steering column and flicked the ignition key. The van's engine immediately burst into life and the driver swivelled around in the cramped space, all the time keeping his body from appearing above the dashboard. Now bent over, below his steering wheel, his feet firmly in the driver's footwell, he dipped the clutch and selected first gear. The big van began to move forward, appearing to those closely watching that it was driverless.

Ricocheting off the lorry parked next to it, as the driver was driving 'blind', the vehicle began to gather pace. After travelling away from the surrounding parked lorries, the driver sensed he had moved past where the police were stationed. Gaining in confidence, he quickly adopted his normal driving position and headed for the exit onto the motorway. He smashed into the side of a police car parked side on to deter his exit. This foolhardy attempt to escape was doomed to fail, even if he had made it onto the motorway. The police had other ideas!

The armed officers realised they could not allow him to leave the services as it would have put the lives of other motorway users at risk. Instinctively, all the armed officers opened fire at once. A hail of high-calibre bullets instantly deflated all the tyres. The van could now only crawl to a halt as all the wheel rims sparked after making contact with tarmac, their tyres shredded. The suspected trafficker simply did not appreciate that surrender was his best option if he wanted to survive. Then he made another miscalculation. He reached across into the compartment on the passenger seat side of his van and pulled out his pistol.

None of the police could quite understand what he was trying to achieve as he was obviously outgunned. The time for giving him instructions or warnings had long passed. He exited his cab firing randomly in all directions before he was shot several times from several different angles. Police cars now converged towards the scene, but still at a safe distance. The armed police were in control and would only let their colleagues advance when they deemed it safe to do so. They approached from different directions, still in a state of readiness, unsure if the driver was accompanied.

Closer inspection of the cab revealed a half-eaten double cheeseburger and fries on the passenger seat and a Coke cup in the drinks holder. As the emergency services personnel began to move forward en masse, the armed officer in charge instructed everyone to wait and at the same time called for silence. He did not want to delay attempting to rescue what he suspected might still be a van full of migrants, but he could not rule out the presence of another armed trafficker in the back. Unlikely, but he had to be sure.

Against a background of distant traffic hurtling up and down the M5, a slow rhythmical knocking could be heard coming from the main body of the large van. Without further delay an armed officer moved to the back and, operating the push-up-pull-out lever locks, the back doors swung open. Once again the Heckler and Koch guns were readied, but they were not required.

Even hardened police officers were ill prepared for what confronted them as they peered into the van. Most of the bodies were stone cold with their mouths gaping open; they had been gasping for air until their last breath. Some had their faces pressed to the cold steel floor of the van's bed where it met the back doors, hoping against hope that they would find air to sustain them. The only sign of life was a young man, close to the doors, holding a small plastic bottle by the base. He was the cause of the rhythmical banging using the screw top end on the doors as a final desperate attempt to draw attention to their plight. The rescuers were not to know that he had been the 'captain' on the perilous sea crossing.

Paramedics, who had been patiently waiting, required no invitation to attend to the migrants as soon as they were given the all-clear, quickly jumping up into the back of the van. For almost all of the migrants, help had come too late. The only survivor was the young man who had bravely tried to raise the alarm. Still clutching the small long-since-emptied water bottle, he was given oxygen as he lay on a stretcher. He only had enough strength to pull the mask from his face. A police officer moved closer as it was obvious the man wanted to speak: 'Monsieur La Liberté. Him bad man!' Those words were the last he spoke.

*

Strensham Services (Northbound) was a hive of activity as a fleet of ambulances arrived to remove the bodies from the van, one by one. Scene of Crime Officers were soon examining the vehicle where it had been abandoned and also taking many photographs, including many of the dead trafficker sprawled on the tarmac. Even though those who witnessed the shooting knew it was entirely justified, an investigation would be held by the Independent Office for Police Conduct.

Later that morning a low loader took the van away, now relieved of its "passengers", for further examination. Earlier, the police officers who had raised the alarm checked the registration and realised the van had been cloned. It did indeed belong to a large white van registered to an address in Birmingham, but not to the van that was in the lorry park.

The incident at the services was the lead item on the national TV news stations later that day and also the newspaper headlines the following morning. West Midlands Police made several arrests in connection with the trafficking. The father and brother of the man shot dead were among them. Their transport company, Fox and Sons, ceased trading shortly afterwards.

DCI Burrows found it gratifying that the Devon and Cornwall Police were given credit for their part in the investigation, but took no solace in the fact that so many people had lost their lives.

SIX

Not for the first time, King and Harris had to interview the spouse or partner of a recently deceased person who had not died of natural causes. These interviews were never easy – and this one would be no different – but were an essential part of the investigation. Very often the information the detectives received from talking to a bereaved partner would prove invaluable in their efforts to find the perpetrator, if foul play was confirmed.

As the inspector and his sergeant drove down the street, a police constable on sentry duty outside gave an early indication as to the location of the Freemans' house.

'Mrs Joan Freeman?' King asked as a red-eyed woman answered his ring. He introduced himself and Sergeant Harris, expressed their condolences and apologised for intruding on her grief.

'Can't this wait? You can see my mother is distressed!' a voice brusquely enquired as soon as the detectives had crossed the threshold. A man in his mid-twenties appeared in the hallway from the adjacent lounge and it was obvious he was in a belligerent mood.

'My apologies, inspector, this is our son, Ben. Sorry, I mean my son,' Mrs Freeman sheepishly offered.

'I'm afraid it can't wait, sir. I've already apologised to your mother, but as we are treating your father's death as suspicious, we have to investigate it without further delay.' King was used to dealing with relatives who suddenly found themselves in tragic situations and was not fazed by hostility; in fact he understood the protectiveness of Ben Freeman towards his mother. At Mrs Freeman's request all four moved to the lounge and sat down on opposite sides of the room to observe social distancing.

'Perhaps you'd like to tell us what happened this morning?' The question brought back painful memories of that morning when she had left her husband alone at home. She broke down and began sobbing uncontrollably. Her son, also visibly distressed, passed his mother another tissue. The detectives waited patiently for the raw emotion to subside. After a short time she was sufficiently composed to answer.

'I should never have left him on his own, inspector. I only popped out to do some shopping and planned to be back within an hour. I used to take him with me and then about two years ago his demeanour began to change. Before then he was always even-tempered and happy. He started to become moody and forgetful. He began to struggle with normal daily tasks and was often confused as to what to do in certain situations. He would also have bouts of anger towards me and life in general. They were caused by this dreadful disease that was eventually diagnosed as early-onset dementia. He had to stop driving as he simply could no longer remember how to change gear. I briefly thought an automatic would help, but quickly realised his judgement was so poor that he would be dangerous on the road.'

'Presumably he had to leave his employment?' King enquired.

'He had worked at Dartmoor Prison in Princetown for many years and at the same time he was also a member of the Army Reserve. He joined up with his mates back in 2010. This allowed him to keep his prison job and also do other things. His reserve role even took him overseas.

'In 2019 when he was first diagnosed, he was only forty-two, he was medically retired from the prison service and couldn't continue as a reservist. I was pleased he left the Army as after the tour in Iraq he started suffering bouts of depression, which I think were due to his experiences in the Gulf. Latterly, as his dementia got worse, he was largely housebound.' The detectives noted she was already referring to him in the past tense.

'So, what happened this morning?' King nudged the interview forward.

'I really shouldn't have left him alone, but as I mentioned, I couldn't even take him shopping anymore as he couldn't even cope with pushing the trolley around the supermarket.' She began to sob into her already wet handkerchief. Her son placed a box of tissues on the table in front of her and bit his lip to prevent himself making any further unhelpful comments; he now realised this had to be done and the sooner it was over the better.

'So, lately I have been leaving him for an hour, one day each week, while I do the food shop. I leave him in front of the telly and stress that he shouldn't answer the door to anyone; the trouble is he forgets. I reassured myself that if someone called he probably wouldn't be able to remember how to open the front door anyway.

'When I got back just after ten o'clock everything in the house seemed normal, apart from the fact he was missing. I did notice straightaway that I couldn't find his slippers and his coat was still hanging on the hook in the hallway. It's as if he just walked out, which he may have done before he was found in the...' She tailed off as the thought of what had happened to her husband overwhelmed her.

Sergeant Harris allowed her a little time to recover before asking: 'Was he capable of opening the front door if it was locked?'

'Sometimes he could if he remembered how to operate the lock, which is just a standard Yale latch.'

The inspector then took the interview in a different direction: 'What was your husband's mood recently? Was he depressed at all?' The reason behind his question was self-evident.

'He suffers from vascular dementia, inspector, caused by reduced blood flow to the brain. A while back, he went through an angry phase that I mentioned earlier, as he knew he couldn't do what he used to do. More recently he had become depressed about his condition; he found it difficult to understand what was happening to him and became very frustrated.'

'Has he ever talked about taking his own life?'

'No, I'm not sure he could think that clearly.'

The inspector felt there was little more to be gained from continuing the interview. He looked at his sergeant inviting her to ask any final question. She had one. Harris probed: 'Do you know if he had any enemies, possibly linked to his role in Dartmoor Prison? Either inmates or colleagues?'

'He didn't talk much about his prison work, but he was aware he could be attacked as some prisoners get what he called "stir-crazy". When that happens they tend to lash out at the warders. He told me that he was involved in a particularly nasty incident when two prisoners were actually fighting, but he never went into any detail.'

'What about any friends whose assistance he may have sought to help him end his life?'

'There's no one really. We tended to keep ourselves to ourselves lately. He had some really good mates, but since his dementia he doesn't always recognise people, so stopped seeing them.'

'Thank you for speaking to us, Mrs Freeman. We will continue investigating your husband's sad death and keep you informed of any developments. We'll see ourselves out.' With that, King stood up, nodding in the direction of the son as both the detectives left.

Once outside, King asked his sergeant for her view on what they had heard: 'Well, sir, because of his depression, I don't think we can rule out he arranged to end his own life with the help of someone; he certainly didn't act alone as we deduced from what we found in the woods and from what his wife has told us.'

'I liked your last question, Lucy, as I was wondering the same thing. In his prison work he must have come across some unsavoury characters who may have blamed him for the punishment meted out following the altercation Mrs Freeman spoke about, or simply from the frustration at being locked up for most of the day, every day. Fix up a meeting with the governor and find out if any recently released prisoners had a grudge against Mr Freeman.

'You said earlier you wanted to call in and see your mother as she was feeling unwell, so if you drop me back at the station, I'll catch up with Sam and Alex. If you contact the prison tonight to make the appointment with the governor, in the morning you can go straight to the prison from home.'

SEVEN

Shortly after the events at Plymbridge Woods and Slapton Sands were unfolding – the latter culminating in the devastating deaths of all the migrants and trafficker at Strensham Services – a family in Woolwell, on the north-east fringe of Plymouth, were settling down for an evening in front of the television.

'You've just won a quarter of a million pounds!' Jeremy Clarkson announced on *Who Wants to be a Millionaire?* to a delighted contestant. The family of three were sitting on the sofa in front of a real log fire in the lounge at their palatial home, which was called "Bonanza". The house name had been chosen by the owner for two reasons: his love of the 1960s television Western of the same name and for its meaning of a sudden increase in wealth. They were watching the programme on catch-up TV while they waited for their takeaway to be delivered. Just then the doorbell rang.

'Pause it please, honey, and I'll get the curry,' said Robert Dangerfield, a self-made millionaire who owned an estate agency business with six offices operating in South Devon. His fortune was made from selling expensive houses, not from a game show. He went from the lounge into the substantial hallway and walked the few paces to the front door. It had a peephole, but this was a man never troubled by self-doubt and he did not bother using it as, although a little early, he assumed their food had arrived; soon after, he wished he had.

He opened the door and a sawn-off double-barrelled shotgun was thrust into his belly. Seldom fazed, this was a whole new experience for the slightly brash, self-confident property sales tycoon. He was shocked as he staggered backwards after being confronted by two figures, both clad from head to toe in black. The gunman was wearing a "Joker" full face mask – with its extravagant wide red grin – but there was nothing remotely funny about masquerading as Batman's adversary. His accomplice had on a simple black balaclava with holes for his mouth and eyes.

Dangerfield quickly regained his normal composure after the shock of their entrance. He took a pace towards the intruders, not daunted by the weapon.

He was not used to being bossed about and certainly not in his own home.

The blast from one barrel of the shotgun reverberated around the whole house as the pellets from the cartridge ripped into his side. He reeled back across the hallway and crumpled into a heap on the parquet flooring. He had not taken the full force of the gunshot, but enough to cause severe damage to the left-hand side of his upper body. The pellets that missed him ripped into the partially glazed kitchen door behind where he had originally been standing. The glass panel at the top of the door shattered and the bottom panel was now pockmarked and in parts splintered.

His wife, Annie, and eleven-year-old son, Dominic, had now emerged panic-stricken from the lounge, he clinging to his mother, having witnessed the aftermath of the shooting with shock, horror and disbelief. At first, both looked incredulously at Robert Dangerfield slumped on the floor with blood forming a pool next to him on the highly polished wood. They then looked in the direction of the front door at the two would-be robbers who were still standing defiantly in the hall.

Mrs Dangerfield rushed to her husband's side and tried to stem the bleeding while their son, transfixed by terror, stood in the doorway to the lounge.

'What have you done, you bastard?' she screamed, half accusing and half begging the man with the gun.

The robber in the "Joker" mask snarled: 'He deserved it. You'll get the same if you don't do as I say. Where's the safe?'

She ignored him, still intent on helping her semi-conscious husband.

'The safe, bitch! Now!' the main robber insisted, his anger rising.

She pointed with her bloodied hand towards the lounge and the man stepped forward and roughly yanked her upright by grabbing a handful of her hair. He then began prodding her aggressively with the barrel of his gun towards the lounge.

'Combination or the lad gets the other barrel!'

Dominic, who had not moved as if mesmerized by the shooting, was by now becoming hysterical as the full horror of the attack sunk in. His mother knew she had to calm him and also do what had forcefully been demanded. They returned to the lounge, the young Dangerfield clutching his mother's waist, while the gunman's partner raced up the stairs intent, it transpired, on filling a Tesco carrier bag with whatever valuable items he could find.

At the top he quickly found the master bedroom, which he knew was likely to offer the richest pickings, and headed straight for the dressing table. He took out his bag and began stuffing it with the contents of a jewellery box. He then threw the bag onto the bed and began pulling out the drawers of furniture in the room and emptying them on the floor, hoping to find some other valuable items that the owners may have secreted. Next he wrenched open the doors of two wardrobes, frantically grabbing handfuls of clothes and underwear, looking for possible hiding places, and scattering them randomly behind him until they were strewn around the room. A diamond necklace clattered against a skirting board and was hastily retrieved and thrust into the bag.

The robber was now racing from room to room grabbing whatever he could find, leaving a trail of rejected items scattered behind him. He wanted small expensive things and bagged a computer tablet, a Kindle, a Fitbit and a laptop. Tempted as he was, he rejected the latest Sony PlayStation as it was too bulky to carry in what he knew would be a hasty getaway.

Robert Dangerfield lay in a pool of blood on the hall floor, drifting in and out of consciousness, while holding his intestines into his body with both hands as blood oozed through his fingers. Even in his perilous state, he was still conscious of what was happening, but was powerless to stop it.

His wife half carried, half dragged her son back into the lounge and went straight to an original Robert Lenkiewicz painting hanging to one side of the substantial fireplace. It was hinged and as she pulled at one side of the painting it swung away from the wall to reveal the main target of the robbery.

'Come on, come on!' urged the gunman as she poked the keypad with her index finger, her son still with his arms around her waist. The safe door clicked open and she stood back clutching Dominic close to her. Envelopes and documents were quickly inspected and discarded by the "Joker"; he was more interested in the rolls of notes, two Rolex watches and a diamond ring, which he eagerly stuffed into the pockets of his black hoodie.

His partner came bounding down the stairs with his Tesco bag laden with the stolen items and went straight out of the open front door, ignoring the prostrate owner. The "Joker" had one last demand: 'Your mobile!' he shouted. She glanced in the direction of the table in front of the sofa where two mobiles were side by side; he picked up both and forcefully threw them in the roaring fire to prevent her alerting the police. He then picked up the house phone in his left hand – his right was still holding the shotgun – traced the landline connection to its junction box and ripped out the wires. For good measure, he threw that phone on the fire as well.

Unaware of what his next move might be, Mrs Dangerfield and her son were now cowering on the sofa. As a parting act of bravado, the robber pointed his gun at the seventy-seven-inch Sony TV fixed to the wall over the fireplace and pulled the trigger: the noise was deafening as the screen exploded into a thousand shards over the carpet. With the occupants suitably traumatised, he ran out of the front door, ignoring the still barely conscious owner who continued to clasp his abdomen with both hands.

When she was sure they had gone the mother turned to face her scared son.

'Dominic, where's your mobile?' but her son was so distressed his mother had to shake him by the shoulders to get him to respond. 'Your mobile! Where is it?'

'Kit... kitchen,' he muttered. She ran from the room, quickly returning with the mobile and a tea towel she had hastily grabbed off the Rangemaster cooker where it was drying. First she took her husband's hands away from his stomach and pressed the towels against the wound, before returning them to the bloodied compress.

'Ambulance, please!' she shrieked into the phone before calming herself and giving the operator her name, address and the reason for the emergency call. She sat on the floor next to her husband, with her son hanging onto her with his arms now around her neck as if his very life depended on it.

It seemed like an age to her, but in reality it was only a matter of minutes before four police cars, two-tones blaring and blue lights flashing, swept into the driveway closely followed by two ambulances with competing sirens. Alerted by the emergency operator that someone had been shot, six officers from the Armed Response Unit fanned out around the house, one moving each side of the front door. They cautiously entered, weapons at the ready, and when told by Mrs Dangerfield that the robbers had gone, urgently beckoned in the paramedics to treat the injured man. The armed officers continued to search the house to ensure the thieves had indeed left.

The ambulance crew quickly attended to Robert Dangerfield while a policewoman comforted his shocked son. The paramedics took twenty minutes to stabilise the stricken man before placing him on a stretcher and wheeling him from the house. His wife and son were not allowed to travel in the ambulance, but followed it to Derriford Hospital in one of the police cars, after a paramedic had spoken to two uniformed officers. They sensed that the wounded man may be lucky to survive the attack and thought it appropriate that his wife should be by her husband's side.

As the ambulance swept out of the property, a bewildered Deliveroo driver arrived with the takeaway. He was politely informed that the Dangerfields would not be eating tonight.

*

After his visit to Mrs Freeman, King had only just returned to the main police station where, very late that afternoon, he was discussing the people-trafficking incident with Hammond and Dyson. He told them that in the morning he had arranged to see John Gleeson, the forensic pathologist, who had examined the body of Daniel Freeman after his death in Plymbridge Woods. He also said that DS Harris was planning on speaking with the governor of Dartmoor Prison at Princetown the following morning. Harris had gone to see her mother who was unwell.

DCI Burrows was still at his desk when alerted to the attack at the Dangerfields' house. He rang King and allocated the incident to him, asking that he attend the scene of the robbery and shooting as soon as possible. King's discussion with Hammond and Dyson was curtailed on this news from DCI Burrows. He knew he had to immediately visit the scene as gun crimes in the city were rare events and demanded his prompt attention.

'Okay, you two, one last job for us today: an armed robbery. Sam, you drive; we're heading for "Bonanza", Dartmoor View in Woolwell. Looks like a late finish!'

EIGHT

Detectives King, Dyson and Hammond turned into the entrance leading to a long drive, passing an illuminated sign announcing that the property was "Bonanza". Even without the signage, they were in no doubt they were at the right place. The substantial front of the mock-Georgian house was illuminated with arc lamps, and Scene of Crime Officers, wearing white protective clothing, were conducting a painstaking search of the part of the drive closest to the house.

Dyson stopped their car a discreet distance from them and all three walked a slightly circuitous route to the front door to avoid compromising the area. As well as the SOCOs, who were busy noting what they had found and searching for evidence, many uniformed officers were also still present. King was greeted by a uniformed sergeant he knew and he updated the detectives on what had happened. The sergeant also expressed his personal opinion: having seen the injured owner, he would be lucky to survive.

King thanked the sergeant for the update and turned to his DCs: 'Did you notice the CCTV camera on the front of the house? Some homeowners want a camera to be highly visible to deter thieves, while others want it to be discreetly hidden to alert them of anyone entering their property when no one is home; the Dangerfields fell into the latter category. Alex, track down the CCTV recorder. I think you'll find the cable coming into the house through a hole in the frame of the window directly above the front door. Follow that cable and you'll find the recording device. Have a look at what's on it if you can and see if it gives us a lead on the suspects. Come on, Sam, let's take a look inside the house.'

With that, all three crossed the threshold after putting on blue plastic overshoes. As they entered the hallway they could see a pool of blood, some smeared across the floor. They walked carefully around the perimeter of the hall and while Hammond went in search of the CCTV recording equipment, King and Dyson entered the lounge. As they surveyed the scene that confronted them, King sucked on a sherbet lemon. The hinged painting that when closed covered the safe was still open, as was the safe door. Some documents were strewn on the floor. Over the fireplace only the outer casing of the huge TV remained, the wall fixing clearly visible as its screen had been shattered apparently by a blast from a shotgun. Many shards of glass littered the rug in front of the fire, twinkling in the light cast by the chandelier.

After several minutes, King's sherbet lemon had all but dissolved. As the detectives took in the destruction and general disarray in the lounge, the inspector finally spoke: 'I think we've seen enough here. Let's take a look upstairs.'

They entered the master bedroom and observed SOCOs who were busy taking photographs of every aspect of the room. One was gently flicking a dark-coloured fingerprint powder over the surface of the expensive white dressing table and empty jewellery box to better show any fingerprints. Drawers from the two chests along an adjacent wall were empty and their contents had been discarded on the bed or scattered on the floor.

When they returned downstairs, DC Hammond told his inspector that he had found the CCTV recorder, which was linked to a laptop in the study. He offered to show the other two detectives the recording immediately before the emergency vehicles arrived. He rewound the sequence and all three watched a car pull into the drive and immediately park on the lawn inside the gates. Hammond leaned forward and pressed some keys on the computer keyboard, first to rewind the sequence and then to pause it before the car swung onto the lawn. Although it was nearly dark when the car pulled in, the camera was fitted with night vision, and that, helped by the glare from a nearby street light, enhanced the image. Hammond then zoomed in and the car's registration was clearly visible. Dyson quickly took the initiative and immediately arranged for the information to be relayed to police patrol cars across Devon and Cornwall.

When Hammond let the recording continue, the two black-clad figures could be seen approaching the house, one wearing a "Joker" mask and carrying some sort of gun, while the other was wearing a balaclava. At that point the robbers disappeared from the CCTV image as they entered the house. Hammond verbally noted the time of entry. He then fast-forwarded the recording, once again verbally noting the time they exited. As the detectives watched, the robbers could be seen running down the drive towards their car, first the one carrying a plastic bag and, soon after, the other one following, still holding what was now clearly visible: a short-barrelled shotgun.

'So, sir, the whole robbery took approximately eleven minutes.'

'Well done, Alex. Okay, Sam, Alex and I will finish up here. I'd like you to take the car and drive to Derriford Hospital and speak to Mrs Dangerfield, if she's in a fit state to talk to you. Arrange for a family liaison officer to be there with you. We need to find out exactly what happened here tonight. We'll scrounge a lift back to the station. I'll set up a meeting with our team and DCI Burrows for 8.30 in the morning and we can have a catch-up on the various investigations. Let's hope this doesn't turn out to be a murder investigation.'

*

Even on a sunny day, there was no mistaking the bleak, grim buildings that made up Dartmoor Prison. The high granite walls incarcerated over 600 Category C male prisoners, and Sergeant Harris was about to enter this male-dominated domain. However, the male domination was not total; the governor was a woman!

Sergeant Harris had an appointment with her and had to undergo several stringent security checks before being shown into an anteroom. The governor opened the door to her office and welcomed Harris to the prison. She had been informed about the nature of the investigation and after offering the sergeant refreshment, which was politely declined, and then a seat, they quickly got down to business.

'Daniel Freeman was a prison officer here until two years ago. He was medically retired as he was diagnosed with early-onset dementia. I understand that your line of enquiry is that he has met an untimely death and you want to see if there is a link with my prison?'

'Yes, that's correct. We suspect he died either due to assisted suicide or he was murdered. Either way, we are trying to establish motive and we wondered if he had made enemies with any of the prisoners, who may have wished him harm?'

'Sergeant, my prison is for inmates who cannot be trusted in an open prison, but who are recognised as being unlikely to make an escape attempt. However, to be here they would have committed a crime, which could have involved violence, arson, drug dealing, and threat of violence or sex-related offences. So, not bad enough to be Category B, but too serious to be Category D. The prisoners in the last category I mentioned would serve their sentence in an open prison. I apologise if you already knew most of that, sergeant, but I just wanted you to have some perspective on the type of prisoner we have here.

'Let me continue by saying it is not unusual for a prisoner to have a grievance against a prison officer as some like to blame anybody except themselves. Now, to your question: Having been informed of the purpose of your visit, I have spoken with prison officer colleagues about Mr Freeman. Specifically, I asked them if they knew of any prisoners who obviously disliked him or of any altercations which involved him. There were two particular incidents mentioned to me and I recall them both. I have assumed you are not interested in any prisoner that is still with us, so I have dismissed one incident. The other involved two inmates. You will appreciate that he left the service over two years ago, but one officer did recall that Mr Freeman had to break up a fight between two prisoners and both then turned their anger on him. Fellow officers quelled the disturbance and I subsequently reviewed the incident, which resulted in ninety days being added to the sentences of both inmates.'

'Presumably they were not very happy with that outcome?' Harris queried.

'Correct. Such was their reaction – they had to be forcefully restrained – that I ordered them to be placed separately in solitary confinement for fifteen days. As this is a criminal investigation, I will provide you with a copy of the file that was prepared following the investigation. They blamed Freeman for intervening in their quarrel and subsequent punishment. They maintained that they were not really fighting and thought he had been unnecessarily heavy-handed.' Harris was handed a buff A4 envelope and took out two sheets of paper. She studied them for several minutes and then the governor continued: 'The file will have answered your next question: date of release?'

'I noticed that Reginald Connelly was released three months ago and David Willis last month.'

'That's correct, sergeant. Now it's not for me to link either with the death of Mr Freeman. When I asked my officers they only came up with the names of Connelly and Willis as prisoners who had an obvious grudge against him.'

'Thank you, ma'am. I appreciate your help in our investigation.' As Harris left Dartmoor Prison, she glanced back at the menacing façade. She knew she now had to track down and either eliminate Connelly and Willis from the investigation or possibly arrest one of them on suspicion of murdering Daniel Freeman.

NINE

Malcolm 'The Boatman' Prescott worked for Plym Boat Services in Plymouth at a marina on the Mount Batten peninsula, directly opposite the National Marine Aquarium. The boatyard operates from the southern shore of the River Plym and offers some harbour berths on pontoons, and also a dry stacking service for boats taken out of the water over the winter. The stacking involved using a crane to lift a boat out of the water in a cradle formed by webbing slings rather than chains that would damage the hull. When a boat was lifted out, a machine similar to a forklift truck would raise it into a metal frame as part of a stack, over six bays high, saving valuable space at ground level. It was Prescott's job to stack the boats and when not moving them around, he was required to clean their hulls before treating them with anti-fouling paint.

His working day usually ended at 5 p.m., but on this particular day he was working late as an owner required his boat to be back in the water the following morning, so he could leave on the high tide. He had completed the anti-fouling work, and all that remained was to lift the six-berth vessel back into the water, ready for collection. The tide was coming in so his timing was perfect. By the time he was ready to return it to the water it was dark and most boatyard workers and pleasure cruising sailors had left for the day. Although he had to complete the task under floodlights, in many ways it was easier as there were no cars or people to consider as he manoeuvred the huge eight-wheeled cradle crane, with the boat slung underneath. After carefully positioning the crane so that it straddled the slipway, he gently lowered it into the river.

He completed the tricky task and slowly returned the crane to the yard. In order to finish the job, he secured the boat to the dock ready for collection the next morning. He then locked the portable cabin office and switched off the yard floodlights, making his way in the semi-darkness to the staff car park; his ten-year-old four-door saloon was the only car left.

He opened the driver's door and was baffled when the interior light did not come on automatically. He thought that perhaps the bulb had gone and made a mental note to replace it the following day. He got in, pulled on his seat belt and started the engine. Apart from no interior light, he also noticed a strange smell in the car and could not think what had caused it, possibly some anti-fouling chemical on his clothes, not that the smells were particularly alike.

Suddenly, he felt the cold barrel of a pistol pressed against the right side of his neck from behind. He froze at first from shock and then from fear, not daring to move. Wide-eyed, he swivelled his gaze to look in his rear-view mirror, while keeping his head stock-still. A face eerily, slowly appeared, barely illuminated by the light from the dashboard.

'Remember me, Greg?' came a voice from the back seat in the semi-darkness.

'You! I thought you were dead!' Prescott was incredulous at the apparition that had just appeared in the mirror.

'No, I'm very much alive, no thanks to you and the others; now it's payback time.'

Prescott began blubbering, pleading for his life: 'It wasn't my idea to abandon you, it was the others. I wanted to help, but Frankie said to leave you, so I just ran for cover or I'd have been shot or blown up.'

The man in the back replied coldly: 'Life is about making choices and you made a wrong one. Now you have to pay for that act of self-interest and cowardice.'

Prescott braced himself and waited for a bullet in the neck. The man did not pull the trigger or release the barrel pressure. Instead, he instructed the petrified Prescott to drive to the top of the slipway. As ordered, he stopped his car at the top of the slope leading down into the river. Without warning, the back-seat passenger, using his free left hand – his right still pressing the gun barrel to Prescott's neck – quickly clasped a rag over his nose and mouth. The strange smell he had sniffed as he got into the car was chloroform.

He briefly lost consciousness and a short time later dreamt that he was sitting on the edge of a swimming pool, fanned by a gentle breeze with cool water swirling around his feet. As he regained consciousness and opened his eyes, his dream became a living nightmare! He suddenly remembered sitting in his car, which was now moving steadily down towards the water. Both the driver and passenger door windows were fully open. To his horror, he watched the rippling water, twinkling in the glare of a marina light, reach the bottom of the windscreen and then rapidly pour in through the open windows. He realised he was alone; his nemesis had gone.

His first action should have been to yank on the handbrake or stamp on the foot brake, but he was still in shock and not thinking clearly; he just wanted to get out. He tried to open his door, but the pressure of the river was too great. He then tried to lever himself out, but his seatbelt held him firm. The water had crept over his waist. He fumbled for the switch on the driver's door that operated the windows. He reasoned that if he could shut them and prevent more water pouring in, it would give him more time to escape. He quickly abandoned that strategy as they did not move; the ignition was not turned on.

In the darkness both his hands reached for the release button of his seatbelt. He found it and pressed it as hard as he could; the belt separated from its holding. Thinking that death by drowning was a horrible way to die and he was about to escape that fate, he briefly relaxed.

His euphoria was short-lived.

Although it had come apart from its anchor, it only moved a few inches. He could not work out why it would not fully release. His fingers fumbled in the water and he felt the knots of a rope that had securely fastened the belt to the underside of the driver's seat.

Water was now gushing into the cabin as the car went deeper into the river. He yanked at the rope with all the strength he could summon, but that just tightened the knots still further. As water crept up his neck, he tipped his head back, lifting his chin to keep his airways above the rising water. He was praying for a miracle to save him; it never happened. His car slipped further into the dark murky waters and became completely submerged. Only a few bubbles could be seen on the surface as the last of the air inside the car was squeezed out.

The man watched from the edge of the harbour wall without emotion as the car slipped beneath the water. He reflected on his good planning and execution: choosing the time when the tide was rising; remembering just how easy it had been to break into Prescott's car and hide in the back, after setting the interior light switch to a central position so it would not come on automatically when he opened the door, and possibly expose him; how he reached over from the back seat to lock the door again, so as not to alert the owner.

With a gun to his neck, it was easy to get him to drive to the top of the slipway. He had only applied a small amount of chloroform to the rag he held over his face as he wanted him to be conscious as he met his end.

With the engine still running and with the man slumped in his seat, it was easy to get out, open the driver's door and electronically wind down both front windows. The rope was the last part of his plan. Pulling out the ignition key, he tossed it into the water. Then he noiselessly shut the car door before reaching in through the open passenger door window to release the handbrake. He moved to the back of the vehicle and with gloved hands encouraged the car to start moving. He only wished that Prescott would regain consciousness before he slipped below the water; his wish had been granted.

He waited for a few minutes just to satisfy himself his task had been a complete success. As the car vanished from view he watched the bubbles on the surface in the dim light. They came from the air that was left in the car and from Prescott's last breath. Waiting was not some sort of macabre voyeurism. He knew that Prescott's only chance of escape would have been for him to stop struggling, which only further intensified the effect of the inertia seat belt. If he had relaxed and gently pulled the belt from his chest, he may have been able to extricate himself by sliding out of the artificially anchored harness. This would not have been an easy task and was made impossible by a state of panic. The man, satisfied that there was to be no great escape, nodded to himself, turned and walked slowly out of the deserted boatyard to his car.

*

High tide on the Plym had been at midnight the night before and by daybreak, the receding water had gradually exposed the roof of the car, alerting an early morning fisherman. Police cars and an ambulance were quickly at the top of the slipway and police divers entered the water. A winch was used to pull the car back up the slipway and onto the flat surface of the boatyard. As it came out, water gushed from the open windows.

DCI Burrows assigned Inspector Best and his team of detectives to the inevitable investigation. If the inspector had any thoughts that the man meant to take his own life they were quickly dispelled by the presence of the rope. There was no doubt: this was premeditated murder.

TEN

All the detectives in King's team, including him, were at their desks soon after 8 a.m. as they knew they had a busy day ahead. Detective Chief Inspector Burrows had asked for a meeting at 8.30 that morning, to discuss the hanging in Plymbridge Woods and the armed robbery, both of which had the potential to become murder investigations. He also wanted an update on the people-trafficking crime. The DCI had a further meeting planned with DI Best and his team straight after this meeting.

King had convened his own pre-meeting to set out the order in which the various cases would be reported on and who would take the lead. At precisely 8.30 all five detectives were gathered around the oval table in the conference room.

Burrows had been appointed as Senior Investigating Officer due to the seriousness of the crimes they were dealing with. As SIO he had to use a variety of skills: investigative ability, crime knowledge and resource management. He was very much dependent on his two inspectors – King and Best – to meet the first two, while he was in the best position to decide on the other.

He opened the meeting: 'Thank you all for coming. Over the last two days we have had a spate of serious crimes in our area and I know you will have heard the tragic news that sixteen illegal immigrants were found dead in the back of the van that picked them up at Slapton Sands. Add to that a hanging, which may develop into a murder investigation, an armed robbery that threatens the life of a homeowner, and a drowning we are treating as murder. Inspector Best and his team are dealing with that last case, which happened in Mount Batten marina last evening.

'I am the Senior Investigating Officer for all three and my main function will be to allocate resources. The most appropriate way I can do that is to be kept well informed as the cases proceed. As ever, I will be relying heavily on both inspectors to carry out the appropriate scrutiny of the evidence and to keep me updated on developments.

'I'm also aware that the detective teams are dealing with other cases, which I need to know about as they will require resourcing too. My primary concern is that the most serious crimes receive the appropriate amount of investigative time. To that end, I will hold regular meetings with the inspectors, both individually and together. So, the purpose of this meeting is to let me know where you are with the cases currently being investigated. Could you start, Richard?'

'Certainly, sir. As you acknowledge, we have a number of investigations underway and as we have been working independently on some, it will be useful for all of us to find out the latest position on each.'

Burrows interjected: 'My apologies for assigning the armed robbery to you at short notice last night. As your team now has the hanging and robbery investigations, I've assigned Inspector Best and his team to deal with the drowning murder.' King nodded his understanding, acknowledging his boss had little scope when allocating police time as police numbers had been reduced over several years.

'As you mentioned the armed robbery in Woolwell, sir, we'll start with that investigation and I'll ask DC Dyson to update us.'

Dyson began: 'I attended the scene of the robbery with Inspector King and DC Hammond. I then went to Derriford Hospital to speak with the victim's wife, Mrs Dangerfield, and even though her husband was in the Intensive Care Unit, she wanted to help. She told me that shortly before 6 p.m. the doorbell rang and, as they were expecting a takeaway to be delivered, her husband answered the door.

'She heard raised voices in the hall followed by a loud bang as a gun discharged. She rushed from the lounge and was confronted by two men. She was horrified to see that her husband was lying injured and bleeding on the floor. He was barely conscious. The men were dressed in black from head to toe and had face coverings on; one was wearing a balaclava and the other a full-face plastic mask with blackened eyes and a broad red grin. From her description I assume he was wearing a "Joker" mask, the Batman adversary.

'Mrs Dangerfield then challenged the man with the gun. She remembered him saying: "He deserved it!" before he demanded she open the safe, threatening to shoot their son if she didn't. Apparently, the other man rushed upstairs.

'She thinks the gunman had a slight Irish accent, but wasn't sure as she was terrified at the time and was more concerned about protecting their young son. The robbers got away with Rolex watches and other jewellery, plus a substantial amount of cash.'

King thanked his DC: 'We later received a message as to what had happened to the car used by the robbers. At about 6.30 p.m. it was reported to be on fire to the east of the city in Southway – a few miles from the scene of the robbery – and was burnt out by the time the Fire and Rescue Service attended. It had been stolen earlier that afternoon from a city-centre side street, which wouldn't have had CCTV coverage, but we're checking nearby cameras for more information. We'll keep you up to date as we get it, sir.'

DCI Burrows asked: 'What's the condition of Mr Dangerfield?'

Dyson responded: 'He is still in intensive care, but the doctors treating him think he will survive the attack. However, he will need several operations to repair the wound in his side.'

King then outlined what they had found in Plymbridge Woods and his suspicion that it was either assisted suicide or premeditated murder: 'In my opinion, it's more likely to be the former as what possible motive could someone have to kill Mr

Freeman who was suffering from dementia? We know that he had worked at Dartmoor Prison as a prison officer, and we wanted to check if there was any link between his former job and his death. Sergeant Harris has been following that line of inquiry.' He then handed over to his sergeant for an update on her meeting with the prison governor.

Harris outlined what had happened on her visit to Dartmoor Prison: 'I spoke with the governor and she identified two former prisoners who had reason to bear a grudge against Mr Freeman. She told me about an incident they were involved in with him, which resulted in ninety days being added to their sentences. They blamed him for the extra three months they had to serve. Both were fairly recently released, and we are trying to locate and interview them about where they were when Mr Freeman was taken from his home.'

'Thank you, Sergeant Harris. Any questions, sir?' King asked his boss.

'Definitely worth pursuing, but any other lines of inquiry?'

King continued: 'From evidence gathered at the scene we are fairly sure the victim was accompanied there. We think that the second person walks with the aid of a stick, possibly wearing a prosthetic. Also, from a tyre track close to the hanging, we may have a lead on the type of vehicle that took both of them to the woods. After this meeting, we will be speaking with Pathologist Gleeson who has completed his post-mortem on Mr Freeman. That may give us further information on the case.'

'Please let me know if anything develops.' Burrows requested.

'Will do, sir. The other case is the people-trafficking near Torcross. Sadly, we now know how that ended, but we're still determined to find out as much as we can. It may be that anything we uncover could be fed back to the French authorities, who may be able to identify the traffickers and put an end to their evil trade. DC Hammond can update us.'

Hammond stood up to address the meeting and moved over to a screen: 'DC Dyson and I found two pieces of crucial evidence during the course of our investigation. After an eyewitness came forward we were able to look at dash cam footage.' With that he pressed a handheld remote device and the dash cam images appeared on a screen behind him.

'From that we were able to identify the van and its registration. We all now know the tragic outcome at Strensham Services on the M5. Apart from the trafficker who was shot dead at the services, our colleagues in the West Midland Police have made several arrests.

'DC Dyson found a satellite phone in the abandoned RIB and that has been passed to our Cyber Unit. We are hopeful the information on the phone will at least tell us where the traffickers' trip began. As I mentioned, we can then liaise with the French Police.'

'Any questions, sir?' King prompted.

'No, that all seems well under control. I just hope they are able to identify all the migrants and inform their families; not an easy task. If you do uncover any information which could be useful for our French counterparts, see me first and I will make the initial contact after informing the chief constable. Well done to all those involved.'

The inspector nodded his thanks: 'That's where we are, sir, with the investigations and I'll keep you updated on developments.'

'Thank you all.' The DCI left the room leaving King to assign jobs. Normally he preferred his team to work in pairs, but knew it would be quicker to address the various issues if he gave individuals specific tasks.

'Right, I'm going to see the pathologist about the post-mortem on Freeman; Lucy, see what progress we have made in tracking down the two ex-cons; Sam, contact the family liaison support officer assigned to the Dangerfield family and check on Mr Dangerfield's condition. What he can tell us may be crucial. Also ask his wife if she has remembered anything else about the attack. Then, check if there were any CCTV cameras around the area where the abandoned and burnt-out car was left. Alex, follow up with the Cyber Unit on the satellite phone found in the RIB. We are too late to stop the deaths of the migrants, but any information to prevent more tragedies and help catch the traffickers in France has got to be worthwhile. Any questions?' King was in a determined mood and was pleased his team had a number of leads to pursue.

'Sam, we are going to the same place, so I'll share a car with you. See you all back here at 8.30

tomorrow morning. In the meantime, if you think more urgent action is needed before then after your follow-up, let me know.'

ELEVEN

Inspector King had arranged to meet forensic pathologist, John Gleeson, in the local hospital mortuary. DC Dyson drove them both to the hospital. While she headed for the Intensive Care Unit, he went to the mortuary on the sub-ground floor. He knew the way as he had been there many times before.

As he entered the main laboratory – having donned slipover plastic covering on his feet, white coat and hairnet – in the middle of the room lying on a marble slab was a body covered by a white sheet. Gleeson sat at a computer on the far side of the room similarly dressed to King. He looked up as the inspector approached.

'Hello, Richard. I'm a busy man, as no doubt you are too, so let's get down to business,' the pathologist said in a no-nonsense manner that did not give offence.

'Suits me, John. So what have you got for me?'

'Interesting case, our Mr Freeman. Death by hanging falls into one of two categories: so-called 'typical hangings' and 'atypical hangings'. In the first, the knot of the ligature will be at the nape of the neck – the back of the neck near the hairline – whereas in an atypical hanging the knot of the ligature will be anywhere but the nape. Mr Freeman's was an atypical hanging. This would suggest to me that the rope was placed around his neck by someone else. However, I can't be sure of that, but I am minded to be influenced by the other circumstances surrounding this case. The fact that there was no vehicle left at the scene does indicate that outside assistance was given.'

'He could have taken a taxi?' King said testing the hypothesis.

'You're right, he could have, but the other evidence you found would tend to suggest he was accompanied. If he was helped, it would appear he accepted it willingly as I haven't found any signs of a struggle.'

'So what will you be putting on the death certificate as the cause?'

'I will be informing the coroner that the death was either an assisted dying or unlawful killing. As there were no other signs on the body of a struggle, I am inclined to the former, but can't rule out the latter. Of course, it will be for the coroner to decide at the inquest into Mr Freeman's death, but I would think a likely verdict would be unlawful killing. You know as well as I do, Richard, assisting someone to end their life is a criminal offence. The other factor to take into account was Mr Freeman's mental state. As he was suffering from dementia it would be difficult to convince the coroner or a jury that he had agreed to end his life.'

'Thanks, John. Anything else?'

'Yes, one other thing I noticed, Richard, is he has a small tattoo on the inside of his right wrist. It's in script and I'd say the letters are twelve-point size, so about half a centimetre large; let me show you.'

Gleeson moved across to the marble slab and pulled back a corner of the covering sheet to partly reveal the body of Daniel Freeman. The white pallor of his skin did not surprise King. Despite seeing many dead bodies in his career, he never became blasé.

The pathologist held the right hand of the corpse and turned it sideways to show the underside of his forearm: 'You can see the tattoo reads: "Celer et Audax". I did Latin at school so I know it means "Swift and Bold", but I don't know what it relates to. Perhaps it could be some sort of regimental motto?'

King had seen enough. He never stayed longer in the morgue than he had to. He thanked Gleeson and left.

*

DC Dyson once again visited the ICU at Derriford Hospital and spoke to Mrs Dangerfield, who was having a cup of tea in an anteroom. Clearly, she had not slept since her husband was brought in soon after six o'clock the previous evening. She was alone as her son was being cared for by a relative. The detective had arranged for the family support officer to be present and they both arrived at the same time. The detective began by gently asking about her husband's condition, and was told he was still in intensive care, but the surgeons were optimistic he would recover. Dyson noted the omission of the word "fully".

When quietly prompted to add anything to what she had already told the police the night before, Mrs Dangerfield closed her eyes to relive in her mind the horror of the previous evening. She opened them and looked at the detective.

'The more I think about it the more convinced I am of the gunman's accent. It was definitely Irish and also I noticed he was wearing black trainers and they were spattered with small white dots.' Dyson made a note and thanked the remarkably brave wife and left wishing her husband a speedy recovery. She knew that the surgeons would be able to estimate how long the physical healing process would take; the mental scars would last a lifetime.

*

Following the devastating news of the lorry deaths, DC Hammond turned his attention to the satellite phone and called into the Cyber Unit to speak with the police cyber expert, with whom he had left the traffickers' phone.

'Just about to ring you, Alex,' announced a cheery individual who spent his days in front of a bank of computer screens.

'I've examined the phone you gave me that was found in the RIB and can tell you that it left the French coast at a place called Anse Saint-Martin.' He then switched to one of the screens in front of him and brought up Google Earth. The initial screen showed the northern French coast and the Channel Islands. He quickly enlarged the picture, homing in on the cove he had referred to, with a car park shown nearby.

'You can see that the road to the cove is the only way in and out. That's where the journey, or should I say the Channel crossing, started. The unfortunate migrants would first have had to be transported to the departure point.'

'Did you manage to get anything else from the phone?'

'The device was switched on at around 11.30 p.m., I assume when it was on its way to the coast. It indicates it came from the direction of Cherbourg, which is about sixteen miles to the east of the cove. I can also confirm something you already know – that its course was set for Slapton Sands. Nothing else, sorry, Alex.'

Hammond thanked him for the information but was not quite sure how he was going to use it. He decided to ring his boss.

'I've just spoken with the cyber guys about the satellite phone, sir, and we now know the part of the coast where the migrants boarded the RIB. I'll prepare a report for you and the DCI and let you have it ASAP.'

'While you're on, Alex, I'd like your help in the hanging investigation. The victim has a tattoo on his arm and I'd like to find out to what it relates. It's "Celer et Audax", which is Latin for "Swift and Bold". Sounds like some sort of regimental motto. Let me know as soon as you've cracked it.' Before he ended the call, he spelled out the Latin name letter by letter.

*

Sergeant Harris was on the track of Reginald Connelly and David Willis, who were both released from Dartmoor Prison in the last few months, in connection with the death of Daniel Freeman. Connelly was known to be sleeping rough in Exeter, while Willis was now living at an address in Newlyn, south-west Cornwall.

Tracking down Reginald Connelly was not easy, but after visiting several places where rough sleepers met during the day, Exeter Police found him. Having confirmed his identity, he was then asked about his whereabouts on the day of the hanging. Through an alcoholic haze he gave vague answers to the questions, as every day to him was the same as any other. When he stood up, unsteady due to excess drink, the officers decided that this dishevelled alcoholic was not the man their colleagues in Plymouth were looking for.

*

Harris contacted Truro Police as they were less than an hour from David Willis's last known address. Getting them to follow the lead would save her four hours on the road – two hours each way. She explained why she was interested in him. If he became a confirmed suspect, after the initial enquiry, she would then travel down to formally interview him. The sergeant gave them the date and time when the hanging took place, and also provided details of what her inspector had deduced from observations in Plymbridge Woods. In particular, she asked them to check the type of vehicle he owned and, crucially, if he used a walking stick.

A police car was duly despatched from Truro to Newlyn, arriving forty-five minutes later at a flat in a run-down part of the town. They knocked on the door and a middle-aged man, with a dishevelled appearance, answered. When he saw the uniformed officers it quickly became apparent he was not going to be cooperative. Willis had done his time and fiercely objected to any further contact with the police or the prison service. When he saw them standing on his front doorstep, he tried to slam the door shut. A size-eleven police-issue boot prevented him succeeding.

They decided to arrest him, not for his belligerent attitude, but because of what they saw standing in a battered umbrella stand in the hallway: a walking stick.

TWELVE

A Spar convenience store in Plymouth on the west side of the city was open twenty-four hours a day. The number of customers using the shop reduced markedly towards the late evening and beyond, so one member of staff could usually cope with serving as well as topping up the shelves. Throughout the day most customers were compliant with wearing a face covering in accordance with the government's Coronavirus guidelines. The customer who entered just after eleven o'clock that evening also had his face covered, but not with the surgical mask variety.

The man had loitered outside the shop for a few minutes with a clear view of the inside. He was nonchalantly smoking a cigarette, waiting for his opportunity to strike. The assistant left the protection of her secure Perspex-enclosed booth for a moment to pick up a packet of biscuits that had fallen off a shelf; the would-be robber saw his chance. He glanced furtively around and pulled on his mask before barging into the shop. Using his left hand, he grabbed the female assistant by her hair and frogmarched her back to her booth. His right hand was already holding a gun.

'Open the till now!' the man wearing a "Joker" mask demanded of the startled assistant. She was now visibly shaking as she was forced back behind the counter. The sawn-off shotgun toted by the robber was not needed to frighten the young woman; his menacing mask and manner were sufficient. She had watched *Joker*, the psychological thriller, several times and knew there was nothing remotely funny about this man.

'There... there's not much as I empty it into the strong box under the counter every hour, and my manager is the only one who knows the code to open it,' she whimpered and pointed down to her left, her head still being forced back by the robber's forceful grip of her hair.

When she had opened the till, he released the grip on her hair and prodded her with his gun, forcing her back further into the limited space behind the counter, so he could reach in and grab what few notes it contained. Angered by what little money there was, he used the butt of his gun to smash a display of scratch cards on the counter, before ripping open the opaque screen fronting the tobacco cabinet and stuffing random cigarette packets into a bag he retrieved from one of the pockets of his black hoodie. He held the gun in his right hand – shorn of two-thirds of its barrels it was considerably lighter – with his index finger wrapped around the trigger. He pointed it at the trembling assistant as he grabbed bottles of Southern Comfort and Chivas Regal off a nearby shelf and, with some difficulty, thrust them one-handed into his bag that he had placed on the floor.

Still angered by the lack of rich pickings, with one defiant parting gesture he looked up to the corner of the serving booth at a security camera that was permanently trained on paying customers. With a snarl, he lifted his gun and blasted the device. Such was his arrogance, he was unconcerned that the gunshot may have alerted passers-by; he left the shop, still wearing his mask and laden with his bulging bag. A car quickly appeared from around the corner, braking hard to stop directly opposite the shop. The "Joker" climbed in and the car roared off.

The sound of the gunshot still reverberated around the store and seemed to linger for several seconds. The traumatised shop assistant rang 999 and armed officers were at the scene within a few minutes.

*

The following morning after the store robbery, a uniformed officer, PC Sugden, who had been one of the first to arrive at the Spar shop after the armed police, asked to speak with DI King as soon as he arrived at the central police station in Plymouth. Although the officer's shift had already ended, he waited as he wanted to pass on some information at this early opportunity. He was aware that the inspector was investigating the so-called "Bonanza Robbery" that had taken place two nights before. No detective had yet attended the store robbery the previous evening and the PC felt the need to give information to the wily detective, face to face. King was happy to oblige.

King said: 'Of course, constable, I'd like to hear what happened.'

'Well, sir, just after 11 p.m. a man entered the Spar store in Devonport, brandishing a sawn-off shotgun. He demanded money and the terrified assistant opened the till. Fortunately, it is emptied into a safe every hour, so there weren't many notes. The robber stole some cash, some packs of cigarettes and two bottles of whisky. Apparently he was angry at the small amount in the till, so he blasted the security camera. He then got into a getaway car, driven by an accomplice, and drove off at high speed.

'A man walking his dog close to the shop had heard the gunshot and saw the robbers leave. He noted the registration number of the car and all units were alerted. It was later found at St Budeaux about a mile to the north of the robbery. It had been torched.'

'Did the security camera footage survive the blast?' asked King.

'Oh yes, the camera was completely destroyed, but the recording was saved.'

'This is all very interesting, constable, but why did you specifically want to tell me about the robbery?'

'When I was having lunch in the staff restaurant with DC Dyson yesterday, she told me about the "Bonanza Robbery". From what she told me, I think it's the same fella and his mate.'

'Why do you say that?'

'Two reasons, sir: firstly, a sawn-off shotgun was used in both robberies and using that type of weapon in a robbery is very rare in Plymouth. Secondly, because the robber was wearing a "Joker" mask. Over lunch, DC Dyson mentioned to me the armed robber in the "Bonanza Robbery" wore the same type of mask. I don't know if it'll help, but I think both robberies could be linked.'

'Good work, constable. Can you let DC Dyson have the camera footage please? I know you're off duty now, but it would be very helpful, so please send it to her computer before you leave. I'll see DCI Burrows and tell him of the suspected link between the crimes, and that my detectives will take on the investigation of the Spar store robbery. Thanks again.'

*

Soon after King's chat with PC Sugden, the rest of his team arrived at the police station for the prearranged early morning meeting. They exchanged greetings, but noticing their boss was sitting in his chair staring at the ceiling and was sucking a sweet, they did not interrupt.

'Grab a coffee you three and let's update each other on our investigations. Sam, I've had a very interesting chat with the PC you had a lunch with yesterday. Apparently a convenience store was robbed late last night. He attended and gave me some very useful information. He's off duty now, but said he'd send you a copy of the footage to your computer from the shop's CCTV before he left; it should make for interesting viewing. Check your inbox and you can show us at the meeting.

'Alex, I'd like us to watch again what was recorded by the CCTV at the "Bonanza" property. Get it put onto your laptop and we'll view it at the meeting as I want us to compare that recording with the one Sam's bringing.'

'Will do, sir, and I want to suggest follow-up action on the traffickers after speaking with our cyber colleagues.'

'Okay, we can do that alongside the other updates. Lucy, find out from Truro Police what's happening about the arrest of the suspect with the walking stick. I've been thinking about the "Bonanza" job and something PC Sugden told me about the robbery last night. The mask and the gun aren't the only similarities. It's 8.20 now so let's meet here at 8.45. I'll update the DCI on whatever comes out of our meeting.

'You know what, team, investigations begin with the bad people having complete anonymity, then, thanks to your diligence, slowly, but inexorably, we get closer to identifying who they are. I think this coming week is going to be a very good one for us and a very bad one for them.'

THIRTEEN

As arranged, King and his team met in the conference room at 8.45. The inspector was the last to arrive carrying a cup of tepid coffee. DCs Dyson and Hammond had laptops open in front of them and Sergeant Harris was poised, notebook at the ready.

King was in a determined mood: 'We've a lot to get through so let's crack on. I will update the DCI after the meeting. First let's look at the footage from the "Bonanza Robbery" and then the sequence taken by the convenience store camera before it got blasted.'

The DCs swivelled their laptops side by side so King and Harris could compare what was on the screens. Dyson played her sequence. It showed the robber, in his "Joker" mask, bursting into the shop as the young female assistant was replacing something that had fallen from a shelf. There was no sound on the recording, but the detectives could imagine what the gunman was shouting as he grabbed her hair and yanked her head backwards. They watched as he stuffed a bag with cash from the till, cigarettes and bottles of spirits. He then looked straight at the CCTV and the recording ended abruptly as he blasted the camera. Dyson rewound the recording to the point just before he fired and paused the sequence leaving his image on screen.

Hammond then showed the footage from the CCTV at "Bonanza". Once again the detectives watched the robbers park the stolen car inside the entrance and walk towards the house. Like Dyson, Hammond similarly finished with a still image as they approached the porch. All the detectives looked from one to the other and King was the first to speak.

'There's no doubt in my mind that the guy in the "Joker" mask at the scene of both robberies is the same person. He looks the same, not just because of his black clothes and mask, but also his height. He looks to me to be 190 centimetres, or six foot two or three, as he comes towards the porch. In the shop he appears to be above average height. Obviously, the weapon looks identical as far as we can tell, but it's partially obscured in the "Bonanza" image. Anyway, I think we can be fairly sure the "Joker" is the same guy. What other conclusions can be drawn from the two crimes?' His question hung in the air, so he took a sherbet lemon from a bag in his pocket and waited. The other detectives were rather nonplussed, so the inspector continued.

'Let's look beyond the footage. What have we got on this man, and his accomplice? If I were a betting man, which I'm not, I'd wager that at the moment they are feeling fairly confident, hence the two crimes in quick succession. When thieves sense that they can't be caught and are out of reach to the police, they increase their offending and possibly start making mistakes; they get cocky. My guess is they'll do another robbery in the next few days.

'I've had a few thoughts that I'd like to share with you. Apart from the "Joker" mask being worn by one of the robbers and also the sawn-off shotgun, what else links the two crimes? I can think of two things: firstly, there is the fact that a car was stolen to help them commit the crimes. Those cars were taken from more or less the same part of the city, close to Southway. They were abandoned and set alight in a different part of Plymouth from where they were stolen, but they were torched not far from each other in Tamerton Foliot. So I see a pattern emerging.

'The other important point is something Sam reported after speaking with Mrs Dangerfield, the robbery victim's wife. Can you remember, Sam, what the wife said after she challenged the robber in her hallway?'

'I can, sir, he said: "He deserved it!"'

'He deserved it. What does that tell us? It tells us that the victim was known to the robber. Why else would he say he deserved it if he didn't know him? So, Sam, I'd like you to check on Mr Dangerfield's progress and, crucially, ask his doctor when you can interview him. We need to ask him if he recalls any very disgruntled customers, or maybe employees in his estate agency business, who might have wished to do him harm. Also ask Mrs Dangerfield if her husband isn't well enough to be interviewed. She may be able to help us. Don't forget the Irish accent she mentioned when you first interviewed her. If she can think of a person with a grudge and he has that accent, it will give us a solid link.

'Back to my first point: in order to catch these robbers, we need to be alert to any future cars reported stolen between 4 p.m. and 6 p.m. from the same area of the city as the other car thefts. If we get a report of a stolen vehicle from that area between those times it might, I stress might, be the prelude to another robbery. If a report comes in of a car theft, we must mobilise every patrol car and alert CCTV operators monitoring the city's cameras, to be on the lookout for the vehicle. If located it should be monitored, not stopped. If we can track it, hopefully before a robbery, so much the better, but if we can't, we could possibly catch them in the act. As always, armed police will be on standby as we know the "Joker" carries a weapon. If we can't locate the stolen vehicle before or during another robbery, then we must scour the city after the robbery is reported and find them before they set it alight. I will inform DCI Burrows what we have planned and seek his permission for the police helicopter to be on stand-by to assist.

'All I have said is purely speculation and may be a tad fanciful. It must not distract us from the ongoing investigations into both robberies. By putting our colleagues on notice, it will help us to be in a state of readiness to act when speed of response will be crucial.

'Right, let's move on to Lucy and the man with the walking stick we suspect was involved in the death of Mr Freeman.'

'I've spoken with the Truro Police, sir, who have interviewed him and he has given "no comment" answers to all questions. He seems to be a very bitter man who feels he is being victimised as an ex-con, so he's refusing to cooperate. He might well have sought retribution for Freeman's role in extending his stay in prison. The police will try to get some answers out of him later this morning and let me know what happens. I don't presently see the need to travel down there, but if he starts talking, I will. The other thing to note, sir, is although he uses a walking stick, he does not wear a prosthetic. I'll let you know what develops.'

'Thank you, Lucy. Alex, any update on the trafficking investigation?'

'Yes, sir. After the tragic deaths of all the migrants, I have prepared a report highlighting where the traffickers loaded the RIB with the migrants. Our cyber team looked through the historical data on the satellite phone we found in the RIB. It could be that the cove it was launched from is the regular place the traffickers use. On Google Earth it looks an ideal spot. It's isolated and has a road down to the beach that I suspect is only used during the day by beachgoers. At night there is nothing at the cove to attract people. Therefore, it is a perfect place for the traffickers to operate. It also has a good-sized car park that can easily accommodate a lorry and a vehicle with a RIB on a trailer. I don't think the traffickers would risk sending a boat to collect the migrants from the beach as the French Police patrol all along that stretch of coast as they know it is a likely departure point for migrants.

'In my report, sir, I have suggested that their police may like to fix a movement-sensitive covert-surveillance camera, fitted with night vision, that will trigger an alarm at the nearest local gendarmerie if motion is detected after dark. As I estimate it must take, say, fifteen minutes from arrival at the car park to get the migrants into a RIB; the early warning should give the police time to catch the traffickers in the act. A police boat launched from Cherbourg, just along the coast, could be there in a matter of minutes. As there is only one road in and out of Anse Saint-Martin cove, the traffickers would be trapped if the police approached by road and sea. Without wishing to tell them their job, sir, I have advised that armed police attend as we know these men are ruthless.

'I know the DCI wanted to make the initial contact with his French counterpart, so I have taken the liberty of finding out the name of the gendarme in charge of that part of the coast – she is based in Cherbourg – and marked the report for her attention. The whole report is written in English, but I have also attached a translation into French. If he is in agreement, the DCI could mail my report to her, after making a courtesy call.'

'Any update on the traffickers here?'

'I understand the van that was used, which had false plates, is actually owned by a small haulage firm called Fox and Sons. The man shot dead at Strensham Services was one of the sons. The other son and father have been arrested and charged.'

'What about the other task I set you to find out about the origin of the tattoo on Freeman's wrist?'

'I found the answer to that, sir, just before we came into this meeting. "Celer et Audax" is Latin and translates as "Swift and Bold" and is the regimental motto of The Rifles regiment in Exeter. That's all I've got at the moment, sir.'

'Very thorough, Alex, well done. I'll put your proposals about contacting the French authorities to DCI Burrows. That brings me to the hanging in Plymbridge Woods. As mentioned earlier, Lucy is pursuing the suspect held by Truro Police and I am reviewing all the evidence. I've also spoken with the pathologist and he has asked to see me with Inspector Best after this meeting. I'll wait to hear what he wants to talk to us about before reporting to DCI Burrows. Thank you all.'

*

King returned to his desk to find Inspector Best sitting in his seat reading a report from a folder about the hanging in Plymbridge Woods that King had left for him.

'Hi, Jim. I see you've read the report on the hanging. What do you think John Gleeson wants to see us about?'

'Not sure, Richard. The DCI gave me the drowning case in Mount Batten yesterday and I know John was carrying out a post-mortem on the dead man, but I don't know why he wants to see us both.'

'Let's find out, shall we?'

*

'Ah, gentlemen, no doubt you are wondering why I wanted to see you both together. Follow me please.' The two inspectors followed the pathologist into an adjoining room, which was like stepping into a fridge. Best shivered and Gleeson commented that the temperature had to be that cold to stop decomposition of the bodies, which were stored in the room. He went over to a wall of lockers, similar to what would be found in any changing room gymnasium; only, the locker doors here were a metre square and the locker itself over two metres long inside. He opened the door of the third one down, fourth one along. He pulled out a slightly concave tray to reveal a white shroud that was evidently covering a corpse.

'This is the body of Daniel Mark Freeman who was found hanging in Plymbridge Woods. I've already shown Inspector King what the victim had tattooed on the inside of his right wrist.' With that he pulled back the edge of the shroud to reveal Freeman's right arm. He turned it over and showed them the tattoo: 'Celer et Audax'. King understood why the pathologist adopted formal names when he was in his lab in the presence of other detectives, but was wondering why he was showing him the tattoo again.

'For Inspector Best's benefit, the translation from the Latin is: "Swift and Bold". I've left it to Inspector King to find out the derivation.' He straightened the shroud and smoothly slid the body back into its refrigerated mortuary cabinet.

'Follow me please, gentlemen.' He then moved along the row of doors and stopped in front of one, checked the name shown on a card slipped into a holder, opened the small door and pulled out a tray with another body, similarly covered by a white shroud.

'This, gentlemen, is the body of Malcolm Edward Prescott who drowned in the River Plym yesterday evening as Inspector Best already knows. While examining the body an interesting fact appeared.' He pulled back the edge of the shroud to show the victim's right arm and turned it over to reveal the inside of his right wrist. The detectives both leaned forward and to their utter amazement the same tattoo, identical in every detail, was shown on Prescott's wrist.

FOURTEEN

Following the revelation by Pathologist Gleeson that the two deaths were linked, the inspectors urgently needed to speak with DCI Burrows. A meeting was hastily arranged and King explained the discovery of an identical tattoo on the wrists of the dead men.

Burrows decided that King and Best should now work together on the cases rather than reallocating one case to each. Best left the meeting after agreeing with King to meet him again immediately afterwards. King remained behind to update the DCI on his team's other investigations. He particularly wanted to pass Hammond's report to Burrows and explain his suggestions designed to catch the French traffickers. After leaving his boss, King found Jim Best, once again, waiting for him by his desk.

'Sorry to keep you, Jim. In view of what John Gleeson showed us, I think we should speak with the widow of Mr Freeman again as Mr Prescott had no known next of kin. If it's okay with you, I'd like Sergeant Harris to come with us as she attended the first interview.' Best readily agreed.

*

For the second time King and Harris arrived at Joan Freeman's house, this time accompanied by Inspector Best. Sergeant Harris rang the doorbell. Ben Freeman opened the door with a similarly inhospitable greeting as the first time they called: 'Not you two again! And now you've brought someone else with you! Can't you leave my mother in peace as she's still grieving for my dad?' With that he slammed the door shut.

Harris was usually slow to anger, but it was evident that the son's manner had greatly irritated her. She moved forward, her rigid straight index finger at the ready to press the doorbell again with what would probably have been a longer ring than the first.

However, before her finger could reach the bell button, her inspector gently restrained her outstretched arm with his left hand placed lightly on her forearm. He slowly shook his head, sending out a clear message for her not to press it again. She knew that he could be fearsome and formidable with people who were uncooperative. She stood back with Inspector Best to let her boss put the stroppy son in his place. King stepped forward and gave the door a gentle tap with his crooked index finger. The son once again jerked the door open with a face like thunder, clearly intent on denying them access.

'We are sorry to call on you and your mother again, Ben, but we have continued to investigate the death of your father and have reason to believe it may be linked to another death, and we want to ask Mrs Freeman if she could help us. By the way, this is Inspector Best who is dealing with the linked investigation. I can assure you that in answering our further questions, should your mother become distressed, you have my word that we will terminate the interview immediately. Can we come in please?'

King's manner completely defused the previous confrontation avoiding the necessity of a more strident insistence, which was his fall-back position. His conciliatory tone had the desired effect as the son stood back and fully opened the door to allow the detectives to enter. Harris was, not for the first time, in awe of her boss and quietly reflected on appreciating when to be assertive and when a more conciliatory approach may be the better option. Clearly King, in this case, had chosen the right one.

Mrs Freeman occupied the same seat on the sofa as she had when they had originally spoken to her soon after her husband's death. Her son was perched on the arm of the sofa, less in scrutiny and more in interest of what his mother had to say. Sergeant Harris was poised to take notes. After introductions, King was keen to find out more.

'We are sorry to intrude further on your grief, Mrs Freeman, but there has been a development while investigating your husband's death. I have told Ben that we hope you can help us and it is not our intention to cause you further distress.'

He never once referred to her husband's death as murder or suicide. She was clutching a white handkerchief in her right hand and nodded her agreement to continue with the interview.

'Thank you, Mrs Freeman, we will try and keep this short. When we last spoke, you mentioned that Mr Freeman worked at Dartmoor Prison and was also an Army reservist. Please could you tell us more about his time at work and in the Army and also about any close colleagues?'

Mrs Freeman wanted to cooperate and give the detectives as much information as possible, if it helped find out what had happened to her husband: 'Dan had worked for the prison service, mainly at Dartmoor Prison, since around 1995 until 2019. Although he quite liked his work, and it was well paid, he wanted, as he put it, more adventure in his life. So, in 2010, he, and six of his mates, all decided to become reservists for the Army. They joined the 6th Battalion, The Rifles based in Exeter. By joining the British Army they thought they could have the best of both worlds by retaining their civilian jobs, whilst spending time on Army duties. When he joined, he was told that reservists spent around thirty days a year on duty, and their basic training would be included in that time. That's pretty much what had happened, although when he was sent abroad, that increased his overall annual days with the regiment for that year.'

'You said he joined up with his mates; can you remember their names?'

'Oh yes, inspector, as occasionally they, with their wives and girlfriends, would all get together for drinks and possibly a meal as well. The mates first got to know each other at school, so they were all about the same age. They called themselves the

Class of '88. Although they each followed their own career after leaving school, some went off to university, while others got jobs, they continued their friendship. Dan called them his "blood brothers". He told me that on one of their frequent pub crawls with all his mates, somebody mentioned about joining the Army as reservists because they could keep their jobs and be released for a few weeks here and there. They hoped if they all joined up at the same time they could do their basic training together and also, hopefully, as Dan put it, go on manoeuvres together. Obviously, the pay they received would also be a bonus.

'I can tell you the names of all of six of them. I think it was Carl, that's Carl Brackley, who suggested they should give each other nicknames, which is rather ironic as he was the only friend not to get one! He was the one that also initially dubbed the group The Magnificent Seven. They even wrote to each other in a code that only they knew. I could never understand the messages on Christmas cards from his mates. My Dan said it was something to do with missing out letters in the alphabet. In truth, I thought it was a bit childish.

'Anyway, let me see, there was Malcolm Prescott and because he worked in a boatyard next to the River Plym, he was nicknamed The Boatman. Malc never

married and actually lives on a houseboat moored on the River Tamar. His work

tends to be seasonal, which gives him the opportunity to spend time in the Army.'

King chose not to add to her grief by telling her of his demise.

'Bob Higgins is another friend in the group; they called him Hurricane after the famous snooker player from Northern Ireland. Although he is a Janner, having been born and raised in Plymouth, he moved to Somerset to be closer to a girl he met while on Army duty. I don't think it worked out and they parted. Dan said he didn't come back to Plymouth as he subcontracts work from a big company that sells TVs and computers in Yeovil. I think he mainly fixes satellite dishes to houses. He left the Army soon after he got back from the tour in Iraq. He doesn't keep in touch anymore. When I asked Dan why, he said Hurricane fell out with his mates, but wouldn't say what it was over.

'Another of the mates is Derek Clayton. After he left school, and during his gap year before going to Exeter Uni, Derek sailed solo from Plymouth in Devon to Plymouth, Massachusetts to recreate the famous voyage taken by the Pilgrim Fathers nearly 400 years ago; sooner him than me. Because of his feat, they nicknamed him The Pilgrim. Dan thought he was something to do with survival courses run as team-building exercises for businesses. Apparently, he was often out on Dartmoor in all weathers. He also used to teach parachuting, so he was a real action man. Sadly, he was killed when the regiment was on a mission in Iraq that was all rather hush-hush. I knew Derek was born on Tresco in the Scilly Isles and was a proud Scillonian. Dan told me he wanted to retire to the island of his birth; unfortunately, he never fulfilled his wish.

'Then there was Colin Franks, who they simply dubbed Frankie. He sort of became the unofficial leader of the group, probably because he is a very confident person, although I found him to be a little brusque. Dan told me that on a couple of occasions when the mates were out socialising and having a discussion, Frankie didn't like being contradicted. He certainly liked to get his own way. Just before the tour in Iraq he was made up to corporal, which was quite an accolade considering he was only a reservist. When Dan and I first knew him he was dating a beautiful young woman, called Bonnie, and eventually they got married. He was some sort of financial consultant, so was never short of money.

'Greg Bryson, another friend they simply called Bill after the American travel writer. Greg is a self-employed graphic designer so, again, he could easily take time off to do Army work. I think he got married and lives on the outskirts of Plymouth. You'll have to forgive me, inspector, as some of what I'm telling you was only passed on to me by Dan.' As she mentioned his name, she paused and gently blew her nose. It was obvious to the detectives this was to prevent her breaking down as she wanted to finish giving them all the information she could remember.

'Carl Brackley, as I mentioned earlier, was the only one without a nickname as they couldn't think what to call him. Carl was a part owner of a service garage over Ivybridge way. Many a time he was called on to make minor repairs to vehicles whilst on duty with the Army. His wife tragically died of cancer two or three years ago. So sad that, along with Derek, he never made it back from Iraq.

'So, that leaves my Dan. He was simply nicknamed Danny Boy. At first he really enjoyed being a reservist, but after the short tour in Iraq, he was never the same again. Then his dementia started a year or so ago and he's steadily gone downhill ever since.

'Regrettably, as I mentioned before, Derek and Carl were killed in Iraq in January 2018 when all the friends, and other reservists, were sent out there for a month to help fight the insurgents. Dan didn't want to talk about the incident when his two mates were killed. I was told by someone else it was an improvised explosive device that killed them. I didn't press him, as I was concerned that reliving it may lead to post-traumatic stress. In fact, I suspect the incident may have triggered his dementia. I can't prove it and, anyway, I've already had a settlement from the Army as he was medically retired.'

King sensed that Mrs Freeman had finished talking about all the friends and then asked: 'Did they all have the same tattoo on the inside of their right wrist?'

'Yes. Dan told me it was when they were celebrating the successful completion of their basic training and they went on a pub crawl in Exeter. Apparently, after several pints, one of them suggested they all get the regimental motto tattooed on their arm. Once they had their tattoos done, The Boatman, that's Malc Prescott, suggested that they should get their wrists pricked, close to the tattoos, to draw a small amount of blood. Dan said that they all then smeared each other's arms. That's when Dan said they became "blood brothers".'

Mrs Freeman seemed more than happy to talk about her husband and his friends. King thought there was something cathartic in her reminiscences and he wasn't about to interrupt her again. Neither, for that matter, was her son. She was now in full flow.

'The mates didn't often fall out, except on one occasion, which I can vividly remember. It was at a Christmas disco at the barracks when Derek, who was drunk at the time, came on strong to Colin's then girlfriend, Bonnie, on the dance floor. I noticed that they had started dancing to a fast number, and when that ended they stayed on the floor for a slow number during which Derek's hands, what shall I say, began to wander. Bonnie took offence, broke away and slapped Derek's face. Colin, who was also the worse for wear, had seen what led to the slap and walked over, pulled his girlfriend away, and hit Derek full in his face. The other five mates pulled them apart and Colin and Bonnie left. It all seemed to be forgotten, but I wasn't sure Colin was prepared to forget the incident that easily; nor, come to that, was Derek. Sorry, inspector, I'm rambling.'

'That's fine, Mrs Freeman. One last question: was Dan still in touch with all of the mates who survived the tour in Iraq?'

'Well, he was until about fourteen months ago. As his dementia got worse he saw less and less of them, which is hardly surprising as he struggled to remember who they were. But even before then, Dan never mentioned Bob Higgins. Even before he moved away, I got the impression Hurricane didn't seem to want to know his mates anymore. It's a shame really, as after two of them were killed, I thought it would have brought the other five closer together.'

The detectives had achieved what they wanted from the interview and left, thanking Mrs Freeman and her son on their way out.

*

On their way back to the central police station with Harris driving, King popped a sherbet lemon into his mouth and became deep in thought: 'What do you think, Jim?'

'The link between the two investigations is becoming clearer, Richard. The most pressing thing is to find out about the other mates and maybe warn them to be on their guard.'

'I agree, Jim.' King then turned to his sergeant: 'Lucy, when we get back to the station, contact The Rifles in Exeter and arrange a visit. From memory I think you'll find the regiment at Wyvern Barracks, close to the Royal Devon and Exeter Hospital. Find out what you can about all the men Mrs Freeman mentioned. We already know the fate of four of the seven mates and now we need to know if the other three are still alive and, if so, where they're living. I'm sure the Army will have their addresses. We need those names and addresses as a matter of urgency. Let's get back to the station and, hopefully, you can make that appointment to visit the barracks later today or better still get the information by phone or mail. I think progress in our investigation hinges on us, to coin a phrase, being swift and bold!'

Almost as an afterthought he added: 'Oh, Lucy, you can thank Truro Police and tell them to release Willis. He's no longer a suspect.'

*

Back at his desk and all alone, King reflected on not paying more attention to Freeman's tattoo after it had first been brought to his attention by the pathologist after the post-mortem. Freeman's wife had mentioned that her husband had served as a reservist, but at that time there was no link between his death and his Army service. The inspector was consoled to a degree by the fact that very little time had elapsed between the hanging and the drowning, when the link was revealed. That did not stop him muttering: 'Wasted time!' to himself. There again, he also knew it was pointless to dwell on such regrets.

FIFTEEN

DC Dyson was once more at Derriford Hospital to check on the condition of Robert Dangerfield. As he was still in the Intensive Care Unit, now in an induced coma, she knew that she would not be able to interview him. However, she was still hopeful his wife might be of further help with the armed robbery investigation. Mrs Dangerfield was still on her vigil outside the ICU in a small area next to a coffee vending machine. Dyson thought she looked as if she still had not slept since the robbery. There again, from knowledge of her parents, Dyson knew that occasional naps did wonders for the body and human spirit.

'How is he?' Dyson enquired.

'Much the same I'm afraid, although that's a good thing, as at one point I thought I'd lost him. The surgeons are now hopeful he will get better in time, but they aren't saying how long that will be.'

'I was hoping to be able to ask him about the robbery and was wondering if he had any idea of anyone who might have a grudge against him? That thought was triggered by something you said when we last spoke, which may suggest he knew the robber.'

'Really? What did I say?'

'When you challenged the gunman he said: "He deserves it!" My inspector thinks that suggests he knew Mr Dangerfield and your husband therefore might know him. Because of the tone, it could imply a grudge. Can you think of anyone who has reason to bear a grievance against your husband? Possibly a house deal that turned sour? Maybe in the recent past?'

'Very occasionally a sale may not go smoothly, but never because Bob did anything wrong. Buying or selling a property can be a very stressful time and emotions can end up running high. Generally, clients are very happy with the service we provide.

'Hang on a minute, come to think of it there was a recent prospective purchaser who was very irate when the sale of a property went to another buyer. He accused Bob of being involved in gazumping. My husband is too honourable to do such a thing and, anyway, he values our reputation as an agency too highly to contemplate getting involved in that practice or, for that matter, contract races.'

'What was his complaint?'

'He made an offer below the asking price. Bob put it to the vendor and the offer wasn't accepted. When the chap found out about a subsequent higher offer, he said my husband should have told him about it.'

'Can you remember the name of the man?'

'I can't offhand, but Bob would remember...' she didn't finish as the reality of her situation returned, remembering her husband was lying in a bed with tubes leading into and out of his body.

Dyson thought she had gone as far as she could in the circumstances and decided to pursue the investigation at the couple's estate agency in Plymouth.

'Not to worry, Mrs Dangerfield. Can I ask where your main office is in Plymouth? Is that the one in Mutley Plain?'

'Yes, that's the one. If you go there, ask to speak with Gerald Payne, he's the manager.'

'Thank you and I hope your husband continues to improve.'

*

Not long after leaving the hospital, Dyson was walking into Dangerfield's estate agency, a stone's throw from Plymouth city centre, when she was approached by a smartly dressed man.

'Could I speak with Mr Payne please?'

'You're speaking to him. How can I help?'

Dyson mentioned the investigation of the robbery at the Dangerfield house and her very recent visit to the hospital. She told him what Joan Dangerfield had said about the irate buyer and wondered if he could give her more details.

'I certainly could as he verbally abused me right here in the shop; very embarrassing. The property we were selling, which he was interested in, was on the market for £1.2 million and he made an offer of £1.1 million. It was not accepted by the vendors and soon after they were offered the full asking price. Obviously, they accepted and we took the house off the market. The man who made the first offer said that if he had been told, he would have come back with an offer of £1.3 million. Mr Dangerfield apologised, but said it was up to the sellers to accept or reject an offer and they were happy to sell for the asking price. The man got more and more angry, at which point Mr D told him that if he had informed the man of the higher offer, he would be guilty of exactly the same thing as he was being accused of, namely gazumping.

'It transpired that the angry man was acting as an agent for someone else and he was going to lose a lot of commission if he didn't close the purchase. In front of the whole shop he shouted that it had cost him £10,000, so I guess he was getting 1% of the purchase price. He was politely asked to leave and as he left he was swearing and said he would "get even" with Mr D.'

'What's the person's name?'

'Normally we wouldn't divulge that information, but as you are a police officer and because of what happened to Mr Dangerfield, his name is Mr Thomas, Mr Eric Thomas.'

'Did he by chance have an Irish accent?'

'With a name like Thomas, detective! His ancestry probably links across the Welsh rather than the Irish border. No, sorry, he didn't have an Irish accent.'

The helpful manager then gave Dyson his address and as she left he called after her: 'I hope you catch the man who shot Mr D.'

*

Dyson rang King and told him about her visit to the hospital and the estate agency. He told her to call at the address supplied by the helpful Mr Payne but, bearing in mind Mr Dangerfield had been shot, she must have armed officers in support.

Dyson arrived at the house, which was a semi-detached property on an estate to the north of Plymouth city centre. It would have been a complete overreaction if the police had swooped on the house. However, she had done as Inspector King had insisted. Dyson requested the armed officers to position themselves discreetly out of sight as it was only speculation that Mr Thomas was involved in the robbery. She was expecting something more palatial than a semi-detached house as the man was involved in a property purchase valued at a million pounds plus. There again, she told herself, he was only acting as an agent for someone else. The door was answered by a man with slicked-back hair, wearing a suit and an open-necked white shirt.

'Mr Thomas? Mr Eric Thomas?' the diminutive detective asked.

'That's right. What's the problem?'

'I am Detective Constable Dyson from Plymouth Police and am investigating a robbery at the home of Mr Robert Dangerfield. I have been informed you had an altercation with him in his shop on Mutley Plain recently. Is that correct, sir?' Thomas was not best pleased at the implied accusation: 'I don't fucking believe it! First he loses me ten grand and now the bastard's accusing me of robbing him!'

'Mr Dangerfield is not in a position to accuse anybody of anything, sir, as he's unconscious in the Intensive Care Unit at Derriford Hospital.'

'Serves him right. Now fuck off and stop wasting my time.' With that he reached into his jacket pocket.

Before he could pull his hand out, armed officers appeared on either side of Dyson with their Glock pistols drawn and held chest high at arm's length. Dyson backed away and let them take control. They took no chances where there was a possibility of a weapon being involved in an arrest.

One officer yelled: 'Do not pull your hand out of your pocket! Repeat, leave your right hand where it is! Come out and lie face down on the ground! Lie face down now!'

The shock tactic had the desired effect as, wisely, Thomas followed the instruction. The orders did not stop there: 'Take your hand out of your pocket very slowly and then put both hands behind your back!'

Thomas obeyed the instruction and was duly handcuffed. As it turned out, a search of his pocket revealed the man was simply reaching for his mobile phone. However, in view of the outburst about Mr Dangerfield and his hostile reaction to her enquiry, Dyson decided to interview him under caution at the station.

*

Later at Plymouth Police Station, Mr Thomas was released without charge after providing a strong alibi about his whereabouts on the night of the robbery. He had gone through a speed trap on the outskirts of Barnstaple – over two hours' drive from Plymouth – at precisely the time the robbery took place. Photographic evidence confirmed he was driving the car. He left the station with his bravado fully restored, threatening to sue for wrongful arrest.

When Dyson later reported the whole incident to her inspector, she told him that she was convinced he was not the "Joker". When asked why, she said apart from his foolproof alibi, he didn't have an Irish accent and he was no more than 180 centimetres tall! She said that according to the CCTV footage, the "Joker" was at least twenty centimetres taller.

As she had drawn a blank with Eric Thomas, she still wanted to speak with Mr Dangerfield about anyone who might have a grievance against him. Her tenacity would eventually be rewarded.

SIXTEEN

The people-traffickers, based in Cherbourg, heard on the French news that the migrants they had taken to Anse Saint-Martin cove two nights before had all perished in the lorry taking them to their final destination. They did not care as they had been paid. The small gang of four was led by a man known to the migrants only as 'Monsieur la Liberté'. They did not know it, but "Mr Freedom", far from being the gatekeeper to a better life, was the pathway to them becoming modern-day slaves. He was not only involved in their transportation but was also the key figure in making all the arrangements, from selection to payment.

His next payday was planned for the high tide the night after next. He was getting greedy by fixing one trip so closely followed by another. His greed also extended to wanting a bigger rigid inflatable boat. A larger RIB meant more people, leading to increased profit. When he first started his illicit trade, he had often stolen a RIB, but began to realise a reported theft might alert the authorities. Besides, the traffickers were making so much money from each trip they could afford to legitimately buy a used boat and trailer without raising suspicion. The head trafficker reasoned that if his purchase was lawful and bought to order, they might as well get a bigger RIB than the one they used for the last trip. Besides, cost was not a factor as there was an inexhaustible supply of migrants willing to pay a lot of money to get to the UK. Overheads were a fraction of the revenue.

The migrants for the next voyage had been identified. Many of their families had usually sold most of what few possessions they had in order to pay the exorbitant fare, in the hope their family member would settle in the UK, with a well-paid job, and send money home.

The RIB and trailer had been bought in Le Havre over 200 kilometres to the east of Cherbourg. This boat, which had seen better days, was built with a dozen seats and, with those removed, it would hold more than twenty people. Capacity was the key element in this operation, not comfort. The €750 it cost was less than a tenth of what one migrant was paying to secure their passage.

As the latest batch of migrants secretly assembled in a warehouse on the outskirts of Cherbourg, the traffickers' battered 4x4, pulling a boat trailer, had already left half an hour before the lorry was due to depart. It was after midnight and there was very little traffic as the Nissan, with the RIB on the trailer, headed for the cove at Anse Saint-Martin. 'Monsieur la Liberté' thought it safe to use the same departure point that had been used on three previous occasions. He liked it as it was not far from Cherbourg, offered seclusion and its gently shelving beach made launching the flat-bottomed RIB very easy.

The two traffickers in the Nissan arrived at the deserted and dark cove. After backing the trailer as close to the beach as they could, they removed the green tarpaulin that had covered the RIB on its journey to the coast, folded it and put it in the back of the 4x4. With some difficulty they manhandled the large boat onto the beach close to the water. They knew there was no fear of it being washed away as high tide had passed half an hour before.

As they waited, one took out a packet of Gauloises and lit up. They could see the lights of the lorry in the distance on the road down to the cove. It was now laden with its human cargo and, as usual, was being driven recklessly.

It swept into the car park and backed up next to the 4x4. The two traffickers who were already there eagerly opened the back doors. As on most trips, some migrants fell out gasping for air. They were all quickly ushered towards the RIB. A quick check with a torch app from a mobile phone shone into the back of the lorry picked out two migrants slumped at the front who were not moving.

The lead trafficker pulled himself into the back of the lorry and began swearing in French: 'Merde! Merde! Merde! Déplacez-vous salauds!' As he got no response, he started kicking them, but they still would not move. Holding the torch to their faces for closer inspection revealed they were either unconscious or dead. He shouted towards the other traffickers: 'Obtenir de l'eau!' and one rushed to the 4x4, quickly returning with a small bottle of water. "Mr Freedom" unscrewed and discarded the cap. He grabbed the nearest migrant by her hair, jerking her head back, and tipped some water into her gaping mouth. She spluttered, and as she revived, two of the traffickers dragged her out and frogmarched her to the boat.

The second migrant did not respond to the water treatment and was still barely conscious. The traffickers knew that valuable time was being lost but could not leave him in the car park or take him back in the lorry. The ringleader decided he should be carried aboard, but not before he slapped him twice across the face, more in frustration than as an attempt at revival. The groggy migrant, dazed from the slaps, was unceremoniously carried to join the others.

As was the usual practice of the traffickers, a "captain" had earlier been appointed, for a reduced fare, and a satellite phone was thrust into his hand. He was then given basic instructions on how to operate the outboard motor attached to the back of the RIB.

The unloading delay, added to the time it took to get all twenty-one migrants on board, irritated the four men, but as it was past midnight, on a deserted and isolated cove, they were not particularly concerned. They knew that the French police had to patrol a 150-kilometre stretch of coastline in an attempt to stop illegal immigration to the UK. They had one last job to do before returning to Cherbourg. The RIB was side on to the water, the outboard motor was idling and the traffickers were ready for the launch. All four traffickers started pushing the RIB towards deeper water.

'Mr Freedom' suddenly raised his hand: '*Ecoutez! Est-ce un hélicoptère?*' he said, telling his men to listen. They stopped pulling and pushing the RIB, looked skyward and listened. As the wind was blowing away from the beach as well as the direction of flight, the sound of the rotor blades was initially barely audible; the helicopter was a lot closer than the lead trafficker had first thought. He pulled out a pistol from his waistband.

From high above, a piercing spotlight illuminated the car park. Realising they were caught in the act, three traffickers left the RIB, two running to the 4x4 and one to the lorry. They were not to know that the arrival of the Nissan at the car park twenty-five minutes before had triggered an alarm in the Cherbourg Gendarmerie. The discreetly hidden camera was fixed on a pole opposite the entrance to the car park. It was fitted with a motion sensor and night vision scope just as DC Hammond had advised. Although the officer, whose job it was to monitor CCTV in Cherbourg and surrounding areas, had false alerts in the past from this camera – as wildlife occasionally activated the alarm – on this occasion, viewing the images on her screen, there was no doubt she was witnessing an illegal act. She immediately informed her emergency contact.

The French police had been in a state of readiness for two nights as they knew that the traffickers favoured operating when the tide was at its highest around midnight. Not only was the helicopter ready and waiting, so were the Gendarmerie Nationale. As part of the French armed forces, they had armoured vehicles and also a maritime section. All had been mobilised as soon as they had been notified that the first traffickers had entered the car park. The ringleader was the only one not to panic and run for a vehicle as he knew the one exit from the cove would already be blocked by the police.

'*Sortez du bateau! Sortez du bateau!*' he shouted at the migrants in the boat who were confused about what was happening. He wanted them to get out of the RIB and began gesturing with his pistol. However, they had paid a fortune for the voyage and were not about to readily adhere to his demands. Realising time was against him and needing a dramatic act to get them out, he shot the "captain". The migrant slumped onto the side of the boat with blood oozing from his chest wound.

"Mr Freedom" then pointed the gun towards the rest of the migrants in a 'who's next?' manner. They quickly got out. When the last one fell out onto the beach, the trafficker then immediately jumped into the RIB, keeping his gun trained on the migrants who were now huddled together in the dark, many ruing the police intervention; their one-way ticket was now null and void.

Bending down, he grabbed the right leg of the dead "captain" and levered him unceremoniously over the side of the RIB and into the water. With his right hand holding his gun and the other on the tiller, he increased the throttle and headed away from the cove.

The helicopter was tracking the 4x4, closely followed by the lorry, up the access road. The pilot was ready for the traffickers to abandon their vehicles and make a run for it as they realised their position was hopeless. He was proved to be right.

The RIB was now powering out to sea as "Mr Freedom" thought it was his best chance to avoid arrest. With one hand on the tiller, he reached into the boat and picked up the satellite phone the "captain" had dropped when he was shot. He wanted to keep the RIB heading out to sea before deciding his next move. Pressing the tiller between his right upper arm and his right side, he freed both hands to operate the phone. He considered various options before settling on the one that he thought gave him the best chance to escape. He changed course and headed due west, aiming for the headland to his left and set a course for St Anne, the northernmost island of the Channel Islands archipelago. Fortunately for him, the sea that night was relatively calm and although the night was pitch black, he was relying on the satellite phone to keep him on course.

Meanwhile, the 4x4, still closely followed by the lorry, was speeding up the road from the coast, the traffickers realising their illegal trade had been compromised, but unsure how they had been ambushed. Up ahead, at the junction where the beach road joined the main road to Cherbourg, a phalanx of police vehicles blocked their escape route. The two traffickers in the speeding 4x4 suddenly saw the roadblock and braked hard; the lorry did not! The lorry driver was catapulted headfirst into the windscreen as his vehicle concertinaed the back of the Nissan. The traffickers in front had managed to open the doors and leap out before the crash and started running in opposite directions. For one of the men, caught in the beam of the helicopter's spotlight, there was no escape; gendarmes quickly arrested him.

The other man stumbled through bracken in the darkness and eventually took shelter in a barn full of hay bales, trying to hide from the probing shaft of light from above. The gendarmes initially fanned out, all with torches, with weapons drawn. A police dog picked up the man's scent and its handler alerted the others. They cautiously closed in on the barn. The trafficker, peering out of a crack in the timber wall, could tell from the flickering torches, the gendarmes were getting closer.

Cries of 'Ici!' echoed around outside the barn. As a last desperate attempt to evade capture, he took out his lighter. In his panic, he had not fully thought through his distraction tactic. The flaw in his plan quickly became apparent as the flames eagerly devoured the dry hay around him. What he had not factored in was how to get out of the burning barn! As the fire intensified, he realised he had cut off his escape route as the door into the barn was the only exit, and that was on the other side of what now was an inferno.

His clothes were now alight as he ran screaming from the building. He had run only ten paces, when two gendarmes pounced on him. They used their thick coats to smother the flames. Their act of selflessness was more than the trafficker deserved.

Back out at sea, the ringleader was content with his plan. The RIB was cutting through the water and he had the satellite phone in one hand whilst steering with the other, and there was no sign of the helicopter. When he eventually reached St Anne, he would decide his next move. He had some good friends that would come and collect him and then he could resume his illicit and highly lucrative trade. Next time, he thought to himself, he would use a different cove.

Just as he began to feel pleased with his escape plan, he thought he could hear the sound of a boat engine behind him. Glancing back he could just detect what looked like a flashing blue light approaching out of the darkness, some distance away. He sensed the Maritime Gendarmerie were heading his way, but he could not work out how they were tracking him in the pitch dark? Then he realised: it was his satellite phone that had pinpointed his position!

He glanced at the sat phone and could see he was close to Pointe de Jareheu, a promontory fairly close by. He changed his course and abandoned his plan. He was just able to make out the shore directly ahead and steered the RIB at speed towards the shoreline. He braced himself for the impact as the bottom of the boat skidded up the beach. He was thrown forward into the bottom of the RIB, but quickly found his footing and began running into trees that bordered the shore.

It was not just a single boat that was tracking him as two police boats soon flanked his abandoned RIB.

Eight armed gendarmes ran up the beach in pursuit of the trafficker. They were unaware that he was the ringleader.

As the coast gave way to higher ground that was impossible to climb, they gradually cornered him. Even then he was defiant. With his back to the cliff he was apparently resigned to his arrest. He held his arms above his head. As one gendarme cautiously approached, the trafficker suddenly pulled his gun from behind his back, where he had concealed it in his trouser belt, and fired. A hail of gunfire followed and bullets riddled the trafficker's body. With a superficial gunshot wound to his shoulder, the gendarme survived; Monsieur la Liberté was less fortunate!

*

Early the next morning, the Chief of Police in Cherbourg contacted the Chief Constable of Devon and Cornwall Police to update him on the events of the previous evening, and the successful outcome of preventing over twenty migrants from crossing the Channel. He also commended DC Hammond for his initiative and his suspicions the traffickers might use the same cove again as a departure point. DCI Burrows informed Inspector King of the commendation and also personally spoke to Hammond to congratulate him.

Not normally an intense individual, there was no mistaking his utter determination to bring the "Joker", and his accomplice, to justice.

*

It was now 5.30 p.m. and two days on from the convenience store robbery. King and Harris waited at the central police station. No cars had been reported stolen from anywhere in the city. The clock ticked on and as it reached 5.45 p.m., King was about to call it a day when his sergeant's mobile rang. She listened intently and then pushed the disconnect button: 'Sir, a Ford Fiesta has been reported stolen from Crownhill, not far from Southway. All patrol cars have been informed and CCTV operators are actively checking the city for it. The registration number is: Whiskey, Foxtrot, 61, Oscar, Echo, Charlie.'

King's hunch had been right and as he stood up, taking his jacket off the back of his chair he enthused: 'Come on, Lucy, let's join in the hunt. Right, "Joker", get ready for your last laugh!'

EIGHTEEN

The robbers had previously attacked a private residence and a convenience store, and they now were targeting a petrol station with an integral store. Their reasoning was that a bigger shop had more customers and therefore a fuller till. Notwithstanding the pandemic, when a much higher percentage of transactions were by card, there were still enough customers who used cash.

The "Joker" knew it would be busier than the convenience store. On that occasion he was able to choose his moment to strike when there were no other customers around. The petrol station was open twenty-four hours and customers were constantly pulling in to fill up. However, from observation, and from the website for the garage showing 'popular times', he had noticed there tended to be a lull at this particular station just after six o'clock in the evening.

At 6.05 p.m. a blue Ford Fiesta parked in a layby about fifty metres away from the Forder Valley petrol station and store on the outskirts of Plymouth. The two men in the car watched as cars pulled in and out. At one point when there were only two cars left in the petrol station, the accomplice drove the Fiesta to the entrance and parked, blocking any other vehicles from entering. The robbers had chosen the station as it was fairly isolated and had a clearly defined entry and exit.

The accomplice got out of the car and lifted the bonnet, signalling to other road users he had a problem. He was not wearing his balaclava, but an anti-Covid mask hid his identity from the prying CCTV cameras. The "Joker" sat in the passenger seat for a few moments waiting for the last customer to pay and leave. The unsuspecting customer eventually returned to his car and drove out. A few other cars coming along Forder Valley began indicating, signalling their intention to pull in for petrol, but then driving on when they realised the entrance was blocked. The "Joker" reached for his trademark mask, got out of the car and walked towards the shop.

*

'Would it be possible to speak with Mr Dangerfield for a few minutes please?' Dyson asked one of the doctors in the ICU. She was told that he was about to be moved to a ward, so she could see him, but only for five minutes. She was already wearing a Covid protection mask as she was shown into the ICU. Dangerfield was sitting up in bed with his wife by his side. His wife acknowledged Dyson and introduced the detective to her husband.

Dyson did not want to waste the few minutes she had been allowed, so immediately asked him if he knew of anyone who might have a grudge against him. The only person he could think of was Mr Thomas. She told him he had already been interviewed and discounted. She wanted to know if there was anyone else, as everything pointed to him knowing the robber or at least, the robber knowing him.

'Well, I never met the man, but I recently had to ask the manager at my shop in Mutley to sack someone for shoddy work.'

The hovering doctor was becoming a little agitated as he was more concerned about patient care rather than solving crimes.

'I'm afraid, detective, that the patient now needs to rest before I can transfer him to the ward.' The doctor was effectively calling a halt to the meeting. Dyson would have liked to have followed up on what she had just been told, but was now keen to contact Alex Hammond.

*

DC Hammond entered the estate agent shop at Mutley Plain just before it was due to close for the day and asked to speak with Mr Payne. Before the manager appeared, Hammond's mobile rang. It was Sam Dyson telling him what she had just been told by Mr Dangerfield. Brief introductions were made and the dapper manager was keen to ask: 'Any joy with Mr Thomas or should I say any anger?' Hammond suppressed a grin.

'We interviewed him, but he had a very good alibi for the evening of the robbery, so he is no longer part of the investigation. My colleague, who is at Derriford Hospital, has just spoken with Mr Dangerfield, and she told me he gave instructions for you to sack someone recently. Is that correct?'

'Now you mention it, I recall that Tom Clancy used to work for us until recently. He was employed to put up "For Sale" signs at properties we were selling and then attach the appropriate additional signage, for example "Sold" or "Sold subject to contract". He'd only been on the job for a few weeks when Mr Dangerfield, who was showing a prospective purchaser a house that overlooked Plymouth Sound, noticed the sale board showed it was "Under Offer". It wasn't, but Clancy had put up the wrong board. The buyer wasn't happy as he thought gazumping was being practised. The seller wasn't too pleased either as the wrong signage would only discourage buyers. Unfortunately, that same day the boss was at another property on our books and the sale sign had actually fallen down as it hadn't been properly fixed. The final straw was a board that read "Sold" when we were still marketing it!

'Mr Dangerfield, who to my knowledge had never met Clancy, told me to dismiss him as he was damaging the reputation of the company. When Clancy came into the shop, I asked him for the keys to the company's van and told him Mr Dangerfield wasn't happy with his work and he was dismissed. He left the shop swearing and threw the van's keys on the floor.'

Hammond then pointedly asked: 'Does he by any chance have an Irish accent?'

'Well, it's not a strong accent, but, yes, he does.'

Hammond waited while Mr Payne accessed a nearby computer and then passed a printout to the detective showing Clancy's address. After thanking the manager he left the shop and immediately phoned Inspector King.

*

The till operator at the petrol station had seen the apparently broken-down car at the entrance and asked her colleague to find out what the problem was. As the automatic door opened and he stepped out of the shop, he was confronted by the "Joker" who hit him full in the face with the butt of the gun. The man fell unconscious onto the forecourt. The robber nonchalantly walked straight to the till holding his gun on his outstretched arm.

'Money!' he demanded thrusting a bag under the plastic shield in front of the till. The woman nervously did as she had been told, grabbing the notes from the till, and then pushed the bag back under the shield. Not only was the robber's mask his trademark, so too was his growing macho urge to blast the security camera, as if taunting the police. He raised his weapon and fired. The till operator dived to the floor only to be showered in bits of shattered camera and ceiling tiles.

The blast was the signal for his accomplice – who appeared to passing motorists to be waiting for a recovery vehicle – to slam down the bonnet of the Fiesta and hurriedly drive to the entrance door. Having traumatised the till operator, the "Joker" calmly stepped over the still unconscious assistant, got in the car and it sped off the forecourt.

*

The robbers drove along Forder Valley Road, observing the speed limit so as not to draw unwanted attention, and then went around the roundabout at the junction joining the main arterial dual carriageway around Plymouth, the so-called Devon Expressway. They removed their masks and began laughing at just how easy it was to steal money. They planned to exit at the next junction and head north to Tamerton Foliot. The accomplice had checked he had his small water bottle filled with petrol. He actually got a buzz from setting cars alight. Did they but know it, the robbers had made a fatal mistake: repetition.

Thanks to Inspector King's plan of alerting all patrol cars, particularly to the north of Plymouth, the Fiesta was soon spotted. By now the latest robbery had been reported, confirming to the police they were now pursuing the getaway car. Other police were alerted, including Sergeant Harris, who quickly informed Inspector King and they were soon heading for Tamerton Foliot.

Police cars and armed units were now converging on the main road out of the city leading north. The robbers were oblivious to the police "net" beginning to surround them. The officers knew the road to the village passed a half-mile stretch with fields on both sides and no turn-offs. Two 4x4s blocked the village end of the road and several police cars were converging from the other end, effectively trapping the "Joker" and his accomplice.

With no traffic coming towards them or following, the robbers sensed something was wrong. Their fears were realised as the police helicopter swooped low overhead and tracked their car with a spotlight. They knew they were trapped. The accomplice stopped the car and got out with his hands in the air, looking up at the helicopter. Police cars were edging towards the Fiesta from both directions. King wanted to be there, but knew he had to keep his distance as the robber was still armed and dangerous.

For some inexplicable reason the "Joker" put on his trademark mask and, carrying his gun in his right hand with his finger on the trigger, quickly flung open the car door. He ran across the grass verge next to the car as the field beyond seemed to be his best route of escape. However, he had not realised that the verge was on top of a bank that fell away to an open ditch. He tumbled down into icy water and inadvertently pulled the trigger. The advancing police abruptly stopped at the sound of the gunshot. The gunman, realising that was the only cartridge he had left, the other having been discharged in the earlier robbery, threw away his weapon and began running across the open field, ripping off his "Joker" mask as he ran.

He was heading for an adjoining road where he planned to hijack a car and make good his escape.

The odds of him executing his plan were heavily stacked against him as he was being tracked by the police helicopter and also several police officers running across the field were gradually gaining on him. If his position was not bad enough, police dog Sabre was not going to let him escape. As the German Shepherd sank his teeth into a criminal's arm, only an instruction from his handler made the dog release its grip. As the "Joker" and Sabre writhed in the grass, several police officers pounced on the robber, unsure if he was carrying a handgun.

As he was led away he suddenly shouted: 'Up the Provos!' as a last defiant gesture. This had been his third armed robbery in only five days, but his thieving days were now over as was his freedom.

The two detectives had witnessed the arrest from a distance. King spoke to his sergeant: 'Well, Lucy, that's one less investigation we'll have to spend time on, apart from the paperwork. Hopefully we can now devote all our energy to catching the person who murdered Freeman and Prescott.'

*

The next day, the detectives made extensive enquiries. The accomplice, Billy Fraser, was very cooperative and told the police that when they were stopped, they had been heading to Tamerton Foliot to burn the car and collect their van. When the van was found it was full of decorating equipment. Fraser was a painter and decorator, occasionally helped by his partner in crime. Dyson then remembered what

Mrs Dangerfield told her when she was interviewed: 'The gunman was wearing black trainers and they were spattered with small white dots.'

Tom Clancy, alias the "Joker", real name Brendan Doyle, was a fugitive from justice. It came as no surprise to King that he was wanted in Northern Ireland for several robberies. He was a long-standing member of the Provisional Irish Republican Army and had only reluctantly accepted the ceasefire brokered in 1998. Being a wanted man in his own country, he had come to Devon six months earlier to escape the Irish police and continue his robbing spree. The money he stole paid for his living expenses, but most was sent back to his native country to help pursue the cause of the Provos. Fraser had no such political affiliations; he was just in it for the money. His 25% cut from the robberies paid for his heroin.

NINETEEN

One month earlier...

Bob Hurricane Higgins, a self-employed electrician, earned his living fitting satellite dishes as a subcontractor for Currys PC World in Yeovil, Somerset. He was born and raised in Plymouth, but had moved to Yeovil to be closer to his girlfriend. They met through the Army as both were reservists, mixing their civilian jobs with Army life. Sadly for him the relationship ended as she found someone else. He decided to stay in Somerset and not return to his home city of Plymouth as he had plenty of work where he was and was well paid.

For the last three days as Higgins went from job to job, unbeknown to him he had been followed from his home to the various properties where he was working. A man had shadowed him throughout this period. If he had been more attentive, he would have seen the same Land Rover Defender parked close to his home or pull away shortly after him. All the stalker was after was an opportunity and on the afternoon of the third day it presented itself.

Higgins drove his leased van up the long drive of a large house to the east of Yeovil in a small village called Bradford Abbas. He stopped on the spacious gravelled area in front of the three-storey house that had seen better days. The seven-bedroom dwelling was built at the turn of the twentieth century and maintenance had been sadly neglected. The present owners apparently preferred to spend their money on modern living and wanted to enjoy the variety of TV programmes available on satellite channels.

Higgins had been subcontracted to fit a satellite dish to the gable end chimney. As the house was a three-storey building, the ridge of the roof was nearly thirty metres from the ground. Fortunately, Higgins was never fazed by heights. He was disappointed the owners appeared to be out, not because he needed access to the house, but when customers were home, he was often given refreshments.

Mature, high rhododendron bushes lined one side of the drive and provided the perfect cover to observe the dish installer without being seen. The man watched carefully as Higgins took the aluminium extension ladder with its three sections from the roof of his van. He had bought them several years before as they could extend to nearly twenty metres; there were few eaves they could not reach. Having got to the level of the eaves, he then used a ridge roof hook ladder to get to the chimney. The perilous part for any roofing job was transferring from the extended ladder to the hook ladder.

If he had not been self-employed and had worked for a big dish installation company instead, he would have had to follow the rigorous health and safety guidelines, including securing himself to his ladder with a harness and fixing the extension ladder temporarily to the adjacent wall of the house to prevent it slipping. But to him, H&S regulations were anathema. They would slow him down and thereby affect his income. Furthermore, if he employed someone to stabilise the ladder by adding their weight to the rung nearest to the ground, his profit margin would take a significant blow. He had been climbing onto roofs for years and had never had a problem, even in rain and icy conditions.

He extended the ladder until the top was beyond and resting on the guttering. He then carried up the hook ladder and expertly lifted the end over the ridge of the roof whilst balanced on the extension.

The man in the bushes watched and waited. Higgins' first task was to fix a bracket to the chimney breast and then attach the dish. As it would be exposed to high winds at that height, he not only used long screws for the bracket plate, but for extra strength, he also ran a wire around the breast and through the plate. He then twisted the ends of the wire together with a pair of pliers carried in a tool belt around his waist.

The man, still hidden by garden foliage, moved closer as he sensed the time for him to act was approaching. Higgins returned to his van to collect the dish he would attach to the bracket, high up on the chimney. He checked he had the right spanner and began his ascent. He held onto the ladder with his left hand and carried the slightly cumbersome, but not heavy, dish in his right. His extension ladder reached beyond the guttering of the roof and he climbed above it to enable him to switch across to the hook ladder. He swung the dish onto the roof as he would need both hands free to transfer himself. With his left foot on the extension and his right on the hook ladder he glanced down, stopping midway through his transfer. There was a man with a walking stick at the bottom of the ladder staring up at him.

'Can I help you, mate?'

'Remember me, Hurricane?'

A look of horror spread across Higgins' face: 'It can't be! You're dead! Listen, Pilgrim, I know I left you, but afterwards I had a real go at Frankie as we were following his fucking orders. Honest to God, ever since, I've deeply regretted not helping you!'

'Actually, The Pilgrim is very much alive, no thanks to you or my other so-called mates! Am I supposed to be impressed that you had a change of heart? I'm afraid that was too little, too late, Hurricane.'

The man pulled down the mask he was wearing to reveal his hideously scarred face. Higgins remained transfixed in disbelief and thought for a moment he was hallucinating. He then saw the man step back a pace and switch his grip to the bottom end of the stick. Placing the hook handle over the last rung on the ladder, he looked up at Higgins who was petrified: 'No! No! Don't do this Pilgrim!

'Goodbye, Hurricane!' Adopting a stance with his left leg in front of his right he pulled with all the strength in his body. The ladder jerked backwards causing the man to drop his stick as he fell back and put out his arms to cushion his fall.

Realising what was happening, the hapless roofer pushed himself off the ladder rung he was standing on and lunged for the guttering in an attempt to prevent himself from plummeting to the ground. He succeeded in grabbing it and for a moment thought he had been reprieved. Sadly for him the cast iron was brittle and its fixings were rusted.

He crashed onto the hard surface of the drive with a sickening thud, his head twisted at a hideous angle to the rest of his body. His extension ladder clattered onto the lawn at the side of the house, propelled there by Higgins' left leg as he leapt for the guttering. Just to compound his folly, a heavy fragment of the gutter followed him down and impaled itself in his chest. He never felt the cast-iron shard; he was already dead.

The man got to his feet, picked up his walking stick and slowly walked down the drive, this time not seeking the cover of the shrubbery.

*

Some weeks later at the inquest into Robert Douglas Higgins death, the coroner spoke gravely about the need to employ good health and safety practices, whether an employee or self-employed. He spoke with a sombre tone and said that if Mr Higgins had worked for a registered company, he would have considered imposing a fine of £20,000 and prosecuting the directors for corporate manslaughter.

However, he could not and although he did not say it for fear of upsetting any relatives of the deceased, he thought Higgins only had himself to blame.

Verdict: Accidental death.

TWENTY

After a more than frustrating wait and the dramatic arrest of the armed robbers the previous evening, Sergeant Harris contacted the barracks in Exeter early the next day and was told someone would see her that afternoon. The Army administrator was returning early from the exercise with his colleagues in Somerset, especially to deal with Harris's request for information. Harris made good progress on the first part of her journey north, before joining the M5 at Junction 31. However, after travelling a few miles along the motorway, the traffic came to a complete standstill.

She listened to BBC Radio Devon and was dismayed to hear of an accident just before Junction 30. She knew that part of the M5 very well and realised that where she was, there were no exits that could have provided a diversion. She knew that she would be late for her appointment at the barracks and telephoned her apologies. She was now at the mercy of the emergency services. From past experience, if there were any fatalities as a result of the accident, the time taken to clear the motorway was likely to double. She also rang her boss to update him on her current position. King told her to ring him as soon as she received the crucial information. He realised that nothing could be done as it had been made clear by the base commander that information about serving personnel could not be released over the phone or by email. King sensed a growing unease that time was not on their side.

It was late afternoon when she was able to ring her boss from the barracks. DCs Dyson and Hammond, DIs Best and King gathered around King's desk and he put Harris on speakerphone.

'Apologies, sir, as it took over three hours for the accident to be cleared. Anyway, I've now spoken with the Army administrator at the barracks and he apologised for the delay. Some of the information he gave me is classified, as it relates to serving personnel, which explains why the base commander insisted on face-to-face contact rather than email or phone.

'I was given a folder that I have in front of me now. I will deal with the records in the order they were passed to me, which was alphabetical. I'll summarise the information I've been given. All the men joined the regiment on the same day in February 2010. Nearly all of their time on duty with the Army was for the same periods. In other words the friends were like a small unit. I was told that as part-time soldiers they still get involved in everything that the Regular Army does, from combat to peacekeeping to humanitarian work. They did basic training and other assignments together for their first eight years in the Army, mainly in Devon. In January 2018, all seven of the friends were posted to Baghdad in Iraq for a month to fight the insurgents. Sadly, our happy band didn't all survive that temporary posting or arrive home in one piece!

'Firstly, Gregory James Bryson is a married man living in Plymouth. He's a self-employed graphic designer. When he joined the Army as a reservist, from the outset he was classed as a Light Cavalry Crewman, as were all his friends. This meant they were trained to operate armoured vehicles so they could move swiftly around the battlefield. He still serves in the Army.

'Carl Brackley was a part owner in a service garage in Plymouth. He too was single. Sadly, while out on patrol outside the Green Zone in Baghdad, the armoured personnel carrier he was travelling in was blown-up by an improvised explosive device and he was killed.

'This is the surprise information, sir. Derek Adam Clayton was not killed in Iraq after all. He is married and used to run a team building company for businesses. As far as I can gather from his Army record he used to take people on Dartmoor on survival courses, exposing them to the rugged outdoors. He was badly injured in the IED attack that killed Carl Brackley. In the Army field hospital in the Green Zone in Baghdad, he had his right foot amputated as a result of the injuries he received in the explosion. He also suffered third-degree burns to the left side of his neck and head. After surgery on the day of the attack, he was then flown back to Derriford Hospital and underwent many skin graft operations on his burns. He was medically retired from the Army early in 2019.'

King queried: 'Sorry to interrupt, Lucy, but, as you know, according to Mrs Freeman, his mates thought he was killed in Iraq. How did they not know he had survived?'

'Yes, sir, as I mentioned earlier, I too was surprised when I heard he was still alive. I don't know why his mates didn't know he hadn't been killed. The only thing I can think of is the records show that all his mates returned to the UK the very next day after the attack.

'There's one other thing, sir. When he returned to the UK, his confidential file shows that he insisted that he wanted no further contact with his friends and didn't want them to know of his survival. The Army psychologist, who deals with a lot of PTSD cases, suggested in Clayton's service record that his self-imposed estrangement was due either to his post-traumatic stress or to his disfigurement, caused by his burns, possibly both those things.

'His service record also shows that when he left the Army, instead of taking a pension, he opted for a lump sum one-off payment. So, as he doesn't receive a pension, the Army doesn't know where he is or even if he's still alive. All they have is his address when he left.

'So, that was Derek Clayton. I'll now move on to another of the mates. Colin Liam Franks is married and lives on the edge of Dartmoor. He is a financial management consultant. Like the others, he has served for ten years as a reservist and was promoted to corporal just prior to the tour of Iraq. He is still active in the Army.

'Daniel Mark Freeman we know about. He retired from the Army on medical grounds not long after returning from Iraq. It was recorded on his record that he was showing signs of early-onset dementia and he was eventually medically retired. Another note in the confidential file on him, made by an Army psychologist, suggests a claim may be made that his dementia was triggered by post-traumatic stress as a result of witnessing what happened to Carl Brackley and Derek Clayton. Of course, we know that Mr Freeman died in Plymbridge Woods.

'Robert Douglas Higgins joined the reservists with his other six friends. His file acknowledges he was very friendly with a female reservist and moved from Plymouth to Yeovil in Somerset to be with her, but they never married. He resigned from the Army soon after returning from Iraq. His Army pension record shows that he tragically died when he recently fell off a ladder; he was a self-employed electrician and was subcontracted to fit satellite dishes. The coroner's verdict was accidental death.'

King interjected: 'In view of what we are dealing with, sergeant, we will need to read the coroner's report.'

'Yes, sir, I have already contacted the Coroner's Office in Yeovil and asked for a copy of the report into the death of Mr Higgins to be emailed to us as a matter of urgency. I've asked one of our admin staff to copy it as soon as it arrives and pass it to you.' King nodded and Harris continued.

'Malcolm Edward Prescott, as we know, worked in a boatyard in Mount Batten. A single man who lived on a houseboat moored on the River Tamar. We believe he was murdered when he was drowned in the River Plym. I have addresses for Bryson and Franks, but not for Clayton. That's all the information I have, sir.'

'Thank you, Lucy. Text me the addresses please and then head on home. It'll be late when you get back, so I'll see you first thing in the morning.'

By the time the detectives had listened to the phone conversation between King and his sergeant it was after 5.30 p.m. As soon as it had ended, DC Dyson printed and passed to King a copy of the coroner's report on Higgins that Harris had requested. He scan-read it as time was pressing and passed it to Inspector Best, while he spoke to the DCs: 'Sam, could you print another copy for you and Alex to read, while Inspector Best and I will now see the DCI. He's been waiting as he knew Sergeant Harris was gathering some vital information.'

Moments later, King and Best were outside the DCI's door and King knocked.

'Come in, inspectors and take a seat. Have you heard from Sergeant Harris?'

'Thank you, sir. I've just had a long conversation with her after her visit to the Army barracks in Exeter. She's told me what she found out from the personnel records and I've also now got a copy of the coroner's report on the death of Higgins with the post-mortem report attached. Apparently he died from a broken neck, among other injuries, which he sustained in his fall from a ladder. I don't think we need to worry about what he died from, rather what happened immediately before he fell to his death.'

The DCI agreed: 'I understand, inspector. Let me guess: the p-m report refers to a tattoo on the inside of his right wrist?' King nodded his confirmation and continued: 'So, they started out as seven mates who joined the Army in 2010. We now know that four are dead, namely: Brackley, Freeman, Higgins and Prescott. The surprising aspect of this investigation is that Derek Clayton didn't die in Iraq as we first thought, he was only maimed. We suspect two of the four friends were murdered in the last few days and we will probably have to reopen the inquest on the cause of death for Mr Higgins.

'We need to urgently contact the three who apparently are still alive and decide if they are suspects or in need of protection. We have addresses for Bryson and Franks, but not for Clayton.

'We now know that, Carl Brackley apart, these deaths are linked and it would seem one of the so-called friends may be directly responsible. We quickly need to find these three men, sir. From what Sergeant Harris has told me, and also from the information provided by Mrs Freeman, it would appear that we are dealing with someone who has committed premeditated murders. I would go further and categorise the deaths as assassinations!'

TWENTY-ONE

The unfortunate road traffic accident, which had delayed Sergeant Harris on her way to Exeter, was to have tragic consequences. Following her report to her colleagues, she knew Inspector King would make it a priority to locate the surviving three men, either treating them as suspects or detaining them for their own protection. Arrangements were hastily made for uniformed police to visit the known addresses of Colin Franks and Greg Bryson, while the detectives tried to locate Derek Clayton's address. It was after 6 p.m. by the time officers had been assigned to visit the houses of Franks and Bryson. They were accompanied by armed officers as at least one of the three was possibly an assassin.

*

"Best of Both Worlds" is the self-proclaimed accolade of Wrangaton Golf Club. Situated on the southern slopes of Dartmoor National Park, between Ivybridge and South Brent, the claim is based on the course comprising nine holes on moorland and nine holes on parkland. Golfers are initially required to navigate the rugged terrain the moor offers, including trying to avoid sheep and cattle that have a right to graze. The other half of the course gives way to the privately owned, manicured part on the lower slopes, protected from wandering livestock.

In the golf club car park, Greg Bryson was waiting patiently for his playing partner, Jim Cantwell, to arrive. Bryson was deliberately slightly early as he knew their early-afternoon tee-off time barely allowed enough daylight to complete their round. He was becoming slightly agitated as his mobile rang. He could see from the recognised number it was his golf partner who was ringing him.

'Where are you, Jim, as we need to get off as soon as we can?'

'Sorry, Greg, but I'm bloody fuming. When I came out to get into my car, I found two of my tyres had been punctured. If it had been just the one, I would have accepted that I'd picked up a nail or something, but to have two punctured I knew had to be vandalism, or, should I say, criminal damage. I've been onto the police and they just gave me an incident number. I could have changed one tyre, but with two flats I'm knackered. It's so bloody annoying, but you'll have to play without me I'm afraid, while I get my car sorted out.'

'Tyres punctured! You live in such a nice area, Jim, who would do such a thing?'

'I was gobsmacked! Normally we don't get any vandalism around here. I guess it's some jealous nut.'

'Sorry to hear that, Jim, and no chance even of an investigation! We'll have a game next week.'

Greg Bryson had a decision to make: to play on his own or put his clubs back into the boot of his car until the following week. He reasoned that, as he could see there were not many golfers on the course to delay him, there being so few cars in the car park, he should be able to finish his round before dusk.

He put his mobile in his golf bag and headed for the first tee. His first nine holes were largely uneventful. He had a few pars, a few holes where he was one over par and a few holes he would rather forget. In order to get from the moorland part of the course to his favourite enclosed parkland part, he had to hit over a low wall. This potential obstruction that kept livestock where they belonged was about a hundred metres from the tee. He was relieved when his drive cleared the wall. His relief turned to elation as he eventually completed the tenth hole and then the long eleventh in regulation figures.

As he strode towards the next tee, he thought that this was how golf was meant to be played; good shots and nobody around to hold him up. Although the weather was a little overcast, he was now fairly confident of completing his round before the light faded.

He was feeling pleased about his general play as he stood on the elevated twelfth tee of a par-three hole. This was undoubtedly the "signature hole" on the course as it was by far the most aesthetically pleasing. The joy of hitting the ball high in the air, as the ground fell away, down to the inviting green below, with the fields of South Devon as a backdrop, was irresistible.

Thanks to GPS he was able to check the distance to the pin on his range-finder watch. Looking up, he saw that the clouds were thickening and threatening rain. The sun had gone down over half an hour before and, coupled with the cloud cover, the light was fading faster than he would have liked. As he stood there he also sensed an eerie quietness descend around him. The fact there was no traffic noise was understandable, as he was far from any main roads, but it seemed to him that nature had already gone to sleep for the night.

There were trees either side of the tee with a path to his left leading down to the green. He was about to play his shot with his trusty seven-iron when, in his peripheral vision, he was distracted by movement close to the path through the trees. He stopped and stared in the direction where he thought he had seen something move. Golfers do not like being distracted mid-swing and Bryson was no exception. If he had not been pressed for time he may have wandered over to investigate, but he knew daylight was limited and he needed to quicken his pace, not slow down.

His mild annoyance at the interruption seemed to add extra impetus to his swing and his ball sailed into the distance before dropping from a considerable height – mainly due to the elevation of the tee – a few feet from the hole. He was ecstatic at his superb tee shot as a birdie beckoned after his pars on the previous two holes.

He replaced his club in his bag and pushed his battery-operated trolley towards the path leading down to the green. After about thirty paces the path became steeper. He stopped just before the path began to meander through the trees, remembering how he had been distracted on the tee. In the already dim light, it was darkened further as a huge rain cloud hovered overhead. He felt a strange foreboding before telling himself not to be so stupid. With renewed vigour, he strode towards the gap in the trees: his bravado was short-lived.

Ten paces further on, the path forked. One led down to the hole he was playing and the other up to another tee. A small square plateau was formed at the junction of the paths. He stopped abruptly just before the fork, as although the light was poorer here due to the tree cover, he could make out a figure standing with his hands on his hips and legs apart. Bryson was slightly unnerved by the appearance of the sinister figure.

'Hello. Are you lost?' he enquired, anxious to appear calm, though a sixth sense was warning him to be wary. The figure slowly moved forward until the two men were close, only separated by Bryson's golf trolley.

'Remember me, Greg?'

'Jesus! Bloody hell, I thought you were dead!'

'No, I'm very much alive, no thanks to you; now it's payback time.' The black-clad figure bent down and gripped one wheel of the trolley. With one forceful jerk, he turned it upside down and pitched it into the bracken by the side of the path. Now there was nothing between them. Terror had gripped the now defenceless golfer.

'Now, lis… lis… listen. There was nothing I could do. I didn't want to leave you. The others made me. It's not my fault. Frankie told us to run!'

The man stepped forward and punched Bryson twice full in the face; he fell, virtually unconscious, onto the path. The upturned trolley had spewed out its contents and the attacker, purely by chance, grabbed the same seven-iron that had been used so effectively a few minutes before.

The frenzy with which the club was repeatedly smashed into Bryson's head as he lay dazed on the path meant he would not survive the attack. Even with immediate medical attention, which was not going to happen, his life was over. A trickle of blood zigzagged down the sloping path and formed a pool.

The assailant was out of breath, but still managed to find enough energy to hurl the bloodied club he was holding deep into the nearby trees. He was not worried about secreting his "weapon" nor about its detection, it simply brought closure to his planning; it was the penultimate vengeful act that evening of a very bitter man. It was now almost dark and starting to rain as he walked down to his well-hidden car. His night's work was not over yet.

*

About two hours earlier he had entered the course, some distance from the clubhouse, on the far side. He had parked along a road that crossed the thirteenth fairway and led to the greenkeepers' compound. Now, after getting back to his car, he turned on the interior light and checked that no blood had spattered his clothes, face or hands. He was not particularly bothered if it had as his last plan did not involve direct contact with anyone. He started the engine and congratulated himself on his meticulous planning, from the earlier tyre puncturing through to the killing.

He had followed Bryson for several days and knew he regularly played at Wrangaton Golf Club. The day before he ambushed him, he had checked the golf club's website where members and guests can book a start time. The man noted the time Bryson was playing that day and, crucially, also the name of his playing partner. He then rang the golf shop reporting that he had found a wallet on the course and a credit card revealed it belonged to Jim Cantwell, Bryson's golf partner, and wanted to return it to him. He was readily given his address and the next day parked in his street about twenty minutes before he calculated Cantwell would leave to go to the golf club for his round with Bryson. Fortunately for the assassin, Jim Cantwell's car was parked close to a leylandii hedge on his drive. The conifers provided perfect cover for him to puncture the front and back tyres closest to the hedge with the sharpened end of a screwdriver, turning it into a stiletto blade.

He knew it was only a matter of time before the police would piece together the murders committed on his one-man mission and identify his last victim. The imminent discovery of Bryson's body – as no doubt the police would be alerted when he did not return home – would make the time he had to complete his mission even shorter. It did not matter to him as he had already planned one last task for that evening and the police would be too late to stop him.

As he left the golf course along the rough track, he allowed himself one last thought of Bryson, his former friend, and whispered to himself: 'You asked for that, you bastard. Four down, one to go.'

*

That night, police officers, alerted by Inspector King, arrived at the home of Greg Bryson with armed officers poised discreetly in the background. His very concerned wife was expectantly looking out of the window as they arrived.

'Good evening, Mrs Bryson, is your husband home?'

'No, and I'm sick with worry as he should have been home ages ago. He's not answering his mobile and I've phoned Jim Cantwell, who he was supposed to be playing golf with up at Wrangaton Golf Club. Jim told me he couldn't play because his car had been vandalised, so Greg must have played on his own.

'When you pulled up I thought you were going to tell me something dreadful had happened to him. I was expecting him back before it got dark. Why are you here if it's not to give me bad news?'

'We would like to speak with your husband about an ongoing investigation we are dealing with. When he does return, please ring this number and explain about our visit and we will come straight back. We'll go to the golf course now and see why he's been delayed.' With that, he passed her a piece of paper from his notebook with a telephone number written on it.

When the officers arrived at the golf club car park there was a solitary car remaining and no sign of the owner. If he had collapsed on the course, it would be very difficult to locate him in the darkness on the inhospitable moor. Rain was now falling. They decided to call in the police helicopter and the Dartmoor Search and Rescue Team from Plymouth and both arrived in a little over twenty minutes. Eventually, after an hour, it was the search team who made the gruesome discovery. The police officers who had called on Mrs Byson earlier that evening, returned to the house and this time they did have bad news.

*

Inspector King was aware from contact with the officers who had gone to Bryson's home that he was missing and a search was underway. Although he had already been at work for nearly twelve hours that day, he waited at the station as he suspected it would only be a matter of time before he would receive more tragic news. He was right and headed for Wrangaton Golf Club.

TWENTY-TWO

The same day that Greg Bill Bryson met his fate, the assassin had one last person to feel the wrath of his revenge. He was saving until last the one he hated most. He knew if he did not act swiftly, his task would become that much more difficult as the police would finally make the link between the killings and be actively searching for him. That evening he would complete his mission and return to his home, content in the knowledge his retribution was complete.

The only regret in the plan he was about to execute was he would not directly confront his victim as he had with the others. They had seen their nemesis and had been reminded of what they did, or did not do, to help him when he needed them most. The look of horror on all of their faces as he confronted them showed him that they were being forced to relive that moment when they deserted him. Even though he would not directly be able to remind Franks of the major part he played on that fateful day, the end of his life was a sort of poetic justice as he would die in the same way as he himself had nearly died in Iraq.

*

Colin Frankie Franks was a rich man. He lived with his wife, Bonnie, in a large double-fronted stone mansion, named "Devonia", close to Yelverton on the edge of Dartmoor National Park. He was captain of the local golf club and was also a key figure in the Rotary. The single-track road that only led to their house eventually gave way to solid stone pillar gateposts and electronically operated gates. The drive sloped down from the road and after levelling for the footprint of the building and large back patio, continued falling away down to a high hawthorn hedge along the back boundary of the property. A wooden door halfway along the hedge allowed access onto the moor beyond.

The front-to-back slope created an uninterrupted, beautiful view across the moor, stretching as far as the sea. The rear garden had been tastefully terraced so the steeper areas in the substantial plot were more manageable for their gardener when he was mowing the lawn.

Two brand-new cars were parked on the drive; for him, a massive BMW X5 and for her, a top-of-the-range Tesla. Alongside them was a motorhome that provided better accommodation than some houses. That evening, Bonnie Franks had booked a Pilates class at a gym in Tavistock, a journey that would take her no more than twenty minutes.

'My car's low on fuel, Frankie, do you mind if I borrow the "Beemer"?'

'I tax your car, arrange for it to be serviced and clean the bloody thing. Why can't you manage to put petrol in it? If you must borrow it, don't drive over any potholes and don't drive so close to the hedges as last time it had scratches all down the left side from the roadside bracken!'

'I promise to take extra special care of it. It's only a car for God's sake!'

With that exchange over, he grudgingly tossed her the car keys.

As she opened the front door, movement-activated security lights lit up the whole of the front of the house. She knew she would have no clutch control trouble on the rise up the drive onto the road as the BMW had automatic transmission.

She pushed the starter button, turned on the headlights, selected "drive" with the turn of the dial on the central console and edged slowly forward. She waited patiently as the electronic gates opened as she pressed a button on a fob kept in the drinks holder on the console. As she edged forward, the gradient of the drive got a little steeper and the big 4x4 eased up the slope.

The explosion could be heard for miles around and the dazzling flash that accompanied the loud bang could be seen from far off.

Mrs Franks' body parts were scattered around the garden and even out into the road. The BMW was no longer recognisable as a swish car as its chassis lay twisted and upside down on the manicured lawn. Every window at the front of the house had been shattered by the blast. Only the toughened glass of the mobile home and the Tesla remained intact with the bodywork of both vehicles severely pitted.

Colin Franks had been standing at the lounge window watching his wife leave. As the bomb detonated he was forcefully thrown back against the opposite internal wall. He took several minutes to recover from the blast, partly due to shock. As he regained his composure, he quickly brushed the debris off his body and rushed outside. He could not believe the devastation that confronted him. He was so shocked he could not ring the emergency services. He just sank to his knees with his head in his hands, unable to understand what had just happened. Such was the noise from the explosion it was left to a neighbour, almost half a mile away from the Franks' house, to phone 999.

*

Inspector King was at the murder scene at Wrangaton Golf club. The pathway down to the twelfth green was bathed in light from four arc lamps and Scene of Crime Officers were busy assessing the area. He asked one of the officers who was wearing a white plastic suit to check something on the body. The SOCO shortly returned and confirmed the dead man had a tattoo on the inside of his right wrist. The inspector did not need confirmation of the wording.

His mobile rang. It was Inspector Best who had been called to the home of Colin Franks and his wife. He informed King of the bombing.

'The wife was blown up, Jim?' he asked, incredulous that a bomb had been detonated, and that the wife, and not her husband, had been the victim. Best confirmed that it was Mrs Franks.

'What can I say, Richard? It would appear that Mrs Franks was using her husband's car. We can't rule out that the bomb may have been set off remotely, but our SOCO colleagues think it was Semtex set off on a tilt-switch like the IRA used during the Troubles in Northern Ireland. Apparently, the car was on its way out of the property up quite a steep incline when the bomb detonated.

'All I know is it has completely wrecked the car she was driving and made a right mess of the other car and a motorhome on the drive. The windows at the front of the house were all blown out.'

Best knew that King had more than enough to deal with and after a long day he advised him to go home and they would update each other on their respective investigations the following morning.

'The husband...' King blurted out, but Best was already ahead of him.

'Don't worry, Richard, he has been taken to the police station in Plymouth where I hope to interview him later if he's in a fit state. I will see the DCI and arrange for him to be placed in a safe house. But for now, probably the safest place is at the station. You get some rest and we'll discuss it in the morning.' With that King ended the call and headed off to prepare to speak to yet another grieving spouse.

*

The headline on the front page of the later edition of the *Western Morning News* the next morning screamed at King as he ate his Weetabix and sipped his strong coffee: 'THE DEVON ASSASSIN'.

The article related to the deaths of Freeman, Prescott and Higgins. The press always seemed to find things out even though they were not public knowledge. For once King was happy with press coverage as he knew he may have to rely on the public's help to track down the assassin, who was now confirmed to be Derek Clayton. Surprisingly, the press did not use Clayton's name in the article.

When he had finished his breakfast, he sat in his kitchen and stared into space. Thoughts filled his head: If only Lucy had not been delayed by that accident they would have had more time to alert Bryson and Franks. If only they'd realised they were dealing with assassinations after receiving the information on all of the reservists. If only they'd stopped Bryson before he went off to play golf. If only they had protected Mr and Mrs Franks. If only he'd been quicker to act once the tattoo link had be made. If only...

Not for the first time recently, he chastised himself for dwelling on the past. He knew wallowing in self-pity was futile. It did not last long. He now had to catch a serial assassin in order to bring him to justice and stop him before he struck again. King suspected he was dealing with a psychopath and the bungled bombing meant Franks was still alive.

Why had Clayton killed his ex-mates, each in such a grisly manner? What possible justification could he have for the brutal murders of people who used to be his friends? Why had he killed Mrs Franks and not Mr Franks? A bomb in rural Devon! Nothing made sense. He finished his coffee and went to work, knowing Inspector Best would fill him in on all the gory details of the explosion the previous evening and he would reciprocate with the details of Bryson's murder.

*

After Clayton had finished his business at Wrangaton Golf Club, he drove to the outskirts of Yelverton and parked on one of the many tracks that criss-cross the moor close to his target property. After he had disposed of Higgins a month earlier, he had carefully planned what he was about to do. He knew that time was of the essence as the police would eventually work out what was happening and be determined to hunt him down.

The clouds from earlier in the evening had moved away and the crescent moon offered just enough light for him to see the ground in front. He had to tread carefully as, even with his stick, his prosthetic made walking treacherous due to the uneven and sloping ground. The bracken on the moor, which would have been at least knee-high in the summer, had shrivelled in the colder autumn weather and did not impede his progress. He did not walk along the road he had just left, instead he chose to skirt around behind the big house across open ground, taking extra care as there was no clearly defined path. He did not need to see the nameplate displayed at the front of the property to know the house was "Devonia".

He had reconnoitred the place in daylight the day before, masquerading as a moor walker, and had noticed the back entrance. He also made a mental note that the couple had a dog. Apart from all the equipment he was carrying in his backpack, he also had a dog treat in the shape of a bone; he mused, would a dog really care about the shape of the treat?

He had experience of explosives from his role as an Army reservist and had first-hand, very painful knowledge, of just how devastating a small amount of Semtex could be.

As he opened the gate that led into the back of the property, lights were shining from what he assumed was the kitchen and adjoining dining room. On his recce, he had noted the rest of the back of the house was dedicated to a lounge with bi-fold doors. He could not actually see the Franks due to the slope of the ground, which also meant they could not see him. He made his way to the front knowing the cars on the drive would inform him as to who was at home.

Without any warning a Labradoodle came bounding towards him. Fortunately the dog was in a playful mood and barking in an enthusiastic rather than aggressive manner. The interloper quickly reached into his backpack and gave the hound the doggie treat, which was immediately snaffled; thankfully for Clayton, that ended the barking. In his haste to quieten the dog he dropped the wrapper as he took out the treat. He had a quick look but could not see it in the semi-darkness.

He made his way around to the front of the house on the opposite side to where the lights shone out. The two cars on the drive were what he was hoping to see as it meant both the Franks were at home. He was only interested in one of the cars. He correctly guessed that the big BMW belonged to Colin Franks and, fortunately for Clayton, the car was not visible from the house as it was obscured by a huge mobile home. He suspected there were movement-activated lights at the front of the house. He left his stick right next to the wheel of the mobile home so he could easily locate it after he had done what he had to do. His Army training was proving invaluable as he crawled around the drive to the BMW. He correctly assumed the light sensors were not directed at the ground and he was under their radar.

Gingerly removing the Semtex – a piece the size of a tennis ball – from its box in his backpack, he pushed a detonator into one side of the soft plastic explosive; the other side had a strong magnet skewered into its surface. The fuse was a simple electrical device that would only be activated when gravity moved the liquid metal mercury in the tube and closed the detonator circuit. He very carefully reached under the car with some difficulty, partly due to the slope and partly due to his prosthetic lower limb. The magnet eagerly grabbed the underside, directly below the driver's seat. He set the tilt-switch and crawled back to collect his walking stick.

He retraced his entry path, passing the dog still chewing its treat, and let himself out onto the moor through the back gate, gently closing it behind him. He was not sure exactly when Franks would die. Maybe that evening, maybe in the morning. Ironically, it could be triggered by the police telling him he was a target and him rushing to get away. Clayton was unconcerned. He knew that probably within twenty-four hours the bastard would be dead.

*

The following morning Clayton listened to Radio Devon whilst he sat in his Land Rover. He was angry and frustrated when he heard that it had been the wife who had died; the bomb had missed its intended target. He felt little remorse for Bonnie Franks because, as far as he was concerned, she was just collateral damage. He never forgot her slapping his face on the dance floor at a Christmas disco held at the barracks all those years ago – which all the friends and partners were attending – or the humiliation as her husband smashed his nose with his fist. That night he knew he had had too much to drink, but the assaults by both Frankie and his then girlfriend he believed were unwarranted. Nevertheless, his mission was not retribution for the slap or the punch. He wanted Colin Franks to suffer for something much more serious.

He knew that the failed attempt had made his task more difficult as the police would now be aware of his identity and would obviously provide protection for Colin Franks.

The photograph of the assassin that was eventually circulated on media outlets was provided by the

Army. It was not a good likeness, partly because it was taken before fire scarred the left side of his face. He was helped too as wearing a face covering at any time of the day, in any environment, was not considered to be unusual while Covid-19 was still infecting thousands of people. He no longer went by the name Derek Clayton; that had long since been changed as he knew anonymity was paramount.

He only reflected on the bungled bombing for a short time before turning his attention to finding where Colin Franks would have been moved to. He already had a plan of how he was going to track him down and, when he found him, also how he would meet his end.

TWENTY-THREE

Inspector King was in a reflective mood. Satisfaction over the arrest of Doyle and Fraser two nights earlier, and their inevitable conviction for three armed robberies, had now given way to a sombre mood following the discoveries of the murders of Greg Bryson and Bonnie Franks only the previous evening. King had spoken with DCI Burrows earlier that morning and also separately with his fellow inspector, Jim Best.

Sergeant Harris had asked to speak with King in private. She told him that she realised that if she had been able to get the information from Exeter barracks earlier, the latest murders might have been prevented. King was quick to reassure her that the responsibility was his and his alone. He may have been able to refer the delay in getting the information to a more senior police officer, but chose not to, even though he had sensed it was an urgent and time-sensitive lead. He was not to know that the assassin would strike that very afternoon and evening. Indeed, until Harris had phoned with the critical information, he had assumed Clayton had been killed in Baghdad. Nevertheless, with hindsight, he admonished himself for not taking into protective custody the three other survivors. If he had done that, Greg Bryson and Bonnie Franks might still be alive.

He called his three detectives together again and asked Inspector Best to attend. Best's team were busy on other investigations and he would update them in due course. They all gathered around King's desk rather than using the conference room. A copy of the local newspaper was on his desk showing the headline he had read over breakfast: 'THE DEVON ASSASSIN'. Although it was a stark reminder of what his team were facing, King was happy for the press to raise the profile of the story as he wanted the public to be on the lookout for Clayton. What would be less welcome was coverage in the national media. King knew the murders would most likely attract criticism of the police, but he could defend how they went about the investigation, even explaining the unavoidable delay in getting the vital information from the Army. What some reporters representing the national papers in particular – as opposed to television channels – were likely to bring was unwelcome intrusion into the lives of grieving relatives, which would be more of a hindrance than a help to the ongoing investigation. King also suspected that the string of murders would reflect badly on the area, even though they had all been committed by one person.

'So, we've helped to end the exploits of a French and English trafficking gang, and two men have been arrested in connection with the three armed robberies. With the help of Inspector Best, we can now devote all our attention to catching the so-called Devon Assassin. Seven friends joined the Army in 2010 and now, as far as we know, only two are still alive, Colin Franks and Derek Clayton. Brackley, we know, was definitely killed in Iraq, and the others met their end in a variety of ways all within the last month. We are treating the tragic death of Mrs Franks as murder, albeit mistaken identity. She was about to use her husband's car when the bomb was detonated, possibly fitted with a tilt mechanism: I believe the bomb was meant for her husband.

'The mysterious Derek Clayton would appear to be the man we need to question about all of the deaths, but where is he? The Army has no record of his address and for all we know he has changed his identity. Why would someone systematically murder the people who used to be his friends? We heard from Mrs Freeman that there was an incident in Baghdad and her husband was reluctant to go into details about what happened. Whatever it was, it appears that Clayton became so bitter that he sought to murder all his previous mates and we've already seen that he is totally ruthless.

'Now only two men know what really happened in Iraq: Clayton and Franks. As we believe Franks is now the next target, he has been removed to a safe house. We need to speak with him and that interview will be conducted by Inspector Best and myself. We don't know where the safe house is, so DCI Burrows is arranging for us to be taken to see him in the next half an hour. After we've spoken with him, we will let you know what he had to say.

'While we are gone, I'd like all of you to work on tracking down an address for Clayton from any source you think might prove useful. I suggest you start by trying any relatives; his estranged wife would be a good place to start. Then the Department of Work and Pensions, DVLA, criminal records, financial institutions, TV licencing, hospital visits, dentists, garages, bank card use, Land Registry, local councils and any other avenue you can think of to get a lead as to where he might be hiding. Of course, as I've mentioned already, he might have changed his name, but we don't know that, so it's worth checking various sources. Any questions?' King asked and as no one had any, Sergeant Harris began allocating who would pursue which source in an attempt to find Clayton's address.

Soon a car arrived at the station to take the two inspectors to meet Franks. Colin Franks was now part of the witness protection scheme, run by the National Crime Agency. He was told that he must not make contact with family, friends or relatives in person or by phone. He must not leave the safe house, unless accompanied by a police officer.

*

The car carrying the two inspectors stopped outside a nondescript small detached house on the outskirts of Plymouth. There were no police outside. Their driver said he would wait around the corner and to call him when they were ready to leave.

'Mr Colin Franks?' King asked as a clearly distressed man peered around the partially open door.

'Ye… yes. Who are you?'

'You were informed we were coming. I am Inspector King and this is Inspector Best. We need to talk to you about what happened at your home yesterday.'

The two detectives produced their warrant cards and offered them to Franks through the chain-restrained door. Franks did not say anything, simply released the chain that allowed the door to fully open. He slowly walked down the hall before entering the lounge; King and Best followed making sure they had securely closed the front door. After expressing his condolences, King avoided any reference to the explosion the previous night. He was more interested to know the background as to why one of Franks' former friends would carry out such a heinous crime. There was no point in him prevaricating.

'Why do you think your home was targeted last night, Mr Franks?'

'I don't know, but one of your officers told me I have been put here for my own protection as it would appear someone wanted to kill me.'

'That's how it would appear, sir, and, at the moment, we think it is a person who you served with in the Army.'

'Who? Who can that possibly be? Why would they want to do that?'

'During our investigation we have discovered that you and six of your friends joined the Army as reservists in the early part of 2010. About a month ago, one of those friends, Bob Higgins, fell off a ladder and died. The coroner's verdict at the inquest into his death was that it was accidental. We now believe he may have been murdered. Also, three of your other friends, Daniel Freeman, Greg Bryson and Malcolm Prescott, have all perished and we believe one man is responsible for their deaths: that man is Derek Clayton.' Franks was visibly shocked and his face changed to a deathly white.

'The Pilgrim? The Pilgrim?' he repeated incredulously. 'It can't be! He was killed in Iraq. But even if he was still alive, why on earth would he want to kill his mates?'

'That's what we are hoping you can help us find out, sir, as we need to catch him before he kills again.'

Franks held his head in his hands and was becoming more distressed. Then his shock began turning to anger: 'Why would he want to kill Bonnie?' he demanded. The death of his wife had been traumatic and now he was being told one of his friends had killed her, and his mates were all dead.

King gestured to Best to fetch a drink of water for the shell-shocked Franks. King waited for him to sip some water before continuing. He recapped as, when in shock, some facts may have not sunk in. 'So, Mr Franks, we now know that Clayton didn't die in Iraq and we believe he is responsible for the deaths of your friends and for the death of your wife. As your wife was driving your car, we also think you were the intended target for the bomb.'

'But why? Why would he want to do such terrible things?'

'We've been told you and he had an altercation

at a Christmas disco some years ago, involving your then girlfriend.'

'How the fucking hell do you know about that? It was just a falling out because we'd all had too much to drink. Anyway, you don't kill people over a thing like that.'

'I agree, so what else could make him want to kill your friends and your wife?'

Franks was silent a short while and appeared to be thinking carefully about how he would answer. King and Best waited patiently until Franks eventually continued: 'You probably know that we all became Army reservists some years ago and early in 2018 we were sent to Iraq to fight the insurgents. While we were there, an incident happened in Baghdad, outside of the Green Zone where we were based. All seven of us were out on patrol in an armoured personnel carrier, the type where two sit at the front. Derek Clayton was driving and Carl Brackley was alongside him. The rest of us were sitting in the back.'

'What happened?' King asked and then listened intently to what he thought would be the crux of the whole investigation.

'We were the last in a convoy of six APCs and ours suddenly stopped. Nothing happened for a few seconds then Clayton shouted: "Brace!" There was an explosion and our APC was thrown into the air by an improvised explosive device. Some IEDs are detonated when a vehicle drives over a pressure pad, while others are detonated remotely. As we were stationary at the time of the blast, the insurgents must have been watching and ready to pick us off as we were last in the convoy.'

'What happened next?'

'After the blast, the five of us in the back were left lying on top of each other as the APC was on its side. I knew that when we got out of the vehicle we were likely to be the target of snipers from the nearby buildings. That's the way the insurgents operated. The APC provided us with some cover from the snipers. We ran towards the other APCs in our convoy for protection until air support arrived.'

'What happened to Clayton and Brackley?'

'I was first out and ran to the front of our APC. Half of Carl's head had been blown away by shrapnel, so I knew there was nothing we could do for him. The Pilgrim, that's Derek Clayton, was covered in blood and there was a fire between him and Carl. I was worried that if we stopped to help him we might all perish. I thought he was a goner anyway.'

'Why couldn't Clayton get out of the APC by himself? Was he too badly injured?'

'He mumbled something about his leg being trapped. I knew then it would take time to get him out and we could have all been shot by snipers. As their corporal, I instructed the others to run for cover as I could hear snipers firing at us. We jumped in the back of another APC and left the area. As we did, attack helicopters flew overhead and, we heard later, the insurgents were neutralised.'

'So, you left Clayton to his fate?' King rather bluntly asserted.

'You make it sound as if we abandoned him.'

'All we're trying to understand, sir, is why Clayton feels the need to murder all his former friends.' The inspector had no wish to add to Franks' grief, but he needed to know what had prompted Clayton's killing spree. So far, the explanation by Franks did not point to revenge as a motive.

'I've told you, Inspector King, in the heat of battle, I made a judgement that it was best to try and save the five of us as Carl was already dead and Derek was probably not going to make it. I actually thought he hadn't survived.'

Inspector Best interjected: 'So, Mr Franks, you say you thought Clayton was dead. Did you check in the field hospital later on the day of the incident or the next day to find out if your friend had made it?'

'Look, inspector, we were all pretty shook up. We knew Carl was dead and we thought Derek was as well. As corporal I thought it was a macabre thing to do to go and see your mates lying dead on stretchers in the base morgue. I advised them not to go as I knew that's how soldiers can suffer post-traumatic stress. Anyway, the next day we were flying back to the UK.'

King thanked Mr Franks, once more commiserating and assuring him they had a team of detectives trying to find Derek Clayton. In the meantime he stressed the importance of following all the advice he had been given to keep himself safe.

The inspectors were whisked away from the house and when they were dropped back at the station, King asked Best what he thought of the interview.

'Well, Richard, from his account, I simply don't believe that would have turned Clayton into an assassin. Anyway, why did Clayton wait so long to carry out these murders?'

'I can only think the time delay was down to his recovery period as he needed so many skin graft operations. Also, don't forget the pandemic. I agree with you about his motivation, Jim. When we find Clayton, it will be interesting to hear his recollection of what happened in Baghdad. What made him so bitter he went on a mission to kill his former friends? One thing is for sure: he isn't going away until Franks is dead.'

TWENTY-FOUR

Derek Clayton had unfinished business. He had left his home one month before after planning his revenge mission. He kept his twenty-year-old Army-surplus hard-top Land Rover Defender in a rented garage in Penzance. It contained all he needed for camping on Dartmoor including provisions with a long shelf life. Apart from a tent and sleeping bag, he also carried clothes, tools, rope and a small bottle of chloroform he had acquired courtesy of the Army. The other essential item for him was his 500cc Enfield Army model motorbike, which, with the aid of a ramp, neatly fitted inside the back of the Defender. He had slightly modified the bike to accommodate his prosthetic lower leg.

Clayton knew Dartmoor like the back of his hand. Since his arrival, he had camped close to areas he was familiar with during his Army training. He had used them with his friends when they joined back in 2010. These military areas were often close to tors with Gutter, Sheeps and Cramber Tors his favoured locations as they were the most isolated. Since his arrival, apart from a few walkers, he had seldom seen anybody else and, in any event, because of the military presence from time to time, his Army Defender never looked out of place. Nevertheless, he never stayed for more than two nights in the same location.

This particular evening, he had filled his motorbike with petrol, ensuring beforehand he could pay at the pump to avoid an attendant seeing his face. Even though he used a snood to cover most of it, he knew that once they saw any part of his disfigurement, it would seldom be forgotten. He acquired other fresh provisions from a farm shop on the outskirts of the moor, while milk and bread were bought from a small local Co-op shop, again using self-service. During all these transactions, he wore his snood. The obligatory face coverings due to the pandemic suited his cause admirably.

He had returned on his motorbike and checked that his Defender was untouched. Anyone trying to break in would have received a nasty shock; the door handle was wired to the vehicle's battery! The shock was not enough to kill a potential thief, but would force them to seek easier targets. He always remembered to flick a hidden switch to turn off the power before he opened the door. Clayton knew the chance of a potential thief passing a remote part of the moor, with his vehicle invariably parked out of sight of nearby roads, was very unlikely. Nevertheless, such was his state of mind that his trust in human nature had been irrevocably damaged.

When the weather was atrocious, as often happens on the moor, his sleeping pattern would change and his motorbike would be left outside, covered by a tarpaulin, while he would take shelter in the Defender. That is how he had led his life over the previous month; tonight he was feeling surprisingly sad as he knew his stay on the moor was coming to an end.

This particular night was clear, if a little cold, but the small log fire was sufficient to counter the chill air. After he had eaten his supper of baked beans and bread, he washed the dishes in a nearby stream. The kettle, hanging over his fire on a forked branch, began to boil and he made himself his last drink of the evening. He lay on top of his sleeping bag with his head propped up by his backpack. As he lay there with his mug warming his hand, he began to reflect on the events of the past month.

Soon after he had arrived on the mainland, he visited his old barracks and spoke to one of the administration staff. He told her that he used to be a reservist and had lost touch with his Army mates and wanted to look them up again. She told him that she would not normally give out addresses, but as he had been in the Army, and taking pity on his evident facial disfigurement – on this occasion he deliberately did not wear his snood – she provided him with the information he needed.

He could now begin plotting his revenge on his comrades who had let him down so badly in Iraq and caused him so much misery in his life. He recalled as he lay in hospital on the day of the explosion outside Baghdad, he felt anger and bitterness towards his so-called mates for their selfish act of deserting him.

Pulling Hurricane Higgins off his ladder had been a tricky start as he had to follow him to his jobs for a few days before the perfect opportunity presented itself. Higgins did not sense he was being followed, because he had no reason to be suspicious. The bonus for Clayton was that the 'one-eyed' coroner, as he called him, after reading a report on the inquest, had viewed his death as accidental. He suspected at some stage the police would work out what had happened, but the coroner's verdict had provided him with vital breathing space. However, he knew that the other assassinations needed to follow in fairly quick succession, so the police would not be able to apprehend him or alert his intended targets.

As he finished his last cup of coffee for the evening, he remembered how he had watched the house of Danny Boy Freeman for a few days from a discreet distance and had noticed that whenever Freeman went out, he was accompanied by his wife. He also saw that she had to open the car door for him, help him with his seatbelt and she always drove. On their return, Mrs Freeman also had to open the door and unfasten his seatbelt. Her husband did not help carry in the shopping from the car; she had to make several trips before it was all unloaded. He was led up the front path as a mother would a young child. It was obvious he was suffering from some form of Alzheimer's. As Clayton planned his next move, he only hoped that Danny Boy was sufficiently aware of what was going on to remember what had happened in Iraq.

Early one morning when he was watching the house, Mrs Freeman left to go out on her own. A younger man, whom Clayton assumed was her son, had left earlier. Freeman was alone. He saw his chance and got out of his Land Rover and briskly walked to the front door.

His Defender would not arouse suspicion from any prying neighbours as they knew Freeman was a former member of the Army. Getting him to answer the door was the hardest part of his plan, but Freeman eventually managed to operate the release lever and Clayton, wearing a facemask, pushed open the door. He remembered what he'd said to him: 'Hello, sir. I'm afraid your wife has been hurt in a car accident and I happened to be passing the crash. I witnessed it and as I was giving her first aid, while we waited for an ambulance, she managed to tell me where she lived and asked me to collect you and take you to the hospital where she was being treated. Don't worry about your shoes or coat as you need to get there as soon as possible. I'll take you, but hurry, as she was very badly injured.'

Clayton recalled how he had already visited Plymbridge Woods earlier that morning and found a suitable place away from any paths. He fixed the rope to a sturdy tree and dangled the noose, which he had prepared the previous evening, from an overhanging branch.

Due to his dementia, Freeman had no concept of where he was being taken, only remembering it was to see his wife who was very badly injured. It was only after he had been led to the makeshift gallows in the woods that he had become suspicious; by then it was too late as the noose had been placed over his head. Only when Clayton had made his: 'Remember me, you bastard?' remark, and removed his facemask, did Freeman finally realise what was happening to him.

Pushing him out over the sloping ground, his legs dangled in the air and his hands instinctively grasped the rope around his neck. The weight of his body was too heavy to prevent the rope squashing his windpipe. Eventually he stopped struggling. Clayton slowly walked back to his Defender, which was parked some way from the main car park and out of sight.

Still by his fire at his Dartmoor camp, Clayton put another log on his fire, and continued his reflection. All his planning as to how he would eliminate Malcolm 'The Boatman' Prescott had worked very well. He was particularly satisfied that Prescott was aware of what was happening to him before he drowned.

An inquisitive fox ran past his camp, momentarily interrupting his reminiscences. How typical of Greg 'Bill' Bryson to blame the others as he begged for his life. He had looked into Bryson's eyes on that fateful day in Iraq and all he saw was fear. No attempt was made to help him escape from the damaged vehicle. No words of reassurance that help was on its way. The rage he felt in Iraq at the moment when his comrades abandoned him to die alone on the battlefield returned with full force as he bludgeoned Bryson to death. To Clayton it was not murder, but summary justice.

He sat up and drained his mug of coffee before he readied himself for bed. He had one more person to deal with: the person he loathed the most. The collateral damage to Mrs Franks was unfortunate as the bomb was meant for Frankie. Still, Clayton mused, he was not too disappointed he had missed his target as next time he would have the opportunity to utter his well-used parting words and rehearsed them out loud: 'Remember me, Frankie?'

He had finished his revised planning on how he would get to Franks. In fact he had already actioned the first part of his plan. He had to be up early the following morning to carry out the next phase. As he threw another log on the fire, his last reflection as he got into his sleeping bag was that, in a day or two, his mission would be over. He had planned one final flourish before returning to his island home to live the rest of his days in peaceful obscurity, safe in the knowledge that The Pilgrim's revenge was complete.

PART TWO

TWENTY-FIVE

January 2018, two years earlier, in Baghdad, Iraq

The seven Army reservists had been posted to central Baghdad as part of an international force to counter the insurgency of the so-called Islamic State. Although they had been in the Army for eight years, this was their first overseas posting. The barracks for the troops was the heavily fortified ten-square-kilometre International Zone – formerly simply called the Green Zone – close to the city's airport. Saddam Hussein had been ousted from the site back in 2003 by US military forces. The three-metre-high concrete blast walls completely surrounded the area colloquially known as "The bubble". The compound, bordered on its eastern side by the Tigris River, had four heavily guarded entrances. The rest of Baghdad, outside the protected area, was referred to as the Red Zone and was considered unsafe. The self-titled "Magnificent Seven" were thrust into this hostile environment for the month of January in 2018. On a daily basis the soldiers had to venture out from the relative safety of the Green Zone on routine patrols and also be ready to deal with acts of insurgency.

The commanding officer, whenever possible, tried to keep soldiers from the same battalion together, as he rightly believed their camaraderie would hold them in good stead when confronted by open hostility. He was not to know that over the next month, the mutual trust and friendship of the seven mates would be tested to breaking point.

Six of the group were squaddies – the lowest rank in the Army – and were led by Colin Frankie Franks, who had recently been promoted to the rank of corporal. In their civilian lives, Franks was just one of the group of mates, but he took his new rank seriously and, when on duty, insisted on being referred to as corporal and not by his nickname. The others largely accepted this; after all it was the Army and it demanded discipline. A few thought his insistence at being addressed formally was slightly unnecessary, and this was compounded when he started issuing orders rather than requesting tasks to be carried out.

The seven were assigned an armoured personnel carrier. Derek Clayton offered to be the driver while Carl Brackley volunteered to be his crewman, sitting next to him upfront; these two positions were considered to be the most vulnerable to sniper attacks and roadside bombs. The other five were in the relative safety of the enclosed cabin at the back of the APC. Their daily routine was rising at 6 a.m. and, after breakfast, leaving the safety of the zone to patrol the streets of Baghdad. The city was home to nearly seven million people. Some of the indigenous population welcomed the occupying forces, while others hated them, viewing them as invaders, and were determined to kill as many as they could. The insurgents were fighting against both the new government and the occupying forces. Every day was the same for the soldiers: the relentless heat, the bone-dry dust, the constant fear of attack.

On their third morning – having been allowed two days to acclimatise – the convoy of APCs left the compound with Franks' team at the rear and Derek Clayton driving. The patrol travelled around the streets of Baghdad, ever watchful, and tending to relax a little only when, occasionally, the buildings gave way to an open expanse of ground on both sides of the road, where there were fewer hiding places for insurgents.

They were passing an open stretch of road when suddenly a figure emerged from behind one of the few trees in an otherwise arid and barren landscape. He was about fifty metres from the vehicles and was carrying a rocket-propelled grenade launcher. Before the soldiers had seen him and noticed the danger, the man had raised the weapon so it rested over his shoulder and then fired at the middle of the convoy. The APC would have been no match for the rocket had it hit its intended target. Despite the weapon having a crosshair sight, the attacker was unskilled in the use of modern weaponry. A slight misjudgement in his aim meant the warhead landed about three metres short of the APCs, creating a huge cloud of dust and sand that engulfed the whole convoy. All the soldiers readied themselves to return fire, but were unable to see the gunman through the dust haze.

The cloud began to clear first on the periphery of the blast. As he was at the rear of the convoy, Clayton was the first to see the gunman and could just make him out as he reloaded. In a matter of minutes he would be ready to fire again and, in all probability, after making a minor adjustment to his aim, be able to inflict a direct hit.

Clayton quickly selected first gear and swerved past the vehicle in front, his right foot jammed against the accelerator. The Rolls Royce 240-horsepower engine thrust the fifteen-tonne vehicle forward. The gunman levelled his weapon, and a split second before he pulled the trigger to fire his second grenade, the APC hit him travelling at nearly forty kilometres per hour. He was flung high into the air, his weapon cartwheeling before it became lodged in the tree he had used as cover. The soldiers checked the area for any more explosive surprises, retrieved the weapon from the tree, but left the man as dead or dying from his injuries. They continued their patrol now at a slightly quicker pace than before.

When all the APCs had returned to the compound, all the soldiers, particularly those from the middle of the convoy, hurriedly sought out Clayton to thank him for his daring initiative as undoubtedly he had saved them from serious injury or death. Franks should have been equally grateful, but for some reason, he seemed irritated with Clayton's newly acquired hero status.

*

The following morning, the reservists from Exeter did not join their routine convoy. Instead, they and fourteen other men in full kit climbed into the back of a lorry. Each wore body armour and carried an assault rifle, plus the standard issue life belt that had several pouches attached. These held a pistol, ammunition, two grenades and, importantly, a canteen. The one litre of water barely sustained a soldier out on patrol in the searing heat of the Middle East.

From drone surveillance, a suspected "bomb factory" had been identified and the mission for the men – comprising three teams of seven, each led by a corporal – was to locate and destroy it. After travelling a few kilometres, the lorry stopped in the street a few houses from the target building. The three corporals, having already agreed on how they would approach it, instructed their men accordingly. One team would advance from the left and one from the right. The third team would approach down an alleyway from a road running parallel to the street and would then be directly opposite the suspect building. Franks and his men were on the left flank.

All the men in the three teams were in single file as they moved in on the "factory", each with its corporal at the front. Franks wanted his team to storm the building from their position, attacking from the side rather than relying on a frontal assault from the team centrally positioned. The men gathered around in close order to receive their briefing.

'Right, men. This is how we'll go in. Privates Gregson and Brackley and I will move past the main entrance. The rest of you come in from the other side. On my command, we'll kick the door in and engage any occupants. If it is a "factory", we'll set charges and withdraw.'

Derek Clayton had serious misgivings about the plan: 'Hang on, corporal. I've got a feeling this might be a trap.'

'What makes you say that, private?' asked Franks indignantly.

'It's just too quiet. There's no one around. Usually there are kids playing in the street. No people, no dogs, it just isn't normal. I think they expect us to attack from the front, so I suggest we send a team around the back and check out the building from there. Also, it could be booby-trapped. As soon as the door is opened it could trigger detonation.'

Franks was not minded to heed the advice.

'When I want your opinion, private, I'll ask for it!' the corporal said dismissively, forgetting that he had just asked him.

Franks contacted the other corporals on his radio and told them what he proposed. But the corporal leading the approach directly opposite the building had ideas of his own. He was the antithesis of caution and was too gung-ho for his own good or for the good of the men under his command.

'I hear your plan, Frankie, but as we're in the middle, let us take it head on and the flank teams can give us support.' Franks rather reluctantly agreed and the other corporal on the right flank was apprised of the plan. All three teams readied themselves for the assault and edged closer. When ordered, the seven men in the frontal attack team moved forward down the alleyway, first in single file and then in line abreast once in the street, rifles at the ready. The corporal suddenly rushed forward, kicked the door with the sole of his boot and forced it open.

He took the full force of the explosion and was propelled backwards across the street and unceremoniously dumped against the wall of the building opposite. His tattered uniform could not hide the damage to his body. Some of his men were also caught in the blast and, although badly wounded, they would survive. The soldiers from the flank teams rushed to their aid, while others looked around them, particularly at the rooftops, in anticipation of attack from snipers.

On further brief inspection, the building turned out not to be a bomb factory. The soldiers had been deliberately lured into a trap as Clayton had feared and suspected. The body of the corporal and the wounded were carried back to the lorry and the men returned to the protected zone, heading straight for the field hospital. The men in Franks' team sat in silence on the journey back and each, in his own way, reflected on what had happened. Franks' self-righteous approach had not gone unnoticed, neither had Clayton's advice before the fatal attack. As the soldiers trudged back from the hospital to their barracks, Corporal Franks grabbed Clayton's arm.

'I'd like a word with you, Private Clayton.' Derek Clayton was possibly expecting an apology from his corporal as Franks had ignored his advice and chosen the wrong approach. If they had followed his plan, he would now be lying in the morgue. Franks spoke through gritted teeth.

'Don't you ever question another of my orders. I am the one in charge and the next time I give you an order, I expect you to follow it. Have I made myself clear, private?'

Clayton, who did not show it, was flabbergasted by his corporal's lack of contrition and off-hand manner. He simply replied: 'Crystal, corporal.'

TWENTY-SIX

The failed "bomb factory" mission was the talking point throughout the camp the following day, including Clayton's perceptive reading of the scene prior to the attack. The death of the corporal was also discussed and, unsurprisingly, it had a big impact on the mood of the group of reservists from Exeter. After Franks' promotion, he had tried hard to adapt to the role of corporal. However, he had badly misjudged the impact on some, but not all, of his friends with his overly officious tone. His unnecessarily heavy-handed approach had backfired. He also felt undermined by Clayton over his concerns about the decision for a frontal assault on the "bomb factory".

Despite his evident shortcomings as a leader, he still retained the support of Greg Bryson, Dan Freeman and Malcolm Prescott who thought Clayton should not have openly questioned the order given by Franks, despite the disastrous consequences. However, his standing as a leader would have been improved if he had apologised and started treating all of the men in a more respectful manner. Sadly, to Franks, contrition was a sign of weakness.

*

The team was back in the APC in convoy and once more out on patrol. This time they were instructed to protect the boundary of Baghdad International Airport as civilian and military cargo planes were due to land later that morning. Recent incoming flights had been fired on by insurgents using a surface-to-air missile from the back of a pickup truck. Fortunately, on those occasions they had missed their target, but it seemed only a matter of time before a tragedy occurred. A week before, a passenger jet had come under attack from small arms fire. It was carrying over 150 passengers and was struck by gunfire as it landed, but only one passenger was slightly injured.

The perimeter of the airport extended for many kilometres and it was decided that rather than all the APCs moving in convoy, they should be positioned around the boundaries at the most vulnerable points – where landing aircraft would be in range of the insurgents' weapons – and also where they could quickly respond to any reported attack. Of course, the soldiers were all too aware of their own vulnerability being stationary and isolated. When the scheduled flights for the day had landed, the soldiers could return to their base.

As a military cargo plane was on its approach to the runway, gunfire could be heard coming from an area between the positions of two APCs. Franks' team was the closer and first to respond. They headed for the buildings pinpointed as the source of the firing. When they arrived, three figures could be seen running away.

The soldiers' APC skidded to a stop as the soldiers in the back jumped out and began giving chase. Clayton, who had the best view of the incident from his driving position, spoke on the radio to his corporal telling him he thought they might be children. Clayton and Brackley followed in the APC, eventually stopping opposite an alleyway the shooters had run down pursued by the soldiers. Clayton and Brackley then climbed out and joined in the chase.

Franks and the others were gaining on their quarry. The alleyway gave way to a small square, bordered by buildings on all sides. As the soldiers arrived, they saw the three figures they had been chasing duck into a building with no door on one side of the square. Franks gestured to his men to take up positions either side of the open entrance. He then reached for a grenade from his belt.

Clayton and Brackley arrived soon after the others and quickly assessed what was happening. Clayton shouted: 'Wait, corporal! I think they're just kids playing war games.' Bryson, Freeman and Prescott tutted to themselves at Clayton's latest interference, which they felt was bordering on insubordination.

Undaunted by the interruption, Franks pulled out the pin and threw the grenade into the building and fell to the ground to protect himself from the blast. The explosion spewed out some of the fragmented contents of the room and the soldiers knew it would almost certainly kill all those inside. As the dirt and dust cloud settled, Franks got to his feet and moved forward, rifle at the ready, to check inside the building.

What he and the others found were the disfigured bodies of three children, no older than twelve. The guns they appeared to be carrying were poor imitation Kalashnikovs made of wood.

*

Dinner in the huge canteen on the base that evening was a sombre affair for the group. Not for the first time on this posting the friends were divided. Clayton, Brackley and Higgins sat together, while the other four, who had arrived later, sat well apart from them. The conversations on the tables were markedly different.

Higgins broke the silence on his table.

'Bad business today, that's for sure. Pilgrim, you didn't want Frankie to throw the grenade into the building; so what would you have done?'

'Anything I say in answer to that question, Hurricane, will seem like criticism of what happened. Look, we all make decisions under pressure that, on reflection, might not stand up to closer scrutiny,' Clayton said, seeking to downplay the incident.

'That's sounds like a cop-out to me, Pilgrim!'

Higgins was not satisfied with the answer he had been given, so Clayton tried a different approach.

'For a start, Frankie didn't see what I saw from my driver's position. I saw the three running away and immediately thought they were just kids playing war games. From their stature, they didn't look to me like grown men. Frankie was still in the back of the APC with you and the others at that point, so didn't get the same view as Carl and I had. By the time you all climbed out, the three were further away.

'Now, even if they were kids, it doesn't mean to say they weren't responsible for shooting at the aircraft or that they weren't dangerous. All I was thinking was they might have simply been in the wrong place at the wrong time and run away when they saw us pull up in the APC. Against that scenario, I didn't want Frankie to blast them.'

'That's all very well, but you still haven't told me what you would have done?' Higgins persisted.

'It's not easy to make reasoned judgements on the spur of the moment when day in, day out we are tracking down insurgents. The mind can get fixated. As soldiers we can easily slip into thinking all Iraqis are bad people. We can simply take the view that they all belong to Islamic State and want to kill us.'

'You should have been a politician, Pilgrim. So, come on, tell me what you would have done?' Higgins was getting fed up with what he saw as evasive answers.

'Because I'd told him over the radio that they might be innocent kids, I certainly wouldn't have tossed a grenade into the building!' Higgins was not the only one getting irritated.

'I get that, Pilgrim, but now you're only telling me what you wouldn't have done, not what you would've done?'

'Okay. There were over twenty soldiers there outside the building those kids took shelter in. I would have sent a few of us around the back to block any escape route. It didn't make sense to have all of us focussing on one doorway, even if the three inside were hard-nosed insurgents armed to the teeth. So, I would have sent some around the back and also some to watch our backs. You can never be too careful, as while we were preoccupied with the three in the building, other insurgents could have been surrounding us ready to gun us down from the rooftops or attack us from behind. It should have occurred to Frankie that this could have been a so-called honeytrap. In other words, luring us into a position where snipers could have picked us off.

'You asked what I would have done. I'd have asked if any of our soldiers could speak Kurdish or Arabic. If someone had said they could, I'd have asked them to shout a message, from a safe distance, so the three inside could hear. Something like: "Come out with your hands in the air. Leave any weapons you have behind. Do not make any false moves or you will be shot!" Something along those lines, so the three could then have made a choice. As it was, they weren't given a choice. As they now appear to have been innocent boys at play, they may well have realised it would have been a smart move to come out with their hands in the air. As we now know, they were only carrying imitation weapons. I think given that option, they would have come out and we'd have sent them away with a flea in their ear.'

'And what if no one could speak their lingo? What then?'

'I'd have used the universal language: gunfire! A few warning shots may have made them think again as to what was their best option. Try and make them realise we weren't playing games. They weren't given any options.'

Higgins thought for a moment before speaking: 'Yeah, that's a fair point, Pilgrim. I hadn't thought of tackling them that way. Obviously, neither did Frankie!'

Clayton and Brackley had finished their meal and both nodded to Higgins as they got up and left. Back in their own billet, Clayton bid Brackley goodnight and lay on his bunk. He reflected on what had happened since arriving in Baghdad.

He thought about the reprimand Franks had given him in private after the explosion had killed a corporal. Also, the incident that day when he had tried to warn Franks about the boys. He had been right on both occasions and yet some of his mates seemed more concerned that he had been insubordinate. That saddened him. This was not about him trying to make Franks look inept. Although he had calmly explained his reasoning to Higgins when questioned by him over the latest incident, inside he was seething. This was not simply because he was being cast as the villain, but also because these were supposed to be his mates. A smouldering resentment was starting to build in Clayton and it wouldn't take much for it to catch fire.

Back in the mess tent, Higgins finished eating and, with his coffee mug in hand, went and joined his other mates. The talk on the other table was somewhat different. Bryson spoke to the others: 'We weren't to know they were just kids, and even if we had known, there are a lot of child soldiers out there. Those bastards in Islamic State don't care about ages; if you can fire a gun, they're happy to recruit you to their cause. I think you were right, corporal, to take them out!'

Freeman also offered his support to Franks, more out of sycophancy than belief in the corporal's decision to annihilate the three boys: 'What they were carrying looked like real guns and why did they run away in the first place?'

Prescott was not going to be left out: 'Yeah, in the circumstances, and based on what we had seen and heard, it was an easy mistake to make.'

'Who said it was a mistake?' Franks said glaring at him.

'Sorry, I didn't mean it was a mistake. The mistake was made by them when they ran. If they hadn't, they'd still be alive.' Now that Higgins had joined the other four, he was made welcome. They took it as him showing solidarity with them.

Franks made a casual enquiry: 'So, Hurricane, what was the chat on the other table about?' Higgins was not bright enough to understand the nuance of Franks referring to him by his nickname rather than calling him Private Higgins.

'What I wanted to know was, when The Pilgrim told you to wait before you tossed the grenade into the building, what did he want you to stop for?'

'And what did he say?'

'He said something about not needing all of us focussing on the building as other insurgents could be lurking on the rooftops. We should've covered our backs and some of us should have checked the roofs for snipers, and also the back of the building for a possible escape route.'

'But why didn't he want me to throw the grenade?'

'He thought you should've given them a chance to surrender.'

'And how did he plan to do that? Walk into the building and have a polite conversation with them?' Franks was now sneering.

'No, he said he'd have asked if any of the other soldiers spoke their lingo and if so he'd have told them to come out with their hands in the air. Personally, I thought it was all a bit far-fetched.'

The other friends started to laugh, all except Franks; he did not see anything remotely funny in Higgins' report of his chat with Clayton. He did not want to let the matter drop: 'Anyway, what if we weren't able to communicate with them, what then?'

'Oh, he had an answer for that too as I asked him the same question. He said he would have fired a few warning shots and that might have encouraged the kids to come out. You know, show them this was for real, not a game.'

The men just shrugged and shortly after gradually drifted away leaving Franks on his own, nursing a mug of tepid coffee. Clayton worried him and he could not forget the events of the day. Although the others had laughed at what had been said, he thought there was merit in both the vulnerability to being attacked and, just as important, his alternative approach to the killing of three boys playing war games. Some officers may have learned from that experience and have been more contrite. Others may have viewed Clayton's points as insulting and challenging authority. Franks fell squarely in the latter category. What's more, that was not the first time Clayton had questioned his decisions. Would he choose self-reproach or view Clayton's actions as disobedience? He drained the last of his coffee and spoke quietly to himself: 'Okay, mister smart-arsed Pilgrim, let's see which of us is the better soldier!'

TWENTY-SEVEN

It was the penultimate day of the reservists' tour of duty. The following day they would fly out from Baghdad International Airport, back home to their normal lives and civilian jobs. Before then they had one last patrol and, as they had done many times during the month, Clayton was driving the APC with Carl Brackley alongside him. There had been no more unfortunate incidents following the deaths of the three boys killed by the grenade tossed into the building by Franks. There had been an inquiry and he had been exonerated as the boys appeared to have been carrying weapons. Clayton's alternative method of dealing with the unfortunate incident did not form part of the investigation.

As on previous occasions, the other five reservists climbed into the back of the APC and the six-vehicle convoy left the compound with their APC once more bringing up the rear. They had patrolled this way many times over the past month and it had almost become routine. However, Clayton knew that complacency increased vulnerability. In the environment they were operating in, they simply could not afford to drop their guard.

The convoy meandered through the streets of Baghdad, receiving smiles and sneers in equal measure from the indigenous population. When the soldiers were at the furthest point from their safety zone an eerie silence fell over the area. Once again the telltale signs were evident. No people or dogs on the streets and no noise coming from the buildings on either side of the wide road they were travelling down.

Clayton sensed an attack was imminent, but could do nothing to combat it as he did not know what form it would take. Using his radio, he alerted his corporal who was rather dismissive of his driver's intuition. Franks did not pass on Clayton's misgivings to the soldiers in the other APCs.

Suddenly, a battered football slowly rolled out from an alleyway between the last two vehicles in the convoy. A young lad appeared from the same alleyway and chased after the ball. Clayton was immediately suspicious as he was aware this was a tactic used by the insurgents. He should have continued at the same speed and kept close to the APC in front, but that would have meant running down the boy. Care for the lad overcame his concern of a possible attack and he braked. The boy momentarily disappeared from view, hidden by the front of the APC, before emerging from the other side. He began running back towards the alleyway. Crucially, he was not carrying his football.

Clayton's instincts had been right; it was a trap. He shouted into his radio alerting his colleagues: 'IED! Brace! IED! Brace!' Barely had the last warning left his lips when there was a huge explosion and the fifteen-tonne APC was lifted off the ground and dumped on its side. The remotely controlled bomb had been detonated right under the seat of his crewman. Brackley took the full force of the blast and both he and Clayton would have been thrown out of their vehicle if they had not been restrained by their seat harnesses. Clayton was now sitting with his body parallel to the ground, his right arm resting on the dirt of the road. Brackley was above him slumped to one side in his seat harness with blood dripping from his shrapnel-shattered face onto Clayton's shoulder below.

When Clayton had recovered from the initial impact of the blast and orientated himself, he looked up to his left and saw his crewman's face; or what was left of it! A piece of shrapnel had taken away its right side. Brackley was clearly dead. Clayton then realised his right foot was trapped in the wreckage and although he could not actually see it, he could feel the jagged edges of metal cutting into his flesh and pinning him down. Painful as that was, a more pressing worry for him was the fire burning between him and his dead crewman. He was already feeling the heat on the left side of his lower body through his combat clothing; it was fireproof, but not heat resistant. Worryingly, the flames were intensifying and he could feel the exposed parts of his body – his neck and face – getting hotter, and the hair poking out below his helmet started to singe.

The soldiers in the back of the APC were largely unscathed, save for a few superficial cuts and bruises. Clayton's warning over the radio had prepared them for the blast and they had grabbed hold of the metal bars that formed the inside of the cabin structure. Even so, three of the men ended up on top of each other as the vehicle landed on its side.

The corporal was first to open the steel door at the back, which could not swing open as normal due to the position of the vehicle after the blast, but instead clattered against the back of the APC, as its hinges were now at the bottom of the hatch. Franks was carrying his rifle as he fell out of the APC. He quickly moved to the side of the overturned vehicle. The others grabbed their weapons and clambered out behind him, more concerned about getting to safety than defending themselves. They all knew that a common tactic of the insurgents was for snipers to pick off any survivors from a blast as they ran for cover. Crouching down, Franks indicated to his men to follow him in single file as they edged around the back of the vehicle lying on its side and moved towards the front.

As he was leading, Franks was the first to come alongside his stricken colleagues in the front of the APC. He raised his left hand to indicate to the others to stop. First he looked at Brackley who was clearly dead. He then looked down at Clayton slumped in the driver's seat, his harness holding him in position.

'Help me, Frankie. I can't get out. My foot's trapped and I think I'm losing blood,' he pleaded. Franks glared at him for a few seconds and then simply smiled. He was not leaving him for dead like Brackley, he was leaving him to die.

'You're on your own, Clayton. You're the clever bastard, you work it out!'

'But, Frankie, the flames. Get the extinguisher from the cab. They're scorching my neck!'

Franks was unmoved. He was able, but unwilling, to help. He glanced back through the cloud of dust and debris and shouted to the others.

'Watch out as there are snipers all around. Okay, men follow me. We'll run to the next APC just up the road. Go in single file and leave at three-second intervals to make it difficult for the snipers. That's an order!' With that he ran as fast he could, bent over to make himself a smaller target for any insurgent marksmen. The others were gripped by terror. Fear of being picked off as they ran and fear of being gunned down if they stayed where they were for too long, heightened their anxiety. Added to that, the 'cloud cover' was gradually clearing and they would be even more visible to rebel gunmen.

Freeman was the next to come alongside the two mates to wait the three seconds before running after his corporal. He glanced at Brackley and recoiled in horror and then down to Clayton who pleaded with him for help.

'Danny Boy. My foot's trapped. Put out the flames, they're burning my neck.' Freeman had fear in his eyes and the acrid, nauseating smell of burning flesh nearly made him puke. He looked away, counted out loud: 'One, two, three!' and sprinted to safety.

Prescott came next and from his crouched position his eyes were level with Clayton's who implored: 'Help me, Boatman. I'm trapped.' Prescott heard his plea and looked back at him helplessly, raising his hands in a gesture that said he could not help his friend. He suffered from pyrophobia and as the flames grew higher his fear of fire intensified. He readied himself to run the snipers' gauntlet. Three seconds later he ran.

Bryson was next in line and after seeing Brackley's mutilated body, he was quite clearly traumatised. Clayton tried once more: 'Bill, help me as my foot is stuck. I can't move!' Unfortunately, Bryson was the most weak-willed of individuals and only wanted to do what his corporal had ordered. He looked at the stricken duo: 'Just following orders!' he said and counted to three and ran. Fear was his mover, self-preservation his goal.

As the flames intensified, Clayton heard the noise of a helicopter overhead, which created a cloud of dirt and dust from the road. Unfortunately, it also fanned the flames. A dusty film began to form over Brackley's blood, which had drenched Clayton's shoulder and was starting to congeal.

Higgins was the last to come alongside his wounded colleague and could just make out Clayton's plea over the din of the chopper: 'Hurricane, I'm trapped. Douse the fucking flames!' Higgins looked at Brackley then back to Clayton. The sight of the blood and smell of flesh being eaten by the flames made him retch. Above the racket from the rotor blades he gave his parting reply before he ran: 'Sorry, Pilgrim. I could get shot!'

Only when the last of his friends had deserted him did he realise he had to help himself. He had not searched for his canteen earlier as he expected his mates to get him out; how wrong he was. He fumbled around his waist for his pouches, which had become dislodged in the explosion. The flames continued to lick the skin off his neck and face. Although he could not see what he was searching for as the dust swirled around him, he eventually found his belt and groped for a pouch. In the first was his pistol and in the second a hand grenade. He found what he was looking for in the third: his canteen of water. He wrenched it out of the pouch and quickly unscrewed the top. With his right hand he poured the water down the left side of his face and neck and the flames reduced but were not extinguished. Barely able to breathe through the dust thrown up by the helicopter, with his left hand, he then felt around the body of his dead colleague above him. Eventually he grabbed his canteen and poured more water over his neck and face in an attempt to put out the fire and to soothe his now excruciating burns. Eventually, the flames momentarily flickered and appeared to die out.

He had not noticed it before, possibly due to shock, but the pain from his lower leg was now intensifying. The jagged metal had cut deep into his ankle and the loss of blood was beginning to sap his strength. He knew he was badly injured and badly burned. He felt his life ebbing away as the dust continued to swirl around him.

It was a truly surreal experience for Clayton and he started to hallucinate. One vision kept coming back into his mind: it was the smiling face of Colin Franks looking down on him as he pleaded for his help. As he began to lose consciousness, he had only one regret: he would not live long enough to get even with the bastards who should have helped him. He slowly closed his eyes and waited for death.

TWENTY-EIGHT

Clayton had given up on being rescued following the IED attack. Every one of his mates had shunned his pleas for help. He was badly burned on the left side of his neck and face and he knew he had lost a lot of blood from the wound on his right foot. He could not see it, but he could certainly feel it. He resigned himself to his fate, even though he had heard a chopper overhead and from the downdraught of the rotor blades, he knew rescue was imminent. It had come too late to save his life. Before he slipped into unconsciousness, he glanced up and mourned the passing of his only true mate, Carl Brackley.

*

Not just one helicopter had landed near to the stricken APC, but three. A dozen marines swarmed over it and four worked hard to extricate Clayton. The very first thing they did was to make sure the fire was completely out using an extinguisher from the chopper. The other marines were scanning nearby buildings to ward off any possible attack from insurgents. The four marines around Clayton worked together and bent back the metal that had trapped his leg, eventually managing to ease his foot out past the jagged edges. One used his belt to make a tourniquet, which helped, but their hands were still covered in Clayton's blood. They knew from their experience that in all probability he would lose his foot.

The marines took heart that he was still breathing and they quickly stabilised him. Cold compresses were placed over his burns to reduce pain and swelling. Once they'd cooled the burn area, they waited until they were on board before applying cling film to ensure the wound was kept clean to prevent infection. They could not do that outside as the rotor blades continued to create a dust storm.

The two Apache attack helicopters were first to take off in order to provide protection from any insurgents' attempts to engage the rescue mission. Their fearsome weaponry was a definite deterrent. Clayton was stretchered to the Puma, still unconscious with his legs tied together in a splint. The marines had secured the APC with strong canvas straps, which were attached to the helicopter. They boarded the aircraft and slowly airlifted the damaged APC back to base camp.

*

Dinner that evening in the mess tent on the military base in Baghdad was a very sombre affair for the surviving mates. It would have been subdued enough for all the soldiers in the tent when just one of their colleagues was killed in action, let alone two. The five reservists were sitting together and had collected their main course. Some picked at their food while others were slow to start. Franks had finished his meal before Higgins had even started eating. They all sat in stony silence and throughout the mess tent the only noise was from the clatter of cutlery on the metal trays. Silence in its own way was reverential.

Higgins sat in front of his meal, without touching his knife and fork. After a minute speaking to no one in particular and looking down at his plate he said: 'We should've helped him. Carl was obviously a goner, but The Pilgrim desperately needed our help. We all let him down when he needed us most.'

Franks was in denial: 'What could we have done, Higgins? He was on fire and any delay in getting him out could have cost all of us our lives!'

Hurricane was not about to be placated: 'What could we have done? What could we have done? For starters we could have put out the fucking flames with the water from our canteens. When I got back to barracks, I checked my canteen and do you know what, it was fucking full. That water could have doused the flames and saved his life. Or one of us could have gone back to the APC and fetched the fire extinguisher. We could have tried to free his trapped leg. That's what we could have fucking done! But what did we do? We fucking left him and ran to save ourselves! I'm as much to blame as anyone. The difference is I'm admitting that I was more interested in saving myself.'

Franks' anger was getting close to the surface: 'And while we were rescuing Clayton, with all that was going on, we would have been target practice for the snipers.' The raised voices had attracted the attention of a sergeant eating close to the mates' table.

'Snipers! Snipers! In case you didn't notice, there weren't any fucking snipers!'

Prescott queried: 'If there weren't any snipers, why did we run for cover and not help The Pilgrim?'

Higgins supplied the answer: 'Because we were following a fucking order!'

Franks got to his feet, closely followed by Higgins and the soldiers squared up.

'Don't you try and lay this on me, Higgins. I was doing what I thought was best to save the lives of all of us!'

'Bullshit! The truth is there was one life you weren't interested in saving!'

The sergeant on the adjoining table had heard enough and quickly got to his feet, leaving his partly eaten dinner and stood between them: 'Corporal, enough.' He then beckoned over a military policeman who was eating his dinner quite a distance from where the confrontation was taking place. No one in the tent was speaking before the altercation and now even the clatter of cutlery on metal plates fell silent.

'Take Private Higgins to my tent and stay with him until I join you. Corporal, you follow me.' With that the sergeant marched out, with Franks following closely behind. Outside he eventually stopped well away from the mess tent and turned smartly to address Franks: 'Attention!' he commanded and Franks duly did as he had been ordered and stood stock-still. The sergeant then moved in front of him until their noses were nearly touching.

'What the fucking hell was that all about? In case you haven't worked it out, corporal, the Army is based on discipline, bordering on blind obedience. What sort of spectacle was that when a squaddie questions your authority in front of 200 soldiers? I don't know the rights and wrongs of the incident, but you need to get a grip of the situation or I will. Do I make myself clear, corporal? I'll deal with Higgins. Now get back to your barracks. Dismissed!'

The sergeant then marched purposefully to his tent where the MP and Higgins were waiting in silence with the private standing to attention. The sergeant thanked the MP and dismissed him. Higgins braced himself for the tirade.

'At ease, private. Listen, I know the tensions that can build up in this godforsaken hole. Believe me, I've been out here for two years and know what it's like. But what you did in the mess tent was out of order and I should charge you with insubordination. However, I'm not going to for two reasons: firstly, I asked for a verbal, off the record report from the other corporals in the convoy today about what happened on patrol. You were right in what you said about there being no snipers. Anyway, I would have expected soldiers not to leave a colleague who needed help no matter what state he was in or what danger existed. I'm not here to stand in judgement over what happened today. Each of you will have to reflect on what you did or didn't do to help the injured soldier.

'Secondly, the main reason I'm not going to charge you is that your tour of duty ends tomorrow and I want you on that flight out, not in the slammer. You are a very lucky soldier. Don't you ever question a superior rank again, do you understand? Now get out of my sight.' Higgins about-turned and left the tent, while the sergeant went back to finish his cold meal.

*

The morning after the attack the reservists were packing to leave the base with forty other soldiers returning to the UK. The five mates were in solemn mood. The events of the previous day would live in their memories forever. Corporal Franks had advised that they did not visit the field hospital morgue as he had read that seeing dead colleagues could bring on post-traumatic stress. Freeman, Bryson and Prescott heeded his advice as they were still loyal to their corporal. Higgins also stayed away, but not out of loyalty to Franks – that had gone the day before. Rather, he knew that seeing Brackley and Clayton would only risk a repeat of his angry outburst of accusations that had happened the previous day.

The soldiers boarded lorries to take them to the airport where they took a military flight to Brize

Norton Airport in Oxfordshire. The seats on the plane were not allocated as on civilian flights. Higgins sat apart from his other mates. He had decided that on his return he was resigning from the Army. He would never contact them again as any communication would be a painful reminder of what had happened on that fateful day.

*

Two days after the attack on the APC, Clayton was brought out of an induced coma to find he was in a hospital bed in the Intensive Care Unit at

Derriford Hospital in Plymouth. He had a cage over the end of his bed to keep the blankets off his lower legs. As he regained consciousness he realised he was surrounded by tubes and machines. An Army surgeon was sitting in a chair by his bed.

'Welcome back, Private Clayton. My name is Major Adams and I operated on you when you were brought here. At one point we thought we'd lost you. You're a fighter and no mistake. I need to update you on your condition. I can do that now or, if you would prefer, I'll leave it until you are stronger.'

Clayton found it difficult to speak as his head was swathed in bandages.

'If you would like me to update you now, just raise your right hand. If you would like me to leave it until later, raise your left hand. Right for now, left for later; do you understand?' Clayton nodded his head fractionally and raised his right hand an inch off the bed.

'Just to confirm, you would like to be told now?' Clayton barely nodded.

'When you were brought into the field hospital, you had lost a lot of blood, so they immediately gave you a transfusion. When your condition had been stabilised, you were examined and the surgeon thought there was a chance your foot could be saved. You were flown back here and my colleagues and I had to make a decision on your foot. I'm afraid the tibia was so badly damaged that I had to amputate it halfway up your shin. I'm pleased to say that the operation was a complete success and I have no further concerns about your right leg.'

He paused to check if the patient wanted him to go on. Clayton raised his right hand again.

'The left side of your face and neck were very badly burned. Your helmet and your combat jacket restricted the burn area. Sadly, I was unable to save your left ear, but your hearing will not be impaired. Another surgeon has already started to apply skin grafts and I'm afraid you will need many operations before we can let it heal over on its own. I'm sorry to be so frank with you, Private Clayton. Have you any questions for me?'

Clayton nodded: the surgeon mentioning the word 'frank' had triggered Clayton's memory of the incident. He remembered Franks smiling at him as he begged for help. He recalled each of his mates, first looking at Brackley, then at him as the flames started eating into his flesh. He remembered them counting: 'One, two, three' and then running, ignoring his pleading for them to put out the fire. The surgeon waited patiently for him to ask his question, as the image of Franks' smiling face flashed before Clayton's eyes once more.

He had trouble speaking as only the right side of his mouth was capable of moving: 'My mates in the APC, sir. Are they still in Baghdad?' he slurred.

'No, they flew back home as arranged the day after the incident.'

'Do they know I survived?'

'Well, until yesterday, we weren't sure you would pull through.'

'So, do they know I'm alive, sir?'

'I can't really answer that, private, but my guess is they don't.'

'Thank you, major. That's how I would like it to remain.' With that, Clayton closed his eyes and the medics withdrew. But he had not gone to sleep. He was already planning. He made a vow to himself that he would dedicate the rest of his life to getting even with his so-called mates who had left him to die. Before he drifted off into a drug-induced sleep, he whispered quietly to himself: 'The Pilgrim will have his revenge!'

TWENTY-NINE

Clayton spent two weeks in the Intensive Care Unit at Derriford Hospital in Plymouth, recovering from his foot amputation, before being transferred to the specialist burns unit. He had suffered third-degree burns to the left side of his neck and face. As his epidermis and the dermis had been destroyed by the fire, he needed many skin graft operations at three-weekly intervals. Although that area of his body was swollen and blistered, he was in very little pain as the nerve endings had been destroyed by the fire. He accepted his foot amputation as an occupational hazard and was confident that with a prosthetic, he would be able to walk unaided most of the time. Regrettably he knew that he would never be able to lead the same outdoor life he had previously enjoyed.

As he lay in his hospital bed, day after day, he could not help thinking how different things could have been if his mates had retrieved the fire extinguisher from the APC or at least used the water in their canteens to put out the fire. They had not even attempted to pull him clear of the wreckage.

During the six months he was in hospital receiving treatment, he insisted he did not want to receive any visitors apart from his wife, Bella, and he was emphatic with her that she must not disclose to his friends that he was still alive. She complied, but when she asked why, he declined to give her a reason.

One day Bella Clayton had a chance and very awkward meeting with Dan Freeman's wife, Joan, in the local supermarket. When Mrs Freeman offered her condolences, Bella did not divulge that her husband was still alive. Joan Freeman told her it was sad that the mates had fallen out over an incident that had happened in Iraq. She did not go into detail as her husband had not told her the circumstances.

*

Not only did Clayton not want visitors, he did not want to make small talk with other patients on his ward. For a while after leaving the ICU, he was on a general ward. He became irritated by the constant questions he was asked by other patients – who had found out he had served in Iraq – and sometimes even by their visitors:

'You were injured in Iraq?'

'What's it like now after Saddam was toppled in 2003?'

'How did the people of Iraq receive you? Were they pleased or hostile?'

'Did you mix with the Yanks when you were over there?'

'How did you lose your foot?'

'How did you get burned?'

'Do you get compensation from the Army for your injuries?'

'Can you continue in the Army? Desk job I expect?'

'Are we winning the war on Islamic State do you think?'

Such was his irritation, he asked for the curtains around his cubicle to always be drawn. When a well-intentioned woman from the Women's Royal Voluntary Service fully pulled back the curtains and enquired if Clayton wanted any books, his anger spilled over: 'No, I don't want any fucking books. Kindly put the curtains back where you found them on your way out!' He later asked a nurse to apologise on his behalf for his unacceptable rude behaviour. He was annoyed with himself. Before he was injured, he would never have dreamt of addressing anyone in such a manner, even people he did not like.

After a week or so, the nurses reported to the matron that Clayton's mental health was giving cause for concern as he just wanted to be left alone. They thought that he may be suffering from PTSD. They knew that for most patients, interaction with others was therapeutic; that medical hypothesis did not apply to him.

At the start of his hospitalisation, Bella came to see him every day and did her best to come to terms with her husband's injuries. But gradually, Clayton became less and less communicative and on some of her visits, hardly a word was exchanged between them. After the first month she came to see him every other day and towards the end of his stay in hospital, her visits reduced to once a week. She was finding it increasingly difficult to accept his unwillingness to talk to her. It was not the fact he was disabled and disfigured, they were just gradually growing apart. She spoke with the hospital mental health therapist as she was increasingly worried about her husband's mental state. He was becoming melancholy and monosyllabic. They never discussed how he was feeling or what he was thinking, so she was not to know that he had developed a fixation with thoughts of revenge.

Although it saddened her, she no longer visited him during his final month in hospital. About a week before he was discharged, he was given an undated letter from his wife:

My Dearest Derek

I was devastated when I was first informed by the Army that you'd been badly injured in Iraq. Since your return, as you know, I have visited you regularly in hospital.

As you recover from your wounds, I've noticed your mood has gradually changed. You are becoming more-and-more bitter about what happened to you. You've never told me about the incident. I know it was a dreadful experience for you and you've never complained about your injuries, but something is obviously eating away at your soul.

I'm sorry, Derek, I can't live with you any longer as you're not the man I loved and married. I hope that in time you achieve inner peace and can find a way of enjoying your life once again.

Thank you for the good times, Derek.

Bella

Clayton had not fallen out of love with his wife, but knew and understood that he was no longer a nice person to be around. He did not blame her for deserting him and was surprised she had put up with his moods for as long as she had. Perhaps one day, after he had done what he intended to do, they might get back together and try to rekindle their love for each other, if she had not found someone else. He knew that would be dependent on many things, not least his freedom.

What he was planning would mean that, if caught, a very long prison sentence awaited.

The loss of his marriage was compounded by his team-building business folding. Obviously, in such a venture, Clayton's involvement was the key to its success; his adventurous spirit, his evident skill at all the outdoor activities, his organisational ability and his charisma. He suspected that some customers would be put off by the sight of his disfigured face. Even though the skilful surgeons had implanted a silicone ear to replace the one he lost to the fire, he no longer retained the rugged good looks that his female clients, and some men, clearly admired.

The main reason why he had to close his business was because of his amputation. He simply would have been unable to do half the things he could do before. He had always prided himself on being adept at all the skills he was trying to get others to master. He realised his customers would find it hard to accept their mentor talking them through activities without actually doing them. His prosthetic was barely noticeable when he was just walking, but good as it was, it was not capable of coping with adventurous outdoor pursuits.

As his wife had left him, he sold the marital home and, although she was only entitled to half, he gave Bella two-thirds of the money raised from the sale. It was his way of saying sorry. With his remaining share, together with the lump sum he received in compensation from the Army for his injuries, plus taking his Army pension as a one-off payment, he was financially well placed. He bought a small dilapidated cottage in an isolated location and set about making it his home.

His other purchases included an Army-surplus Defender Land Rover, an old Enfield motorbike and a small boat with outboard motor. He paid the Penzance Harbour Authority in advance for his mooring. He already owned an assortment of camping gear from his business venture, including everything he would need when away from his cottage on his mission. There would be no luxury hotels – although he could have afforded them – or even comfortable guest houses.

Clayton intended to use Dartmoor as a base for his mission. The moor was a second home to him. He had been out in all weathers and he loved the solitude it offered. He planned to be away for about a month if his plans worked out. He could not be precise about the duration of his stay as some of the time he would be watching and planning before taking action. He made sure he had enough food to last him for a longer period if necessary. He would limit his trips to buy supplies to an absolute minimum to avoid being remembered by observant staff or customers.

When he was first discharged from hospital, one of his first tasks was to change his name by deed poll. It cost him a mere £15 and then he was able to tax and insure his car without the authorities being able to link these transactions to his former identity. He complied with the law as he simply did not want to get stopped at a random checkpoint or fall foul of the Automatic Number Plate Recognition system as a car tax dodger; he wanted to be a legitimate road user. He was confident that the chances of the police tracing his change of name were remote. However, while he was on his mission, just to make sure he could not be traced if his Defender was seen, he looked on the Autotrader website and noted the registration of a vehicle for sale that was the same make and model as his own. He then bought false number plates and fitted them to his Land Rover. If the police happened to check his registration, they would discover it indeed belonged to a Defender and registered to a Paul Barrett from Somerset. He also used the same subterfuge for his motorbike.

He kept his Land Rover Defender in a rented double garage in Penzance, which provided the ideal starting point for him. His provisions, acquired over a few days before his departure, were stored in one half of the garage and his Defender in the other half. In the back of the hard-top Land Rover, one side was dedicated to shelving in the form of cubby holes. These were packed with all his changes of clothing, toiletries and provisions he thought he would need for the time he was away from home. In the other side was space for his tent and cooking stove and utensils, leaving sufficient room for his motorbike and an improvised ramp to help him get it into the back.

Having finished his packing and having filled the Defender and Enfield with petrol, including a spare five-litre can of fuel, he edged out of his lock-up. He was on the west coast of Cornwall and was heading for the Dartmoor National Park where he planned to spend his first night and the next month at various locations on the moor. After making camp overnight, early the following morning he planned to head for Yeovil in Somerset: the place where he would find his first target. His life had been ruined; now he was about to ruin the lives of people who had once been his friends.

PART THREE

THIRTY

King and his team, ably assisted by Inspector Best, were now fully dedicated to tracking down the assassin they suspected of five murders during the course of the previous month. DCI Burrows had been appointed as the senior investigating officer and assumed overall control of all the murder cases. This was not because of any lack of confidence in King – who he knew was his best detective – rather this was now a very high-profile investigation and had come to the attention of the chief constable, and, increasingly, the media. They were certainly now hunting a serial killer and this necessitated the control by a senior officer who could allocate the necessary resources.

On the day after Mrs Franks was killed by a bomb, the DCI informed his inspectors that he had made available additional detectives and uniformed officers. Catching the killer was his top priority. Burrows also arranged a meeting with all the detectives at two o'clock that afternoon to bring everyone up to date and decide the next course of action. He knew that his two inspectors had spoken with Colin Franks that morning, while the other detectives were busy trying to track down an address for Derek Clayton from public records.

*

The DCI opened the meeting: 'Good afternoon. As you all know, we have a serial killer at large in Devon and we must make his capture a matter of great urgency. I am aware that it appears the murderer's last victim was almost certainly intended to be Mr Franks, but his wife tragically died in the explosion instead. We have every reason to believe Derek Clayton is the man we are looking for and that he will make another attempt on Mr Franks' life, who is now at a secret location; our task is to apprehend Clayton as our main suspect. I met with Inspectors King and Best prior to this meeting and I'll now hand over to Inspector King to outline our plan of action.'

Whenever King addressed a formal meeting, particularly if his DCI was present, he used rank and surname when referring to detectives; even though his preference was simply to use first names, protocol demanded the formal address.

'Thank you, sir. Apart from the murder of Robert Higgins, the other murders have all happened during the last week. Just to recap: after the death of Daniel Freeman, which at the time was viewed as suspicious, a link was made between his death and that of Malcolm Prescott. We then discovered that the death of Robert Higgins, a month previously, was also linked. The murders of Gregory Bryson and

Bonnie Franks then followed in very quick succession. As the chief said, we believe that Mrs Franks wasn't the intended victim of the bomb.

'Fundamental to our investigations is: why? Why has Clayton apparently become a serial killer? He was a friend of the people who have been killed, so what has happened to him that was so bad he has resorted to multiple murders? If we can establish a motive, it might help us understand how his mind is working.

'But we also need to do two things: firstly, we need evidence – not just supposition – that Clayton murdered the five people and, secondly, we need to catch him!

'To that end, I will assign to each of us a murder enquiry and it will be your responsibility to drill down through the evidence we already have and search for other incriminating evidence, preferably DNA-based, against him. In doing so, be ever mindful that any lead, however small, may lead us to him. Our watchwords therefore are "evidence" and "whereabouts". Whilst following your assigned case, inevitably there will be overlaps as all the victims were once friends. Feel free to liaise with each other and because of the urgency, I want all of us to update DCI Burrows at 8.00 every morning until Clayton is in custody.'

He then addressed each detective in turn: 'So, the allocation of the murders is as follows: Sergeant Harris will pursue the Higgins case. See if you can find the ladders that he fell off and get the bottom rungs checked. If, as we now suspect, Clayton used an implement to pull the ladder away, we might find something to link him to the crime. Bearing in mind his prosthetic lower leg, he may have had difficulty pulling it with his bare hands. I suggest you liaise with the police in Yeovil and see if they can help rather than you having to travel there. If they find something, ask them to collect samples for analysis of anything they find.'

Harris scribbled some notes and nodded her understanding.

'DC Hammond, I'd like you take on the murder enquiry of Gregory Bryson. See if you can locate the murder weapon as it's not been found yet. Clayton is unlikely to have taken it with him, so check the wood surrounding the twelfth hole again. He may not have worn gloves when he bludgeoned Bryson to death, so if we can find it, he may have left his DNA behind. Also, check with his golfing partner who had his tyres punctured. Find out where he lives and ask him and his neighbours again if they remember seeing anything suspicious during yesterday afternoon.

'DC Dyson, I'd like you to investigate further the murder of Mrs Franks. We know Clayton must have visited the property, but presumably didn't enter it by the front driveway. Check for signs of his entry. There aren't many houses close by, but it might be worth asking the distant neighbours if they saw a vehicle parked near to the Franks' place shortly after dusk.

'Inspector Best will follow up on the drowning murder as he was assigned that case at the outset by the DCI. We have already discussed checking any fingerprints or DNA samples from the seatbelt, interior light switch he handled, door handles and the rope that was used to ensure Prescott couldn't escape.

'I will, once again, reconsider the murder of Daniel Freeman. I plan to speak with Pathologist Gleeson about the noose Clayton allegedly used to hang Freeman. I want to make sure that he's checked for DNA from the rope. Knowing John Gleeson, I expect he has already looked for samples.

'Two other things: firstly, we all need to redouble our efforts on eyewitness accounts. I don't just mean anyone actually witnessing the murders, but Clayton must have used some form of transport to get to each murder site, so ask the neighbours if they noticed anyone walking around at the time of the murders or if they saw any vehicle in the area they hadn't seen before or since. If we can identify what means of transport he's using, it may help us track him down. Because of his prosthetic lower leg, it is likely he'll have a limp and people notice things like that. The extra resource made available will be used to do more house-to-house enquiries. Any questions?'

He then turned to his DCI: 'Sir, is there anything you'd like to add?'

'Thank you, Inspector King. These are dreadful crimes and we must bring the perpetrator to justice. Derek Clayton needs to be apprehended urgently. So I would ask all of you to diligently carry out the tasks you've been set and we will have our first review meeting tomorrow morning at eight sharp. If, however, your investigations lead to some significant development before then, please contact Inspector King and we'll act on it immediately.'

*

That same afternoon, Sergeant Harris walked across the detectives' main office and sat down next to Inspector King.

'You asked me to follow up on the Higgins murder, sir, and I have spoken with the company who employed him as a subcontractor. They confirmed the place he visited on the day he fell to his death and also the properties he fixed dishes at on the previous two days. Following your suggestion at our meeting, I asked for those addresses and contact details so I could speak to the customers by phone and ask if they had noticed anyone hanging around at the time their dish was being fitted. It seemed likely that Clayton would have carried out some reconnaissance. One woman said she had noticed a man sitting in an Army-type vehicle parked just along the street. She couldn't see it from her property but had to post a letter and noticed it as she walked by. The driver was just sitting there and he had what looked like a scarf around his face.'

'Could she provide any further description of the vehicle?'

'I asked her that and she was hesitant at first, so I suggested she use Google and search "Army Vehicles" to see if she could identify the type. She did that while I waited on the phone and she was excited to say that she did recognise it from the pictures. It was a Land Rover Defender. But she added it didn't have a canvas covering at the back like in the picture she looked at, but metal like a normal car.'

'Well done, Lucy. I think that's a good enough witness account. So, we think he may be driving around in a hardtop Defender. Let's hope that's the breakthrough we've been looking for. Alert all patrols and let's see if we can catch him.'

THIRTY-ONE

The week before he murdered Higgins, Derek Clayton had arrived on Dartmoor in his Army-surplus Land Rover to begin his revenge mission. It was to be his home for however long it took him to complete his task. Over the coming weeks, he planned to avoid shops as much as possible to minimise the risk of being remembered by staff and other customers. He had plenty of provisions stashed in his Land Rover. Among them was his Army pistol. Crucial to the success of his mission was his trusty Enfield motorbike that fitted neatly into the back of his Land Rover. He had the bike modified to accommodate his prosthetic, so all the controls were operated by his hands or his left foot.

He was a man of simple tastes: cereals and porridge had sustained him for over a month, and would continue to do so. What little occasional shopping he did for essentials like milk, bread and eggs, were all purchased from self-service shops where the machine accepted cash. He brought with him over £2,000 in cash as he was not exactly sure what his outgoings would be. He also had a credit card – but not in the name of Derek Clayton – for use on contactless payments. He wanted to meet as few others as possible; the only people he wanted contact with did not want contact with him!

His preferred face covering was a snood as the wide ring of knitted material covered his neck and face. This was worn to hide his identity and conceal his burn scars, which were likely to be remembered by anyone seeing his full face. Now that the media coverage about the murders and his identity as 'The Devon Assassin' was increasing, he had to be extra careful. He knew that in normal times, constantly wearing a snood would have appeared somewhat strange and out of place. The pandemic that had started earlier in the year gave him the perfect opportunity to hide his identity.

Prior to starting his mission, he had earmarked six sites around the Dartmoor National Park that he would use as bases, never staying for longer than two nights in any location. He had chosen them with great care, drawing on his personal knowledge of the area from his Army training and his business venture. The prerequisites were that the campsite should not be visible from any roads, not close to any footpaths, bridleways or tracks, ideally sheltered by trees – to avoid detection from the air – and be close to a stream. Water was essential for drinking, cooking and ablutions.

He would use the sites in rotation; this was his third visit to the current location during the last month. If ever he thought a site had been compromised, for example by walkers passing close by, he would immediately move to another location. This had only been necessary once since his arrival.

He used his Defender when moving from site to site or when he needed it to transport provisions or a passenger, as he had done when he abducted Freeman. The other occasion when the Land Rover was needed was when he was on a reconnaissance mission, as was the case when he followed Higgins around Yeovil to the places where he was fitting satellite dishes. Clayton knew that someone sitting on a motorbike was more likely to arouse suspicion than someone sitting in a car. When he wanted to move around quickly, possibly over rough terrain, his chosen transport was his Enfield motorbike. The only qualms he had when on his bike was leaving his Defender isolated on the moor. There again, the places he had carefully chosen seldom had people passing, but even if they were and saw his ex-Army transport, it would not have looked particularly out of place.

Although his planning had been meticulous, there was one event he had not planned for, and that was the bomb that had blown up Mrs Franks. However, he was not to be denied his revenge, particularly against the man who bore the main responsibility for what happened to him in Iraq. There were now additional things he had to get that he had not brought with him and they were crucial to his next move.

His current site was in a secluded spot near the Great Mis Tor, which was a few miles to the east of Tavistock. He started his motorbike and headed for the town.

He arrived at an out-of-town supermarket and, wearing his snood and cap, only his eyes were visible. He headed straight for the greetings card section and in particular the selection of "With sympathy" cards. He knew what he was looking for and found something close to what he wanted. His chosen card was embossed with a crucifix. He was not interested in the cross, he just wanted a card with a design that stood out in relief. Quickly moving to the self-service till, he placed a twenty-pound note in the slot and collected his receipt and change.

However, there were other things he needed when he could not avoid being served by a sales assistant. After buying the card, he headed for an electrical shop called "Bright Sparks" just off the High Street, where he selected a micro transmitter and receiver. He was wearing his snood so his anonymity was still preserved. Nevertheless, he was still slightly apprehensive of any direct contact with people due to the media coverage of the murders and the revelation of his identity.

Back at his campsite he parked his Enfield and covered it with a tarpaulin as it had started raining. He climbed into the back of his Land Rover and sat cramped on a small folding camping seat in front of a collapsible table. He placed the card he had bought on it and from his toolbox he kept stored on a shelf, he took out a Stanley knife. He placed the micro transmitter – which was smaller than a 5p piece – receiver and card he had bought earlier on the table. With the sharp blade from the knife, he very carefully made a slit in the embossed design of the card, just big enough to slide in the small device. Unless they had been looking for it, to a casual observer, the insertion could not be detected. He switched on the handheld receiver and it immediately started bleeping as it recognised the transmitter signal.

In order to complete his task, he took out a pen and, writing left-handed to disguise his handwriting, he addressed the envelope: MR C FRANKS, DEVONIA, YELVERTON, WEST DEVON PL20 6AE and stuck on a first-class stamp. All that remained to be done was to take it to the nearest post box, which meant uncovering his motorbike and riding to the village of Merrivale, less than two miles away. Crucially, he made a mental note of the collection time shown on the post box.

After an afternoon coffee and a biscuit back at his camp, he once again headed for Merrivale on his Enfield and parked about a hundred metres from the post box, making sure he could see it from where he was sitting astride his machine. He was fairly confident of where his card would end up that evening, but still wanted to track its progress. Shortly after the stated collection time, a post van arrived and the contents of the box were taken to the van. Clayton then followed it as more collections were made until it eventually headed for the delivery office in Plympton, to the east of Plymouth. The sorting office location was confirmed and he once again returned to the Great Mis Tor and made his evening meal. He was in his sleeping bag in his compact tent by 9 p.m. as he knew he had an early start the following day.

*

The next morning he was awake before dawn, skipped breakfast and headed for Plympton on his motorbike. He had the receiver in his pocket and the map on the device confirmed the location of the condolence card by a flashing red dot, accompanied by an audible intermittent bleep. After about half an hour, the red dot started to move on the map as the van carrying the card left the sorting depot. Once the van had been identified, and Clayton had made visual contact, it was easy for him to follow it on his motorbike. The crux of his plan was that he knew the card would be redirected to where Colin Franks was now living. Every time the van stopped to make a delivery, he had to refer to his receiver and if the red dot on his screen moved at the same time as the post van, he knew the houses that had just received mail were not the safe house.

After an hour of following the van at a discreet distance around the streets of Plymouth, it pulled away from the latest delivery and Clayton prepared to continue his pursuit. This time the red dot on the receiver did not move. It was still blinking, but was now stationary. If he had been closer to the property, he would have seen a bundle of letters delivered to the address, held together by an elastic band, which had been redirected to the house. He realised any redirected mail, particularly any packages, would have been closely scrutinised for possible explosive devices. His condolence card was one of many and had not aroused suspicion.

Having identified the safe house, he did not expect to find a uniformed police officer on duty outside as that would only have drawn attention to it. What he did expect was that there would be covert surveillance and he was right. A man sat in his car pretending to read a newspaper. Clayton already knew how he would deal with him when he came for Franks, even though he had never fired that particular type of weapon.

Before he left, he duly noted the address of the house and also observed the surrounding streets as he would be returning in the near future, when he judged conditions were in his favour. The Pilgrim now knew Franks' secret location.

THIRTY-TWO

All of the detectives were assembled in the conference room the following morning and DCI Burrows joined them sitting in the seat reserved for him at the head of the table. He addressed the expectant meeting: 'Good morning everyone. I hope you had a productive afternoon yesterday. I'd like a progress report from each of you measured against the two watchwords that were highlighted at our meeting yesterday by Inspector King, namely "evidence" and "whereabouts". Please also mention any theories you may have on a possible motive.' He then invited his inspector to begin the meeting.

King began: 'Thank you, sir. After we receive each update, I also want to decide on any follow-up points as they arise, rather than wait until the end of all the reports?'

'Very sensible approach,' Burrows nodded.

'I'd like to start, sir, by mentioning that the team has scanned public records and can find no record of an address for Derek Adam Clayton. In fact we've drawn a complete blank on any information referring to him. From that it seems obvious that he has changed his name.

'Sergeant Harris, I've told the DCI about the eyewitness statement and that we think we have a possible link to the vehicle Clayton is using. Could you update the rest of the team?'

'Certainly, sir. I was tasked with digging deeper into the murder of Robert Higgins. For the benefit of the others, I spoke with the company who employed him as a subcontractor. I thought it worth checking with the customers visited by Higgins in the days prior to his murder. It seemed likely that Clayton would have to follow his victim around until he had the best opportunity to strike. One customer told me at the time he was working at her house, she remembered an Army-type vehicle out in the street. She identified it as a Land Rover. I gave the description to Inspector King yesterday afternoon and he immediately alerted all patrols.

'I also tried to track down Higgins' van and his ladders. Luckily, the ladders were in a police compound in Yeovil waiting for collection by Higgins' next of kin. The van he used was reclaimed by the company he rented it off. I asked one of the detectives from Yeovil Police to check the bottom few rungs of the ladder for a sign of any marks. She came back and said there were some brown marks on the underside of the bottom rung. I asked her to collect a sample and send it to our forensic lab marked for the attention of John Gleeson. I've alerted the pathologist and he'll test it as soon as it arrives.'

King commented: 'So, we think he may be driving an Army Land Rover Defender with a hardtop, not canvas. Nevertheless, let's keep an open mind on whether it was Clayton's. It would be useful to know if any other eyewitnesses had seen the same type of vehicle at another murder site. Let us know what the pathologist finds from the sample please, Sergeant Harris.

'DC Hammond, what about Gregory Bryson?'

'Before I visited the golf club, I asked the DCI if I could have a look at the confidential files Sergeant Harris brought back from the Army barracks in Exeter where the reservists enlisted. I wanted to check if Clayton is right or left-handed; he is right-handed.

'I then went to the golf club and asked the professional if I could borrow three iron clubs as I wanted to test a hypothesis. He kindly took me to the twelfth hole in a golf buggy and went to the exact spot where Mr Bryson's body was found. I then faced the same way I think the killer would have faced and hurled a club into the nearby trees with my right hand. Some of the trees had dropped their leaves, but there were conifers still in leaf. I then repeated the process with the other two clubs and watched their trajectory; the throws approximately covered a thirty-degree arc. I was trying to mimic what our suspect might have done after the frenzy of the assault and hoping he might just have thrown away the club he used to kill Mr Bryson.

'I then set about retrieving the clubs I'd thrown into the trees, which was not an easy task as the ground falls away at that point. I picked up two clubs fairly quickly, but didn't see any sign of the murder weapon. I looked for the third and saw a club stuck fairly high up in the branches of a conifer.

'At first I thought it was the last club I'd thrown, but it wasn't; I found that one a few metres away at the base of another tree. I retrieved the club from the branches with some difficulty as it was so high up. I believe the one I pulled out of the tree is the club that was used to kill Greg Bryson. It's understandable how it was missed initially as it was hidden in the branches and quite some way from the ground. When I brought it down, sure enough, the head of the club was bloodstained. I carefully picked it up wearing a latex glove and on my return took it to the forensic lab. I'm confident they will find Mr Bryson's blood on it and hope they can get a fingerprint or some DNA off the grip.

'Also, after this meeting I am going to interview Jim Cantwell, Mr Bryson's golf partner, who had his tyres punctured, and speak with his neighbours to ask them if they saw anything suspicious.'

King was impressed with Hammond's golf club initiative and told him so. He asked his detective to inform the others when the forensic examination of the seven-iron was completed.

'DC Dyson, what about the bombing?'

'I visited Devonia on Dartmoor, the Franks' house, and found the place was pretty much as it had been left after the bomb went off. Scene of Crime Officers had already examined the site. There was POLICE DO NOT CROSS tape across the entrance and a uniformed officer sat in his car opposite the drive and he recognised me.

'I didn't enter the property from the front but skirted around the outside and found a back entrance with a gate that was unlocked. The latch was missing. If Clayton entered from there, which seems likely, he may have left his DNA. When I got back to the station, I checked and it had already been removed by Scene of Crime Officers and passed to Forensics for closer inspection back at the lab.

'Then I started thinking where Clayton would have parked if he didn't want to approach the property from the front. There are a few dirt tracks fairly close to the house, but wherever he parked I think he would have headed for the back entrance. I also figured he would need his walking stick, which we know he uses, as the ground was quite steep in parts. Sure enough, about ten metres from the gate where the ground was bare were similar impressions to the ones Inspector King found in Plymbridge Woods where Mr Freeman was murdered. I've informed Scene of Crime Officers and they've taken photographs and castings. They'll let me know if they match the other impressions.

'I also found a wrapper from a dog biscuit. Now I know that the Franks have a dog, which I understand is now being cared for by a neighbour, and it is somewhat traumatised by the explosion. It may be nothing to do with our suspect, but I'd be grateful if you could check, sir, with Mr Franks when you see him, if the dog was out in the garden just before the bomb went off. If you could also ask him if he feeds his dog treats.' With that she passed a photo of the wrapper to Inspector King; the original was being examined by Forensics.

'Just a guess, sir, but if the dog was in the garden, giving it a treat could have been a way of keeping it quiet.'

'Well done, DC Dyson. I'll check with Mr Franks as I'm sure we'll be seeing him again shortly. Inspector Best was reviewing the drowning of Malcolm Prescott.'

'I think it's fair to say that whoever killed Mr Prescott was wearing gloves at the time as no prints were found on the car. What I was interested in was the rope that was used to tie his seatbelt to the seat. I asked John Gleeson if it matched the rope used to hang Mr Freeman and he has confirmed it does. Now, that doesn't prove that Clayton is responsible for the two murders, only that it is highly likely the same person killed both Mr Freeman and Mr Prescott. The pathologist is searching for DNA from the ropes and checking if there is a match.'

King continued: 'Thank you, Inspector Best. And that leaves me. Yesterday, I attempted to speak again with Mrs Freeman, but she was away from home, returning today. I have arranged to see her straight after this meeting as I feel she should know we have reason to believe that Derek Clayton is alive and that we are seeking him urgently to assist in our enquiries.

'We think he abducted Mr Freeman in broad daylight. I know we have made house-to-house enquiries, but they were carried out on the afternoon of the hanging and not all the neighbours were home. I want to make door-to-door enquiries at the same time of the morning as we think he was taken from his house. If Clayton did take him, it's reasonable to assume he parked right outside the house. We know

Mr Freeman left in a hurry as he still had his slippers on, so Clayton's car must have been parked there for at least a few minutes.'

He turned to his DCI: 'At our previous briefing, sir, I mentioned about Clayton's motive. What turned an apparently successful, well-liked man into a serial killer? It is pure speculation on my part, but when DI Best and I spoke to Franks, he recounted the incident in Iraq when the IED detonated under the soldiers' vehicle and Clayton's foot was trapped. Franks said to us: "I made a judgement that it was best to try and save the five of us as Carl was already dead and Derek was probably not going to make it." I think that's what sparked Clayton's fury, namely revenge as he thought his mates should have at least tried to save him.

'That's where we are, sir. We have some potential evidence against Clayton and, hopefully, further examination will confirm either way if he's our man. Of course, we've got to catch him first and get a DNA sample! We also have a possible sighting of his vehicle. I'd like Sergeant Harris to provide the rest of us with a picture of a hardtop Land Rover the woman in Yeovil identified as the type she saw parked where Higgins was working. That would be useful when we are speaking to people who may have seen the vehicle he was driving.

'I'm convinced that all of our investigations will get us closer to Clayton. Make no mistake, we are dealing with a very clever, very dangerous man, who is on a mission to murder his ex-mates and he's not going to make it easy for us to catch him.'

THIRTY-THREE

The next morning DCI Burrows and the detectives were once again sitting around the table in the main conference room at the police station at 8.00 a.m. for their daily update. This was the third meeting to specifically discuss the search for Clayton. At the DCI's request, King opened the meeting.

'As you know, all patrols have been alerted to be on the lookout for a grey, hardtop Land Rover Defender. A number of points arose from our early morning briefing yesterday and I'd like an update on them. Sergeant Harris, you were liaising with Yeovil Police and they had promised to send a sample to our forensic people of something they found on the rung of Higgins' ladder?'

'Yes, sir. The sample has been analysed and it is a form of varnish. So, what I think happened is something was hooked under the bottom rung of the ladder, while Higgins was at the top, and was pulled away with such force it left behind varnish from the hook. It is pure speculation, but that hook could have been the handle of a walking stick. We know Clayton has a prosthetic fitted to his lower leg and apparently uses a stick as we've seen from the impressions left behind in Plymbridge Woods and at the Franks' house. When we find him, it's my guess the varnish on his walking stick will match what was found on the ladder rung.'

'Thank you, Sergeant Harris. DC Hammond, what have you discovered about the golf club?'

'After retrieving the club from the woods on the golf course that we think is the weapon used to kill Gregory Bryson, Forensics has confirmed that the blood found on the club head belonged to him. Two DNA samples were taken from the handle and one was obviously from Mr Bryson. So, the other probably belongs to the killer. As with Sergeant Harris's findings with the varnish, when we apprehend Clayton we will see if it's a match.

'I have also spoken with Mr Bryson's golf partner and he hadn't seen any suspicious vehicles around his house just before he was due to leave for the club. However, one of his neighbours did recall seeing an Army vehicle parked further down their road. He could not be certain as he only caught a fleeting glimpse as he turned into his driveway when he got home on the afternoon of Mr Bryson's murder.'

King was encouraged about the possible match: 'Well that tends to support the identification from Sergeant Harris's eyewitness. Nothing changes as all patrols are on alert for the vehicle anyway. Could I ask DC Dyson for her report?'

'Certainly, sir. The walking stick impression I found at the back of the Franks house at Yelverton is confirmed as a match with the one at Plymbridge

Woods. Forensics also examined the latch from the back gate and has a DNA match with that on DC Hammond's golf club. So, although we cannot yet confirm it belongs to Clayton, they do belong to the same person. I know the result of the DNA test is awaited on the dog treat wrapper I found and I suspect the treat was used by Clayton to keep the dog quiet.'

'Thank you, DC Dyson. Inspector Best?'

'I was interested in the rope that was used in the Freeman hanging and the rope used to anchor Prescott's seat belt. Pathologist Gleeson has confirmed a DNA match and, crucially, a match with the golf club handle and the latch already mentioned. We can be sure that the same person carried out the hanging, the drowning and the bombing.'

King added his report: 'That leaves me. I've informed DC Dyson that after speaking with Mr Franks again, he did confirm that their dog was running loose just before the bombing. So, I think the dog treat wrapper is significant and DC Dyson may well be right that it was used to distract the dog.

'Moving on; as planned, I did door-to-door enquiries back at the Freeman place and I'm afraid drew a blank. No one I spoke with remembered seeing him being taken away. Whilst there I felt I should update Mrs Freeman and her son on what we have been investigating, as the media reports will soon be circulating. I arranged for a police family support officer to be with me at their house when I broke the news.

'I told the Freemans to prepare themselves for disclosures that they would find upsetting. Firstly, I said that we now believe Mr Freeman was murdered. I then informed them about the deaths of the other friends. They had only heard about Malcolm Prescott. I told them that Greg Bryson had also been murdered and we have reason to believe Robert Higgins was as well. They were incredulous when I said that Colin Franks is thought to have been the target of the bomb that actually killed his wife.

'I had to wait for that information to register before I broke the devastating news that Derek Clayton wasn't killed in Iraq and that he was the leading suspect in all the murders. As you can imagine, both Mrs Freeman and her son were distraught. I apologised for breaking the news to them, but thought they should know what we are investigating and reassured them that we are doing all we can to apprehend Clayton.'

King then addressed his boss: 'So, on our two watchwords of "evidence" and "whereabouts" where are we, sir? When we can get a sample of Clayton's DNA, and his walking stick, we will have incontrovertible evidence that he's our man, who has murdered five people. As to finding him, we suspect he has changed his name and is driving around in an Army-surplus Land Rover Defender. All patrols are on the lookout for the vehicle and, if he's still in the area, it's only a matter of time before we find him.'

DCI Burrows started to bring the meeting to a close: 'Thank you all for your efforts. I know we have made substantial progress and I hope he will be soon be...' Before he could finish, the door of the conference room opened and a very apologetic PC entered and approached the DCI.

'I'm very sorry to interrupt your meeting, sir, but I thought you would want to know that we have a sighting of the Army vehicle we are seeking.'

THIRTY-FOUR

At the news that Clayton's vehicle may have been spotted, all the detectives quickly left the room. Outside, King spoke to the PC who had delivered news of the sighting, with the other detectives from his team hovering close by. He was told that a patrol had reported an Army Land Rover parked at South Milton Sands close to Thurlestone Golf Club. There was no sign of the driver. King immediately decided he and his team should be there to reinforce the uniformed officers' presence in the hope that they had located Clayton and could witness the end of the terror campaign that had occupied his thoughts for the last week, ever since the murders were linked.

'Right. In two cars and we're heading for the coast!' he told his team. Sergeant Harris drove with King in her car. They did not speak for the first few miles.

'It's too late now, Lucy, to stop patrol cars converging on the car park. They are probably already there and in force!'

Harris looked sideways at King and queried: 'Sir?'

'If the vehicle is Clayton's, what would you say is the best way to alert him and frighten him off?'

Harris did not answer, just tutted.

*

King was right. Other patrols were converging on the top car park on the headland overlooking South Milton Sands, among them an armed response team. They were there well ahead of the detectives. When King and his team eventually arrived, the police were already preventing other car park users from having access to their cars and the part of the South West Coast Path that bordered the car park was also closed. Police cars now outnumbered the half a dozen other vehicles. King thought to himself that if this was Clayton's Land Rover, he would not be returning with so much attention focussed on it. He spoke with a uniformed sergeant and told him to keep a minimum number of his officers to secure the car park, and get the others looking for a man walking with a stick away from the beach along one of the roads that lead to South Milton Sands and along the coast path.

The main National Trust car park, between the beach and a bird sanctuary, situated below the car park the police were controlling, had people gazing in the direction of the activity above them. The four detectives entered the police cordon but kept a safe distance from the apparently abandoned Defender.

Ownership of the vehicle was established through DVLA and it was found to be registered to Brian Kevin Hunt from Bodmin in Cornwall. Efforts to contact him or anyone at his address went unanswered. Police were naturally cautious about approaching the vehicle, wary of the events at the Franks' home. After half an hour there was still no sign of the driver and as the police sergeant controlling the incident thought the vehicle might be booby-trapped, an Army bomb disposal team was called in to check if the Defender was safe to approach.

The detectives remained well away from the vehicle as a bomb disposal expert tentatively approached the Land Rover. He was clad in an armour-plated bomb suit – designed to withstand the pressure generated by an explosion – and he edged closer to the side window. He looked in and reported over his radio that he could see a backpack on the passenger seat.

He knew if it was a bomb and was on a timer, it could detonate at any moment. The other thing that would set it off was movement. He gingerly pulled up the door handle; it was unlocked. Because the Defender was on a slight incline the door swung open and the expert stepped back. Bomb disposal people are intrepid, but they are not foolhardy. It was time for a robot to take over.

A remotely controlled device, with six wheels and caterpillar tracks, no bigger than a wheelbarrow, was directed towards the open passenger door. Fixed to its front was an extendable mechanical hinged arm with a robotic claw attached to the end. The arm was gradually extended until the claw gripped the backpack. The crowd who were behind the cordon a safe distance from the vehicle watched with bated breath. There were gasps as the bag, nudged by the mechanical arm, toppled off the seat. A flask fell out of it onto the ground.

Just then a distant voice could be heard coming from behind the police cordon shouting: 'Hey, that's my Land Rover. What's the problem?' Officers surrounded him and led him away from the other onlookers. It transpired he was a twitcher who had been alerted on a birdwatchers' website that a rare bird had flown in and was feeding in the small sanctuary behind the sand dunes. When he had arrived, he was so excited he not only forgot to take his backpack, he also forgot to lock his vehicle. For over two hours he had been engrossed in watching the bird and was completely oblivious to what was happening half a mile away where he had left his Defender. The police questioned him and found he was indeed Mr Hunt from Bodmin.

As the detectives trudged back to their cars, King stopped and took out a sherbet lemon from his pocket. The other detectives waited as he looked into the distance, sucking on his sweet: 'Well, team, sadly, Mr Hunt is not The Pilgrim and our search goes on!'

*

This time King drove Sergeant Harris back to Plymouth and when they were nearly in the city he asked: 'Are you hungry, Lucy?'

'Yes, sir,' she lied in reply.

'How about I treat you to a fish and chip supper on the Barbican?'

'That would be nice, sir.'

King parked opposite Sutton Harbour and they ambled to the aptly titled Harbourside restaurant. He was a regular at the award-winning fish and chip shop. He asked his sergeant what she would like to eat and went in to order.

'Good evening, inspector. Your usual?'

'Twice please, Ben, and salt and vinegar on both.' After a few minutes he was walking out with two boxes, napkins and two small wooden forks.

'Let's eat these between the harbour and the sea, Lucy. There's a bench I usually sit at and watch the world go by.' They walked more quickly now so their meal would still be hot when they reached the bench opposite the Admiral MacBride pub. The pub was built on the original site of the Mayflower Steps and was named after John MacBride, a naval commander and former MP for Plymouth back in the late eighteenth century. They began eating straightaway, while their meals were still hot.

'It's rather ironic to be sitting here, Lucy.'

'Why do you say that, sir?'

When it came to the protocols of addressing work colleagues while at work in the expected manner, King played by those rules even though he thought being called 'sir' rather formal and a throwback to schooldays.

'Listen, Lucy. When we are alone and off duty, if you are comfortable calling me Richard, I would be okay with that.'

'Okay, sir. Sorry, as old habits die hard. Thank you, Richard.'

'Where were we? Oh yes, the irony of sitting here. Well, we are close to the Mayflower Steps, which is where the Pilgrim Fathers set sail for America in the early seventeenth century, over 400 years ago. The irony is that the man we are desperate to catch, according to Mrs Freeman, is nicknamed The Pilgrim as he once sailed on his own from here to Plymouth, Massachusetts, recreating that voyage. Anyway, enough of history and nicknames.'

They finished eating, King disposing of both wrapping papers, and strolled back to their car. This dinner out with Richard King, given the choice, had not been quite what Harris would have had in mind, but nevertheless, she had thoroughly enjoyed it. As he stopped outside her flat, she leaned across and kissed him on the cheek: 'Thank you for supper, Richard.'

King replied: 'You're very welcome, Lucy. We must do this again sometime. See you in the morning.'

She got out and he drove away.

Before putting the key in the door, she stopped and said to herself: 'Did I really just give my boss a kiss on the cheek? No, I must be dreaming!'

THIRTY-FIVE

Colin Franks had prepared his evening meal and had just sat down in the lounge with his plate of spaghetti bolognaise and cup of tea in front of the TV. It was dark outside. Although his curtains were closed – as advised by the police – he could see an intermittent blue light, but heard no siren. He had also been told not to answer the door, and if he felt he was in danger at any time to press an emergency silent alarm that would alert the police. It was colloquially known as "the panic button". He was reassured that someone from the National Crime Agency had the house he was in under constant surveillance.

He left his meal and moved to the curtains in the front room, pulling them apart no more than a few centimetres to see what was causing the flashing light outside. It was a police car and a uniformed officer was striding up the garden path. There was a loud knocking on the door, ignoring the doorbell. Franks was alarmed by the urgency of the rapping that seemed to go on forever. He moved towards the panic alarm and was in two minds whether to press it or not. The sight of the uniformed officer helped him decide. He cautiously opened the door ajar, as far as the security chain would allow, and peered through the crack. What he saw was an officer in a peaked cap, with black and white chequered headband, yellow high visibility coat – emblazoned with 'Devon and Cornwall Police' – and a black facemask with the police logo on one side. The officer was carrying a box wrapped in brown paper.

'Ye… yes, what is it?' Since the bombing and death of his wife, he had lost all of his bravado.

'I'm sorry to bother you, Mr Franks, but we think the location of this house has been compromised.'

'Where's the chap who is guarding the house?'

'Don't worry, sir, as I've spoken to him and he knows I'm taking you to a safer place. He'll follow on.'

'You said the house has been compromised. Why do you say that? How could that happen?'

'We are not entirely sure, sir, but we intercepted this parcel with your name on, addressed to you here, not to your Yelverton address.' Franks could not see all of the package through the crack, so slipped the chain out of its runner and fully opened the door. The officer held out the shoe-box size parcel with brown wrapping paper loosely covering it. It was dimly lit by the light from the hall, but the name and address were clearly visible. He peered at the box held by the PC, who remained standing on the porch step.

'It was put through the X-ray machine at the sorting office, which revealed there was nothing sinister inside. What we don't understand, sir, is the contents or the note that we found in the box.' With that he slipped off the wrapping paper with one hand and balanced the box on the other. After Franks had removed the lid, he stepped back in horror: the box contained an empty Army canteen water bottle. He was loath to touch it, but had to lift it out to retrieve the note that was just visible between the bottle and the side of the box. He put the canteen back in and opened the folded note, his hands visibly shaking. For the second time that evening he looked horrified as he read it. His face turned white. He reread the message hand printed in capitals:

```
JGNNQ HTCPMKG

VJGRKNITKO'URTQITGUU
KU PGCTNA EQORNGVG.

K'O EQOKPI VQ IGV AQW!

VJG RKNITKO.
```

'He… he knows where I am!'

'Who, sir?'

'That madman, Clayton. The bastard says he's coming to get me!'

'In which case, sir, we need to leave immediately. When I knew your location had been compromised, I arranged for you to be moved to another safe house. So, just grab your coat, sir. Don't worry about your belongings; I'll have them collected and brought to your new location. Leave the box, canteen and note for the detectives to examine.' With that, Franks kicked off his slippers, put on a pair of shoes and grabbed his coat. The PC was already walking down the path to his car. Before he left the house, Franks wondered whether he should press the panic button, reasoning there was little point as he was leaving, but he pressed it anyway.

The uniformed officer was now at the garden gate, looking both ways to see if anybody was lurking in the shadows. He held up his hand for Franks to stay where he was, halfway down the path. When he had carried out a cursory check of the road immediately in front of the house and looked under his BMW – still with blue lights flashing – he was satisfied the area was safe and beckoned Franks forward, opening the passenger door for him to get in. He then moved around to the driver's side, still scanning the street.

He started the 4x4 and accelerated away and turned off the flashing blue lights, explaining to his nervous passenger that he did not want to attract attention.

'I'm taking you to Royal William Yard, sir, to an apartment overlooking the Tamar. Do you know the Yard?'

'Oh yes, my wife and I used the restaurants there.'

'I don't propose to drive through the main entrance as we cannot be too careful. I won't be happy until you are in the apartment. Instead, we'll drive around the back to the car park at Devil's Point and from there we can walk the short distance and come down the metal steps that lead into the Yard.

The apartment is at the far end and by going in the back way, we'll come out close to it. The less time you spend out in the open the better.'

The officer drove slightly faster than the speed limit through Stonehouse and ignored the directions to Royal William Yard. Instead, he followed the road which led him to the isolated car park towards the back. If it had been daylight, they would have looked out to Drake's Island in the middle of Plymouth Sound on their left and across to Cornwall to their right. All they could see at that time of night were twinkling navigational lights across the water.

'Won't be long now, sir, and I'll have you safely tucked up in your new location.'

He drove more slowly now, partly because of the speed humps along the fairly narrow road leading directly to the car park. As the officer expected, although it would have been full to overflowing during the day – as it offered free parking – at night it was deserted. He drove to the part furthest away from the sea and switched off the ignition.

Franks was about to express his gratitude for the swift action taken by the officer to ensure his safety. He reached to his right to undo his seat belt and turned his head slightly towards the PC. A fist smashed him in the face!

THIRTY-SIX

Earlier that evening...

Derek Clayton had a late lunch at his campsite as he knew his evening meal was likely to be delayed by something he had to do. He waited until after dark to execute his plan. He prepared the things he needed to take with him for his backpack: a 500-millilitre filled bottle; a shoebox-size parcel – complete with wrapping paper and its contents ; the receiver he had used to locate Franks; a vacuum-sealed food bag with a treated facecloth inside; a box of matches; and his Army pistol. The most crucial item he needed for the task he had planned was one he intended to steal: namely a police car!

He arrived at Royal William Yard shortly after 5 p.m. on his Enfield and rode along the main thoroughfare to the back of the extensive sixteen-acre site, with his Army backpack containing all he needed to carry out his plan. Royal William Yard was built in the early part of the nineteenth century and was used by the Royal Navy until 1992. It was now home to executive apartments and a range of high-end restaurants. Clayton was not interested in its history past or present. All he was using it for was subterfuge and a place to hide his motorbike while he did what he had to do. It was an ideal location to execute his plan.

At the far end of the site was a steel staircase, which linked the South West Coast Path, thirty metres above the level of the Yard, to the now popular residential and hospitality venue. It was easy to understand the attraction it offered as it bordered the Tamar River and had spectacular views of Cornwall across the estuary.

Apart from the views of Plymouth Sound and Drake's Island from the coast path, the car park above the Yard was always very busy throughout the day as it was free to use. Clayton left his motorbike and helmet under the steel staircase out of sight of any passers-by. He picked up his backpack, put on the baseball cap from his coat pocket, pulled up his snood from around his neck and set off to walk to Plymouth Hoe.

It took him nearly half an hour and he eventually arrived at the deserted waterfront. He knew it well as he and his wife, Bella, had spent many happy hours sitting there after getting coffee and cake from The Coffee Shack kiosk, centrally positioned along the seafront. Sadly, since his wife had left him, they no longer would be reliving those treasured moments.

From his experience, he knew that the kiosk was a favoured place for police patrols all through the day and evening when taking a coffee break. The previous night he had ridden his motorbike to The Hoe around this time and sure enough, after waiting for twenty minutes, a police car parked a short way down from the Shack, and two officers had a coffee each.

That evening, he made sure he was there well ahead of the police officers arriving. He was at the western end of The Hoe and walked down from the road that skirted Plymouth Sound – and was over twenty metres above it – to the stony beach. He stopped at a point that was directly below the approximate spot where he thought the officers would park. He took out the receiver he had used to track Franks, switched it on, and placed it with the screen facing upwards. He then wedged it between two rocks. He knew high tide had been two hours before so would not interfere with what he had planned. He retraced his steps back to the higher level and checked that the device could be seen from the road. Sure enough, as he looked down from the road, he could see the pulsating small red light.

He wandered up and down the road trying not to look suspicious. However, he felt a little conspicuous, but as there was no one else around, it did not unduly bother him. He did not have long to wait as he could see in the distance the yellow and blue chequered livery of the police car slowly coming down the one-way road and eventually parking close to where Clayton had predicted. He had planned to deal with the two officers by disarming them of their yellow Tasers at gunpoint and using them against the officers to immobilise them. As he approached the police car, he could not believe his luck. He had made provision to deal with two patrolmen, but as he got closer, he could see there was only one officer on duty.

*

Police patrolling around Plymouth often took their breaks on Plymouth Hoe, particularly during the early evening when they were usually less busy. That came later when the pubs and night clubs closed. However, since the pandemic had started in February 2020, most nights were quiet as all hospitality venues either had to close early or, during lockdown periods, stay completely closed.

Nearly every evening when they were on duty, PCs Boardman and Flynn parked their BMW 4x4 close to the kiosk on Plymouth Hoe to get a takeaway coffee. This particular night, PC Flynn called in sick just before his shift started. It was too late to get a replacement and, as the previous evening had been largely uneventful, PC Boardman started his shift alone.

He drove around the streets of Plymouth and, apart from stopping a driver for a minor traffic violation, he had very little to do. He was ready for his first coffee of the evening and had headed for The Coffee Shack. He parked about fifty metres past it and was pleased to see there was not a queue. Because of the time of night and cold weather, The Hoe was deserted. He was about to get out and get his drink when there was a tapping on the passenger window. He wound it down electronically and a snood-masked face, topped with a baseball cap, looked in from a metre away, aware of social distancing.

'Oh, officer, I'm glad you're here. I need to report something to you. I was just walking up this way and I glanced over the sea wall and down on the shingle, I thought I could see a small red light going on and off. I'm not sure what it is.'

'Okay, sir, I'd better take a look.' With that he reached for a torch out of the centre console, took the keys out of the ignition, got out and pulled on his chequered-headband hat and big high-visibility bright yellow coat. He walked around his car and looked out over the sea wall. Clayton pointed down to the suspicious object. They both peered into the darkness and could just make out the pulsating red light on the beach below.

The officer was intrigued and took the steps that led down to the beach thirty metres below. He led the way with Clayton following closely behind until he abruptly stopped. He took the pack from his back, undid the main zip and took something out. He quickly caught up with the police officer again. They walked down the last few steps to the beach and then continued in single file until they came to the receiver. The officer shone his torch on the device and squatted down to take a closer look.

Suddenly, a hand holding a facecloth came around from behind his head and was forced against his nose and mouth. He briefly struggled before succumbing to the chloroform. Clayton let the officer gently slide to the shingle and threw the cloth onto the beach. He then, with some difficulty, removed the PC's coat. Fortunately, it was quite a bit bigger than him, so he could wear the coat over his own. He took off his cap, put it in his own coat pocket and replaced it with the officer's hat. Now clad in the police uniform, he checked that the car key was in the pocket of the coat. He then bent down and ripped the radio from the officer's stab vest and hurled it across the shingle. He also took the handcuffs from his belt and put them in his coat pocket. The other item he pocketed was a yellow Taser from a holster on the PCs belt.

He walked back up the path, knowing that the chloroform would take at least an hour to wear off, well before the tide was due to return. As he came back up to street level, he checked there was still no one around and headed for the police car. Once inside, he familiarised himself with the controls, making particular note of the switch that operated the blue lights. He opened the glove box and, as he suspected, there were police-issue face masks in a packet. He took one out and put it on after pulling his snood down around his neck. He placed his backpack on the passenger seat and headed for the so-called safe house.

*

His journey was uninterrupted and took about fifteen minutes. As he neared his destination, he was on the lookout for an occupied car parked nearby. He knew the house had covert protection as he had seen a man sitting in a car, just along from the safe house, when he had ridden by the previous evening after checking on the Hoe.

Sure enough, about three doors down from the house, he once again spotted the unmarked black Ford Mondeo with a man inside looking at his mobile phone. This partially illuminated his face, which Clayton appreciated, but thought it was not a smart move for someone trying to be unobtrusive.

Clayton flicked a switch and the blue lights mounted on the roof of the 4x4 began flashing. As he pulled up immediately opposite the safe house, he checked in the rear-view mirror that his hat and mask obscured most of his face. He walked back to where the National Crime Agency man was sitting in his car. As Clayton approached he lowered his window.

'What's the problem, officer?'

Clayton did not answer, but instead pulled out the Taser from his coat pocket and shot the man in the neck at point-blank range. Immediately, his muscles started contracting as he slumped over the steering wheel. Clayton opened the driver's door, electronically wound the window up, threw the Taser into the car and took the man's mobile. He knew from research that he had enough time to do what he wanted to do before the man had recovered from the 1,200 volts he had received. He slammed the door shut and, checking no one had been alerted by the flashing blue lights, slipped the mobile down a nearby drain.

Immobilising the man had taken less than a minute and as he went back to the police car, he took out the package and put the backpack on the back seat. He walked briskly up the garden path carrying the package and rapped on the front door with his knuckles.

Before the door was opened, albeit on a security chain, he muttered to himself: 'Okay, Frankie, your day of reckoning has arrived!'

THIRTY-SEVEN

'Remember me, Frankie? I'm the one you wouldn't help and left me to die!'

Franks had not realised it was his nemesis who had tricked him, even when he was punched in the face. Clayton had been prepared for Franks recognising him at any point in his subterfuge, perhaps from his voice, although he knew his speech had changed due to the left side of his face now being disfigured. His masquerade had worked.

Franks was dazed from the punch and blood was now running freely from his nose over his mouth and down his chin. He instinctively tried to lift his right hand to wipe away the blood, but its movement was restricted. He looked down and could just make out through his blurred vision that his right wrist was tightly handcuffed to the gear knob of the 4x4. Instead, he used his left sleeve and only succeeded in smearing it across his face and along his sleeve.

The erstwhile helpful police officer had now removed his mask, but even then Franks had difficulty recognising him as he was side-on to the burn scarring on his neck and face.

'You! It can't be! You were killed in Baghdad!'

'I survived, no thanks to you,' Clayton snarled in reply. He had not forgotten what had happened years ago at a Christmas disco: 'As far as punches to the face go, I owed you one from the disco dancefloor; on that score we're now even.'

Suddenly, it dawned on Franks that he was face to face with the man who was responsible for his wife's death: 'You bastard! You utter bastard! You killed my wife!' Franks screamed in a rage at Clayton.

'That was unfortunate. If she'd used her own car that night we wouldn't be having this conversation.' Franks' anger boiled over and he swung several punches, none of which connected as Clayton leaned to his right so he was out of range due to Franks being constrained by the handcuff.

'Is that your best shot, Frankie? You'll have to do a lot better than that!' He was now mocking him, just as he had been mocked by Franks in Iraq. Now out of breath from several futile attempts to punch Clayton, Franks sank into his seat, through a mixture of shock and exhaustion, blood still dripping from his broken nose. Clayton leaned across and spoke menacingly: 'Now I'm going to make you suffer, just as I did.'

The realisation of his position began to sink in: he knew his mates had died and now it was his turn. Fear gripped him and his previous violent and aggressive attack gave way to whimpering. He began to beg, just as Clayton had begged him for help. Although he hated the man who had killed his wife and exposed his shortcomings in Iraq, he wanted to live.

'Listen, Pilgrim, I'm not proud of what happened in Iraq. I was under a lot of pressure. Being a corporal meant I had extra responsibility. I know I should have listened to your advice in Baghdad, but I couldn't appear weak in front of the others. I should have helped you when you were trapped, but I had to save the others! Come on Pilgrim, let's put it behind us and get on with the rest of our lives.' Another trickle of blood from his nose ran into his mouth before his left sleeve could intercept it.

'Don't give me that bullshit, Franks. You knew what you were doing. I pleaded with you to help me, but what did you do? Do you remember? Of course you remember. You smiled at me. You looked into my eyes and you fucking smiled! Then do you recall what you said before you ran for cover?' Clayton did not want him to answer, only to remember what he had said to him as he pleaded for his help.

With that he opened the driver's door and got out. Franks then began frantically pulling at the handcuff to no avail. His right wrist was now bleeding as the cuff having initially chafed his skin now exposed bare flesh. Blood was being smeared across his tattoo that all the mates had had done after their basic training in the Army; "blood brothers" no more.

Clayton took off the police cap and tossed it into the footwell of the 4x4. Next he did the same with his stolen high-visibility coat. Then he reached into the pocket of his own coat and pulled out a 500-millilitre plastic water bottle: but the bottle was not filled with water. As soon as he unscrewed the cap, Franks could smell the petrol.

'No! Don't do this, Pilgrim. Whatever happened in the past, I don't deserve this. You've already had your revenge by killing Bonnie!'

'You're wrong, Frankie. You do deserve this and it's exactly what you let happen to me!'

With that he sprinkled the petrol over the police coat and the front seat. He tossed the empty bottle and its cap into the footwell. Franks again desperately pulled at the handcuff, but the gear knob held firm. He was desperate to work out how he could escape this retribution. He began looking around the inside of the car and in panic pressed the button that activated the blue lights. Clayton was unfazed and made no attempt to turn off the lights as he knew there was no one around to take any notice. He took out a box of matches and, as there was little wind, he knew once lit, the match was unlikely to go out prematurely.

'Don't do this, Clayton, you bastard! Don't do this!'

He had the match poised to strike the matchbox: 'Have you recalled what you said to me when I was trapped in the APC, Franks? You said: "You're on your own, Pilgrim. You're the clever bastard, you work it out!" That's what you said to a mate who was desperate for your help.'

He then paused; Franks knew what was coming next: 'Well, you're on your own now, Frankie. You're the clever bastard, you work it out!' He struck the match and, knowing the petrol vapour would be the first thing to catch alight, he moved to the side of the open car door and tossed it in.

There was a 'whoosh' as the vapour ignited and Clayton slammed the car door shut. This was partly to contain the fire and partly to muffle the screams of Franks as the fire began melting his clothes and eating into his flesh.

Clayton slowly walked away from the contained inferno along a path that led to the back entrance to Royal William Yard, the muffled screams and the flashing blue lights gradually fading as he got further away. He was about to pass through an archway and descend the metal staircase down to the level of the Yard. He looked back in the direction of the police 4x4 and an explosion suddenly lit up the sky as the petrol tank exploded. The blue lights stopped flashing.

He showed no emotion as he descended the metal staircase.

At the bottom, he turned sharply to his right and walked towards the dark corner under the stairs where he had earlier left his motorbike and helmet. He could hear the emergency services sirens wailing in the distance, gradually getting closer to Devil's Point. He started his machine and rode at a sedate fifteen kilometres per hour through the Yard so as not to draw attention to himself. He then skirted the west side of Plymouth, heading north out of the city and on to Dartmoor.

*

Back at his secluded campsite in the lee of Sheepstor, he lit a fire and fried two eggs for his supper, complemented with a chunk of bread and washed down with a mug of tea. After washing the dishes and himself in a nearby stream, he lay on his sleeping bag, close to the fire as the night had grown colder, and reflected on the last month.

Lonely people sometimes talk to themselves and he was no exception: 'Mission accomplished. Tomorrow I return to my cottage.'

THIRTY-EIGHT

Richard King was about to prepare his evening meal when his mobile rang. He was informed that the panic alarm had been activated at Franks' safe house and officers had already been dispatched. He immediately rang Sergeant Harris and told her what had happened. He said that he was heading for the house and asked her to attend. She had nearly finished her meal, but readily agreed. King told her he would pick her up in fifteen minutes.

*

When they arrived at the inappropriately named safe house they saw that there were two police cars outside and the front door was open. A few doors down, a man was sitting in a car with his feet outside on the pavement and he was talking to a uniformed officer. King approached introducing himself and Sergeant Harris and asked him what had happened.

'He was dressed as a copper. Then the bastard tasered me from point-blank range. He also nicked my mobile phone. I've only just recovered.'

The inquiry into how he had allowed himself to be tricked and disabled would wait for another time. The detectives had more pressing matters.

As King and Harris walked up the garden path they were met by a uniformed sergeant who recognised King.

'Good evening, inspector. We were here within five minutes of the panic alarm sounding at the station, but the place was empty and the front door was unlocked. We searched the house, but there was no sign of Mr Franks. We have checked with the neighbours and two said there was a police car outside the house earlier with its blue lights flashing.

'Also, there are reports that a patrol car, driven by PC Boardman, has gone missing. My feeling is that both incidents could be linked. We are looking for the car, but it's not been found yet.' Just then he received a message over his radio into his earpiece. King and Harris waited in the hope of news that it had been traced.

'Apparently, PC Boardman was attacked on the Hoe, but isn't injured, sir. He confirmed his car was stolen by a man he was helping and who then surprised him by using chloroform; he was unconscious for about forty-five minutes. I've just spoken with him over the phone and he said that apart from a little nausea, he has more or less recovered.'

'Did he get a description of the man?' King asked.

'I asked him that, sir. He said he was average height and build and was wearing a snood, which covered his neck and most of his face. He also said he thought he had a slight limp. Apparently he was lured down to the beach on West Hoe as the man had reported seeing a suspicious object. It turned out to be a receiver for a transmitter. When he came round, his radio and the transmitter had gone.'

'Is PC Boardman still on duty?'

'I'll check for you, sir, and let you know.'

King thanked him for the update and as the detectives walked towards the house, King turned to his sergeant: 'So he has a slight limp. That will be because of his prosthetic.'

Once inside, they had a cursory look around the downstairs and noticed the untouched meal and cup of tea in the lounge, with the TV on in the background.

'Obviously left in a hurry,' King commented. He was more interested in what was on the hall table. They both pulled on latex gloves. He examined the wrapping paper, the box and its contents, passing each to his sergeant. Harris looked quizzically at the canteen and the note.

'Thoughts, Lucy?'

'Well, sir, if Clayton has abducted Franks using one of our cars, it begs the question how did he find him? Also, if Clayton brought this box, judging by the address on the wrapping paper, he knew exactly where to come. I'm not sure of the significance of the water bottle canteen and don't understand the note as it's some sort of coded message.'

King took off his latex gloves and took out a sherbet lemon from his coat pocket.

'Well, Lucy, it's obvious that Mr Franks' life is in grave danger. We have every available patrol car and the police helicopter searching for him and the stolen police car. I agree with you that Franks' location was compromised. Although he left in a hurry, there's no sign of a struggle. That might suggest he left at gunpoint or was somehow tricked into going voluntarily.

'The box was brought here as there is no stamp on the wrapping paper. I'm not sure what the Army canteen signifies, but I know what the note says. The message addressed to Franks told him that The Pilgrim was coming to get him; I'll explain later. We'll leave these items for Forensics and hope our colleagues can find Franks and Clayton.'

As they left, the uniformed sergeant was listening intently with his hand against his earpiece. The detectives waited to learn if there were any further developments.

'Two things, inspector: I'm sorry to report that our patrol car has been found burnt out at Devil's Point. I'm afraid there is a body in the car, as yet to be identified, but I've been informed that it was handcuffed to the gear knob. The other thing is what you asked me earlier. PC Boardman is still on duty.'

'I think I can confidently guess the identity of the dead person, sergeant. I was thinking of asking PC Boardman to help us search for the receiver on the beach, but I'm not sure it would be of any help if we could find it. Instead we'll go to where the body was found.'

*

The short journey to Devil's Point was made in complete silence. There was much on their minds, and now it appeared that Clayton had located and killed Colin Franks, they were asking themselves the same questions: how did Clayton locate Franks? Could they have done more to protect him? How the hell could they catch the man who had eluded them for the last week? Where is Clayton staying? Why have there been no sightings of him despite all the patrols and the media having been alerted?

*

As the detectives arrived at Devil's Point, they had to walk the last 200 metres as the road had been closed by the police. Emergency service vehicles were already nearly filling the car park. Scene of Crime Officers were erecting a tent over the burnt-out police car. There was little King and Harris could do, but they were shocked at seeing how Franks had died, which made them even more determined to apprehend Clayton – not that they needed any added motivation.

King remembered something Franks had said at interview: *'The Pilgrim was covered in blood and there was a fire between him and Carl. I was worried that if we stopped to help him we might all perish. I thought he was a goner anyway.'*

The inspector suspected that this was not simply premediated murder; this was like-for-like retribution. King looked in the 4x4 at the incinerated corpse and saw for himself the skeletal remains of Franks' right arm with the wrist securely fastened to the gear knob. He could not work out how Clayton had left the scene. He probably would not have gone back down the entrance road as he might have met the emergency services coming that way. King reasoned that the best way to unobtrusively escape the area would have been through the pedestrian back entrance to Royal William Yard. He beckoned Harris to follow him along the path that led in that direction.

'I said he was clever, Lucy. He creates all the kerfuffle at Devil's Point and I think he then calmly walked to his car parked in the Yard and drove off. Let's walk to the metal stairs and down to the other level.' When they reached the lower level the place was deserted. King mused: 'No point in door-to-door enquiries here.'

They walked back up and along the path, once again passing the 4x4 shell and could just make out Franks' body being removed, or what was left of it. They walked on and eventually got back to King's car. Before getting in, King spoke: 'This whole episode with Franks' protection, and now after what's happened, will be the subject of an inquiry. But, that will be for later. Now we still have a serial killer on the loose and we need to find him.'

'I was thinking that Clayton has been very elusive. No one has reported seeing him. All we've had are a couple of sightings of his Land Rover. Why is that, do you think, Lucy?'

'Well, he tends to operate at night and during the winter there are fewer people out and about. Also, the Covid restrictions mean he could wear a mask at any time and any place, therefore he could more easily hide his identity.'

'I think all those things work in his favour, Lucy, and yet he still has to keep his Defender hidden as that would arouse suspicion, assuming he knows we're looking for it.'

'So, sir, he's either able to garage it or he's in a secluded place somewhere?'

'If the latter, where do you think he might be hiding? Think about what we were told about his former business.'

'Dartmoor?'

'That's my thinking and perhaps I should have thought of it three days ago when our suspect was known to have regularly used the moor. Now, the National Park covers 365 square miles, so it would be a bit like looking for a needle in a haystack, particularly as he will no doubt have chosen a very secluded place. However, that shouldn't have stopped us looking. I think we can discount three-quarters of the moor as he wouldn't want to be travelling miles. In the morning, if the DCI agrees, I'll get the police helicopter to fly over the south-west part of the moor and look for an active campsite, hopefully with a Land Rover parked nearby.'

'That's certainly worth a try, sir.' Harris tried to sound optimistic, but there was no enthusiasm in her voice. King sensed her misgivings.

'I said previously, Lucy, that we are dealing with a very clever and a very ruthless man. From our investigations, it appears that Clayton was treated very badly by his former friends when they were in Iraq. It's hard not to feel some sympathy for him after what he has suffered, but we owe it to all the people he has killed to track him down and force him to face justice for his crimes. Sooner or later, he will make a mistake and when he does, we need to be ready to arrest him. I have a feeling that day is not very far off.'

THIRTY-NINE

The morning after Franks was killed, Inspector King was up very early and called at the safe house to have another look around. He had to work out how Clayton had found out where Franks was living. This was not only to satisfy his own curiosity, but also to gather further evidence against Clayton to ensure his conviction when he was eventually arrested.

He walked around the rooms in the house, asking himself how the location had been compromised. Had Franks contacted someone and his call had somehow been intercepted by Clayton? Was someone followed to the house? Was something delivered, if so what? The wrapping paper and box had been removed by Forensics and he knew they had been delivered personally by Clayton as there was no stamp on the wrapping paper. But there were other items that had been delivered to the house that had not appeared to be suspicious. He picked up all the condolence cards that had been left in a pile on the coffee table in the lounge, rather than being displayed by Franks in the conventional manner. King thought to himself that the cards perhaps were the key to the mystery and he knew just the person to unlock it.

*

King arrived at the station in time to join all the detectives who were attending their morning briefing with DCI Burrows, which he was not looking forward to in view of the events of the previous day. When he arrived the meeting had been cancelled and King was summoned to the DCI's room. There was no warmth in the greeting he received.

'Come in, Inspector King, and sit down. Well, you can imagine how I'm feeling right now. I'm extremely disappointed... no, make that bloody angry... that we allowed Franks to be abducted from right under our noses and then killed. Have you any idea how bad that looks? The chief constable is incandescent and I don't blame her. She has contacted the director of the National Crime Agency, who was charged with protecting Franks, demanding an explanation and wants to know how the location of Mr Franks, who was in protective custody, was compromised leading to his murder? After attending a rather embarrassing press conference with the national press, she has asked for a full report on the hunt for the serial killer. It is not unreasonable for her to expect an arrest as we know who the killer is and we knew in advance who his final victim was going to be.'

King was suitably contrite: 'I share your frustration and annoyance, sir. I too was astounded that Clayton had discovered the location of the safe house. I apologise if what I am about to say sounds as if I'm being wise after the event, as to some extent that is true. It may not help appease the chief constable, but I believe I now know how he did it. I appreciate it's too late to save Franks' life, but this would be crucial evidence against Clayton when he is arrested.'

The DCI had calmed down and was hoping for any positive news he could pass on to the chief constable. 'Okay, Richard, let's hear it.'

'We now know that Clayton hijacked one of our cars last night and used it to abduct and kill Mr Franks. Having spoken with the PC whose car was stolen, we know that he was lured from it at West Hoe by his attention being drawn to a suspicious object on the beach below. It transpired that Clayton had earlier placed a receiver on the shingle, so the LED red light could be seen from the road overlooking the beach. The fact he had a receiver got me thinking that he could somehow have planted a transmitter in the safe house, to identify its location. But how did he get it into the house? I can think of two ways: either hidden amongst the food that was provided for Franks or through the post. I ruled out the food as Clayton wouldn't have been able to identify the supplier.

'However, Franks did get letters that had originally been sent to his home address. I know all his mail was scanned at the sorting depot to ensure it didn't contain any nasty surprises, before being redirected. He received over a dozen cards of condolence and I collected them on my way into work this morning. I called into the forensic lab before this meeting, as I knew John Gleeson starts work at 7.30, and I explained my hunch to him. Sure enough, under closer scrutiny than it was given at the sorting office, he examined all the cards and found a micro transmitter in this one.' He held up the card with the embossed crucifix on the front.

'So, Clayton hid the transmitter in the card and posted it to Franks at his house in Yelverton. He then must have tracked it after it was redirected, first to the sorting office then to the safe house.'

The DCI could see the logic in King's theory, but wanted to know more: 'So, that could explain how he found out where Franks was living; what about the box, canteen and note that I believe were found at the house?'

'I think Clayton used it to convince Franks that his location had been compromised, so he would willingly go with him. Very clever disguise, not only was he wearing PC Boardman's coat and hat, he also had his police car!'

'And the box, canteen and note?'

'The wrapping paper with Franks' name and address on was to convince him he was in imminent danger. In his state of panic, he wouldn't have noticed there was no stamp on it. If he had noticed and he was thinking straight, he would have worked out the messenger was a fraud.

'I can only guess at the significance of the canteen, sir. We were told by Franks that when they were in Iraq together, Clayton was trapped in an armoured personnel carrier after a bomb was detonated. Not only was he badly injured, he was severely burned. Apparently Franks decided to save himself and the other mates leaving Clayton to his fate. I think Franks was being reminded that, at the very least, he could have used his canteen of water to put out the flames. His mates refused to help him too.

'The note is easy to explain. I remembered something Mrs Freeman said to us when we interviewed her and she was talking about how the mates communicated in writing using a code. She said: "My Dan said it was something to do with missing out letters in the alphabet. In truth, I thought it was a bit childish." It didn't take me long to break their simple code: when writing they would simply jump forward two letters from the original message. So "A" becomes "C" and "M" becomes "O". The original note is with Forensics, but I've got a photocopy here, sir. I have scribbled the translation underneath the original message.'

JGNNQ HTCPMKG
Hello Frankie
VJG RKNITKO'U RTQITGUU KU PGCTNA EQORNGVG.
The Pilgrim's progress is nearly complete.
K'O EQOKPI VQ IGV AQW!
I'm coming to get you!
VJG RKNITKO.
The Pilgrim.

'You can appreciate how Franks would have reacted to that note. He probably couldn't get out of the house fast enough!'

'Thank you for your deduction. It sounds to me a bit like a damage limitation report, but I'm grateful to have something positive to tell the chief constable. So, what about apprehending Clayton?'

'I know that's all well and good, sir, as evidence against Clayton, but it doesn't get us any closer to catching him. I've been discussing this with Sergeant Harris and we think the main reason why we haven't had any sightings of him – apart from his Land Rover being placed at the scene of two crimes – is because he may have been camping on Dartmoor. Our reasoning is he knows the moor very well, as he used it for his outdoor survival business. He knew how he could "disappear" on the moor and yet be in striking distance of the people he planned to kill.'

The DCI interjected: 'Dartmoor covers a huge area, inspector!'

'It does, sir, but if I were Clayton, I'd pick the nearest secluded place or places to where he wanted to be to carry out the murders. That's still a big area for us to search, so, subject to your approval, I would like to arrange for the police helicopter to fly over the south-west corner of the moor and see if they can find where he's staying.'

'Approval granted, inspector. How soon can it be in the air?'

'In about two minutes, sir, as I had arranged for it to be on standby awaiting your approval!'

After discussion on stepping up the number of patrols, and the production and distribution of wanted posters, the meeting ended. King left the room suitably chastened.

*

DCI Burrows had received a request from the local BBC news programme *Spotlight*, the local newspaper and radio about the serial killer. King volunteered to do both the interviews as, although Burrows was the senior officer in charge of the investigation, King was the person in possession of all the facts of the case. The interview for television was scheduled for noon in order to catch the lunchtime bulletin. The DCI somewhat reluctantly agreed as he knew his inspector had a very close grasp of all the facts. He also acknowledged a public appeal for information might glean a better response coming from the detective actively involved in the case.

*

After introducing King, the *Spotlight* interviewer briefly catalogued the murders and then asked the question others were asking themselves: 'So, Inspector King, we have a serial killer at large and active in our area, why haven't the police been able to apprehend him?'

'It only became apparent after the murder of Mr Prescott that his murder was linked to that of Mr Freeman. The link was they were all friends and served in the Army together. Subsequently, we discovered that Mr Higgins, another friend and Army reservist, died in a fall from his ladder about a month ago, in Yeovil; we now think he was murdered. The coroner has reopened that case and the verdict of accidental death is being reviewed.'

'And, Inspector King, three further murders have been committed since the death of Mr Prescott.'

'That's correct and we believe that Mrs Franks was not the intended victim when she was killed.' The interviewer had a follow-up question, but King continued: 'The man we are urgently looking for to help us with our enquiries is Derek Clayton and he has two distinguishing features: he wears a prosthetic below the knee on his right leg. He is also badly scarred on the left side of his neck and face from injuries he received when in the Army. We need to locate him as soon as possible.

'We have reason to believe his is driving an Army-type Land Rover Defender. If anyone should see him, please ring 999 immediately. This man is a vicious and ruthless killer. Do not attempt to approach him.'

That signalled the end of the interview and King then did an interview for Radio Devon, more or less word for word the same as the TV interview. The *Western Morning News* local paper was providing regular updates on the murders and had moved on from: 'THE DEVON ASSASSIN STRIKES AGAIN' to 'SERIAL KILLER STILL AT LARGE'.

*

Clayton listened to the radio broadcast while sitting in the Defender. He was quietly seething at King's portrayal of him. He became consumed by the need to tell the inspector his side of the story. So much so, after some thought, he decided to delay his departure. He wanted to give Inspector King a full explanation for his killing spree and, importantly, the root cause. He decided he was going to do that face to face! Still sitting in his Defender, his initial thought was to abduct King after following him home from the police station. He dismissed that idea as too risky. Then he developed what he thought was a better plan.

Later that afternoon, after being angered by the broadcast on the radio, Clayton set out to prepare for his plan, which he would carry out the following day. He crossed the county boundary into Cornwall – marked by the River Tamar – and headed for Saltash, which sits on the banks of the river.

His planning required him to do two things: the first was to buy two identical pieces of clothing, so he went to the market in Saltash and found exactly what he was looking for, paying for them in cash. The second was not so easy to obtain, namely someone to help him. There were two things that person would need: the first was a motorbike and the second was a desire to make easy money.

He rode around the outskirts of the town on the lookout for a person who fitted that profile. It took him over an hour, but eventually he found who he wanted. A youth was sitting alone on a park bench, his scrambler motorbike parked nearby, eating a McDonald's meal as Clayton approached.

FORTY

The day before he killed Franks, Clayton had relocated to a secluded spot on Dartmoor near Sheepstor over a mile from the nearest tarmacked road. This, his last camp, was the closest to Plymouth of all his camps and that suited his planning. He had originally decided to leave the day after disposing of Franks. The final act of his mission had been completed. Now, on the day of his intended departure, he had woken, made himself a late breakfast and then walked to the top of the Sheepstor, only possible with the aid of his walking stick. He loved the wide-open spaces and although it was pleasantly calm, it made no difference to his love of the moor whatever the weather.

As he stood there gazing into the distance, he was not sure for how much longer he would be able to enjoy what it had to offer. After listening to Inspector King's TV interview, broadcast on the radio, he decided to change his plans. He was determined that his story had to be told. After the traumatic events in Iraq and subsequent retribution, he should have finally found some inner peace, but that was not enough. He was the only one left alive who knew the true story of what happened to him and why he had embarked on his killing mission. Despite the police hunting for him, he would stay another day. That afternoon he had recruited a youth to help him with his final farewell at noon the following day.

*

Clayton spent the early morning of the next day walking close to Sheepstor, enjoying his last stroll on the moor. By mid-morning he was back in his secluded campsite and from the embers of his fire, he retrieved a saucepan of boiling water – which he had placed there before his walk – made himself tea in his tin mug and also a flask of coffee. He sat on a nearby boulder and had his final drink before preparing to leave Dartmoor for the last time.

When he had finished his tea, unusually for him, he did not bother washing the mug. He simply threw it into the back of the Land Rover. He then collected other items, including the tarpaulin, and did the same with them. From his spare supply of fuel, he filled the petrol tank of his Enfield motorbike and a small plastic bottle. He used the remainder of the petrol from the can to soak a bundle of his spare clothing, which he then placed on the driver's seat in his Defender. In the back he piled all his possessions that had served him so well over the previous month, except for his motorbike, crash helmet, walking stick, his backpack and another pack that he had only used once since leaving his home. All were placed well away from his dependable vehicle.

He took out a box of matches from his pocket, together with a small rectangular Zip firelighter. He knew, once lit, the firelighter would burn for up to twenty minutes. Opening the driver's door of the Defender, he placed it on the seat and partially covered it with the petrol-soaked clothes. He lit the firelighter and just as one of his shirts burst into flames, he shut the door. Patting the bonnet in silent gratitude, Clayton stepped back. He waited for a few minutes until he was sure the Land Rover was fully alight. He knew the cloud of smoke might attract attention, so only stayed long enough to be sure that his beloved vehicle would be totally destroyed. He did not take any pleasure in its destruction or, for that matter, polluting the moor, but it had to be done for him to successfully execute his plan.

He put on his helmet, slung one backpack onto his back and secured the other on top of the fuel tank with a Velcro strap. As his Land Rover was now billowing black smoke across the moor, he sighed, mounted his motorbike and headed for the Tamar Bridge.

*

'We have a suspicious sighting from the police helicopter, sir!' Sergeant Harris announced to Inspector King. The helicopter crew had been criss-crossing the south-west corner of Dartmoor looking for Clayton, following King's hunch that he may be camping on the moor. When the helicopter crew saw smoke coming from a small copse, close to Sheepstor, they decided to investigate. Landing nearby on flat ground, the navigator jumped down and made his way to the source of the smoke. Although partially destroyed by fire, the vehicle was recognised as a Land Rover Defender. Nearby were the remains of a campfire, but no sign of anybody. The pilot radioed in and the message was quickly passed to Sergeant Harris.

King decided to take his team to the site to investigate further as he quite clearly sensed that they had discovered Clayton's hideout, albeit too late to apprehend him. Hammond and Dyson travelled in their unmarked police car, while King and Harris opted for a patrol car with two uniformed officers who were responding to the alert. The blaring sirens and flashing lights would make their journey that much quicker.

When they arrived, the helicopter was still there, together with another police car, which happened to be on patrol not far from Sheepstor. By now, the Land Rover was smouldering and they realised that the chance of retrieving any evidence from it was remote. The officers from the car and helicopter were using their fire extinguishers with little hope of salvaging much from the vehicle. As the detectives walked around the wreckage, the small indentations left by a walking stick were clearly visible and all but confirmed that this had been Clayton's camp. What they could not understand was why he had set fire to his Defender.

*

In the meantime, DCI Burrows was urgently trying to contact King, but as there was no mobile phone signal where they were, he had to make contact on the police radio. The uniformed driver of the patrol car came rushing over to where the detectives were sifting through the remains of the campfire and surrounding area.

'Inspector King, I have an urgent message from DCI Burrows for you that there's a "jumper" on the bridge across the Tamar River.'

'So, what's that got to do with me?' King quizzically asked.

'The "jumper" is asking for you, sir.'

'Me? What possible connection can I have with someone who wants to jump off a bridge?'

'The police negotiator is talking to him, sir, and apparently his exact words were: "Tell Inspector King that The Pilgrim wants to speak with him!"'

FORTY-ONE

King and Harris quickly got back into the police car that had brought them to the campsite, and left Hammond and Dyson searching for any evidence from the smouldering Defender. King could not quite believe what he had been told. It looked as though the man that had proved so elusive was now waiting to speak with him, standing on the edge of a bridge and about to end his life.

They left Sheepstor to travel the ten miles to the bridge down the A386 and then joining the A38. As they entered the Devon Expressway – as that part of the A38 is called – they were still five kilometres from the bridge, but the westbound traffic was already at a standstill. The police car hurtled down the hard shoulder and eventually the bridges came into view.

The Tamar Bridge is suspended over the River Tamar and marks the county boundary between Devon and Cornwall. It was constructed in 1961 and shares the crossing with its parallel neighbour, the Royal Albert Bridge, which was built to take the railway and designed by the famous architect Isambard Kingdom Brunel a hundred years earlier.

King was not sure which bridge he should be heading to as he had just been told it was a bridge over the Tamar River; he suspected it was the road bridge. As they got closer it was obvious from the gathering of emergency vehicles it was the Tamar Bridge as King had thought. He knew Clayton would not be the first person to end their life jumping from this bridge and, sadly, would not be the last. Now, stationary traffic queues stretched for miles in both directions as the patrol car reached the police cordon.

King quickly got out and was ushered along the bridge, stripped of its traffic. The total span reached over 330 metres and about halfway across there was a small group of people, close to the exact line of the county boundaries. He could see a man dressed in a bright orange hoodie up ahead and wearing a backpack. He was standing on top of the railings that protected the edge of the bridge, and he was holding onto one of the steel support cables with his right hand, leaning away from the bridge at a dangerous angle. The strangely shaped toggles of his hoodie were swaying in the light breeze.

The police negotiator intercepted King as he approached: 'Inspector King?' He nodded. 'The man is threatening to jump unless he can speak to you. I've tried to reason with him, but he is adamant. When you talk to him, try to speak slowly and reason with him that if he comes down, he will be given all the help he needs. Don't raise your voice. If you get into a dialogue with him, show that you are prepared to listen to what he has to say. Use open questions and paraphrase when appropriate. Try to build a rapport with him and show empathy. That's the best way to encourage him to come down.'

King listened to the crash course in negotiating skills, realising he had the unenviable task of trying to stop Clayton jumping just so he could spend the rest of his life in prison! He was apprehensive and at the same time intrigued as he prepared to meet the man who had turned from being a model member of society into a vengeful killer. He moved forward now on his own until he was less than four metres from Clayton. He was not wearing anything on his head, but his snood was pulled up over his ears, the blackness of it standing out against the orange of the hoodie. His only connection to the bridge was by the fingertips of his right hand and his right foot.

'Ah, Inspector King, we meet at last. I recognise you from your picture in the local paper. Allow me to introduce myself. I am The Pilgrim, formerly known as Derek Clayton. I understand you've been looking for me?'

King was impassive: 'I had a message that you wanted to speak with me? What did you want to say?'

'I won't insult your intelligence, as I know you are fully aware of what I have done, if not how I did it.'

'Do you mean pulling Higgins off his ladder with your walking stick; tricking Freeman into going with you to Plymbridge Woods; drugging and drowning Prescott; puncturing the tyres of the car of Bryson's golf partner then bashing Bryson's head in with a seven-iron; the Semtex with the tilt switch at Devonia; the bungled bombing; the transmitter hidden in the condolence card crucifix; the coded note and water canteen to Franks to scare him into leaving the safe house with you; or do you mean the fact that we knew you were driving a Land Rover Defender and were camped near Sheepstor!' King was in no mood to be patronised; he was angry.

The negotiator put her head in her hands at King's approach as that was not at all what she had advocated.

'Well, I'm impressed, Inspector King. You're not as dumb as you look!' This was now getting personal.

'That will save me the trouble of explaining how those bastards died. No doubt you spoke to Franks. This is the main reason for wanting to speak with you, inspector. I wanted you to know what really happened in Iraq in 2018. The truth and not some half-truth from Franks.

'As I'm sure you know, our APC was blown-up and my good mate, Carl Brackley, was sadly killed. I was trapped in the overturned APC and Franks and the others could have saved me from this…' With his free hand he dramatically pulled down the snood to reveal the full horror of his burned neck and face. 'And maybe this…' He pulled up his right trouser leg to reveal his prosthetic.

King showed no emotion nor did he speak as he sensed Clayton had not finished what he wanted to say; he was right.

'When I pleaded for help, do you know what that bastard Franks did? He just smiled at me and told me I was on my own. Each and every one of my so-called mates could have put out the flames with their water canteen and tried to release my trapped foot, but they didn't. Why? Because Franks had more or less ordered them not to help.

'I knew he was beginning to dislike me through no fault of my own. It was his incompetence as a leader that I had unwittingly exposed and his pride was wounded. I didn't set out to make his job more difficult than it was; I was trying to help him, but he took it the wrong way. I never bad-mouthed him, but he just couldn't see that the best way was to seek my help and the help of others. He didn't, as he thought he knew best. The rest of my mates were just gutless individuals who refused to help a friend when he needed them most. If it hadn't been for the marines who rescued me, I would have either burnt or bled to death.

'So, no doubt you have been wondering about my motives, inspector? Well, I'll tell you what motivated me. While my ex-mates continued to enjoy their lives, mine was ruined beyond repair. I lost everything. The woman I love, my Army career, my business, my self-esteem, everything! It didn't have to be like that. They could have helped me, but each and every one of them decided to save themselves. There's your motive, inspector.'

His precarious position holding on with his right hand and balanced on his prosthetic leg was beginning to show the strain. King had no reason to doubt his testimony and now fully understood what had motivated him to exact his revenge.

'Come down and finish your story at the station.' King said matter-of-factly, but Clayton ignored his conciliatory tone.

'So, I survived, but what happened next? Countless operations; I was invalided out of the Army, a career that I loved; my business, which had been thriving before I went to Iraq, folded. Worst of all, my wife, Bella, left me because I'd become a vengeful, introverted man.'

Just then the police helicopter appeared overhead. Clayton raised his voice. partly in annoyance at the intrusion and partly because of the noise from the rotor blades: 'Get rid of that, inspector, or I'll jump!' he threatened.

King turned and shouted in the general direction of the emergency services personnel: 'Tell the chopper to back off.' It quickly banked away and was gone.

Clayton was getting closer to his final farewell: 'You might say they didn't deserve to die. I say they didn't deserve to live.'

King tried to reassure Clayton: 'Sounds to me that there are mitigating factors, so why don't we get your story recorded down at the station.'

'Thank you, inspector, but that's not going to happen. I knew what I was doing and I understand the consequences of my actions. Anyway, you now know why I had to destroy their lives, just as they destroyed mine. I'm glad we finally met Inspector King, but now I must leave you!'

With that he jumped.

FORTY-TWO

There was a collective gasp when Clayton jumped. King did not move, transfixed by a range of emotions. Clayton had killed five people and still evaded justice, yet now King, having heard his version of events in Iraq – which he believed to be the true account – also felt a degree of understanding. Other officers, who were standing behind King, rushed to the railings.

'Inspector, look at this!' the negotiator shouted as she peered over the edge. King slowly turned, not keen on seeing someone plunge to their death. When he reached the iron railings, she moved aside to let him take her place. He put both hands on the top rail and looked down.

He found it difficult to take in what he saw: below him was a yellow canopy, no bigger than a bed sheet, swaying from side to side as Clayton, dangling beneath it – although he could not see him – controlled his descent. The drop from the bridge down to the River Tamar did not give him much time to deploy his parachute and land safely, but he was an accomplished parachutist having been an instructor in his business venture.

King muttered under his breath: 'The clever bastard. I wondered why he was wearing a backpack. The toggles weren't from his hoodie, they were ripcords!' He quickly regained his composure and shouted an instruction to a uniformed sergeant: 'Get the chopper back now. Tell the pilot what's happened and to track the parachutist when he lands!'

Soon the rotor blades could be heard overhead. The police helicopter swooped down towards where the parachutist had just landed in a clearing among the trees on the Cornwall side of the river. King waited long enough to see the orange hoodie-clad figure discard the 'chute and head for the nearby trees.

In less than a minute a motorbike came into view as the rider rode into the middle of the clearing, his hoodie standing out like a beacon, before accelerating in a northerly direction through the trees. Having seen enough, King turned and ran along the deserted bridge shouting instructions to police officers as he ran: 'Your patrol car. We're following him. Take the road to the China Fleet Country Club. Alert other patrols and try to head him off. I think he's using the riverside path. Get this traffic moving. Tell the toll operator to raise the barriers until the tailback has cleared.' Sergeant Harris had run with him and they both jumped into the back of the police 4x4 as it roared along the deserted road to Saltash, before branching down towards the river.

As King had anticipated the rider's destination, the police cars, travelling well above the speed limit, would be able to overtake the motorbike as the rough ground was restricting its speed. There were a few pathways leading up from the riverside path, and King issued instructions that patrol cars should block them all in case he was wrong about the destination and the motorbike changed direction.

The navigator in the helicopter kept the patrol cars informed of the motorbike's route and that it remained on the riverside path. The pilot had occasional visual contact – as the orange hoodie stood out among the backdrop of trees – but when he lost visual contact, there was the assistance from his thermal imaging camera. Although he was on a rough dirt track, the motorbike was still travelling at over fifty kph.

The helicopter crew alerted the pursuing police – who had now got ahead of their quarry on a much faster road parallel to the path – to the fact that about half a mile ahead of the motorbike there was a tarmac path leading up from the river that crossed the riverside track, which would be ideal for the deployment of a stinger device. A patrol car immediately raced to the crossing and, as an officer went to get the stinger out of the back of the car, he could hear the motorbike approaching. It was no more than fifty metres from the cross-over path when the officer hurled the extendable arm with its six-centimetre-long hardened steel spikes across the full width of the tarmac.

As the bike rounded a corner and ran over the spikes, the tyres immediately deflated, leaving it travelling a short distance on its wheel rims before coming to an abrupt stop. The rider was thrown over the handlebars and landed upside down in a hedge, which broke his fall. Four officers moved in to pull him out – somewhat difficult as he had landed in overgrown brambles.

By the time the officers had extricated the rider, checking he was uninjured, King and Harris had arrived in the patrol car. The motorcyclist was sitting on an old fallen tree trunk, still wearing his orange hoodie and his crash helmet. He had been handcuffed, his scrambler motorbike lying in the hedge on the opposite side of the path. The helicopter was still circling overhead.

As the two detectives walked down the path from the road above, King took one look at the forlorn figure and remarked:

'That's not Clayton!'

He did not wait for the rider's identity to be revealed; instead he immediately gave specific instructions to one of the officers who had brought them.

'Tell the chopper pilot that the rider in the woods is not the wanted man. I think the suspect might either be walking to Saltash or be on a motorbike travelling along the A38 in Cornwall and should be about halfway to Liskeard by now. Tell him to alert patrols if he locates the suspect. If no sign of him on the A38, fly across to the A388 to Launceston and look for him riding a motorbike along that road.'

Having issued his instructions, he turned his attention to the handcuffed motorcyclist who he had left sitting on a log recovering from his fall. He still had his crash helmet on.

Sergeant Harris looked on in amazement at her boss: 'How can you be so sure this isn't Clayton, sir?'

'Several reasons, Lucy: first, he was travelling down a dead end. Even if he had come up off the riverside track onto the road, he would have been vulnerable. He's way too smart to put himself in that position. Second, I was suspicious from the outset when from up on the bridge we saw him ride into the middle of the clearing before he roared off along the path. If ever there was a "follow me" gesture, that was it. Third, the person who emerged into the clearing was wearing a crash helmet. If it had been Clayton, would he have wasted time putting on a helmet? Lastly, and the most obvious indication he's not our man, he has two good legs!'

He then addressed the officers on either side of the rider: 'Right, let's have a chat with our decoy.' With that, an officer undid the strap under his helmet and took it off to reveal a youth, no more than twenty, with long hair and wearing a pained expression. King stepped forward: 'And your name is?'

'Wayne Truscott. What's all this about? You could have killed me with that spike thing. I never saw it until it was too late.'

'I am Inspector King. So, what's the story, Wayne?'

'What do you mean, what's the story? I was getting paid to do a job for a geezer that's all.'

'Tell us about this geezer, Wayne.'

'Am I in trouble?'

'That depends.' King said not committing himself.

'On what?'

'Your full cooperation. You tell us all you know and that might be the end of our interest in you, otherwise we'll have this chat at the station. It's your call.' Truscott weighed his options.

'Okay. Yesterday this geezer comes up to me in the park in Saltash, wearing a sort of scarf round his head. He had a crash helmet on so I could only see his eyes. I was eating my McDonald's and he asks me if I want to earn some dosh. I ask him what I have to do and he tells me he's in a daredevils' club with some of his mates and he wants to trick them. I asks him how much dosh? He says 250 quid there and then, and another 250 when I complete the job. He showed me two envelopes stuffed with £20 notes in case I didn't believe him. Well, I'm out of work at the moment so I tells him okay. He then hands me one of the envelopes and tells me to follow him.'

King mused to himself that the police had been focussing on finding a Land Rover Defender and most of the time Clayton was probably riding around on a motorbike: 'What happened then?'

'I get on my scrambler and follows him around the outskirts of the town and down to the river. We ride about half a mile along the riverside path, no one was about, and stop next to a clearing in the trees, about the size of half a footy pitch. We look up at the Tamar Bridge and he says at noon today he's going to parachute off it down to where we were standing. He told me he wanted me to wait here on my scrambler under the trees and out of sight.

'He says when he lands and gets out of his 'chute, he'll give me the rest of the dosh. Then he says I must ride out into the clearing, before heading off down the path and head for the country club at the end of it. When I gets there, that's the job finished. He also gave me this hideous orange hoodie to wear. God knows why, but for 500 quid I'd have worn a dress if he told me to!

'Blow me, at noon he did jump off the bridge just as he said he would and I couldn't believe it! When he landed he was wearing the same ugly orange coloured hoodie as me! I think this was to trick his mates. We looked like a pair of bloody bookends! Did he fool his mates? He hasn't done anything wrong has he?'

King could not blame the lad for not turning down that sort of money: he had been duped just like the police; but he was not going to let him get away entirely scot-free: 'Wrong? I'd say that's an understatement, Wayne. You've helped a potential serious offender evade arrest. So, we'll need you to come to the station and make a statement after all.'

Truscott went white with shock and King beckoned an officer to come forward and escort him to a patrol car. The inspector then turned to his sergeant and the two uniformed officers who had brought them. He waited until Truscott was out of earshot: 'I don't think we can charge Mr Truscott with any offence as he was completely oblivious to Clayton's little charade. No doubt he'll be allowed to keep the 500 pounds for his ride along the river and we'll have to pay him for two new tyres. Any news from the chopper?'

'I'm afraid not, sir.'

'Okay. Let's have a look at the clearing he parachuted into.'

Once there, they saw the abandoned 'chute and after a few minutes found an orange hoodie partly covered in leaves, which was collected as evidence.

King was rather deflated: 'Let's get back to the station; the search for Clayton continues.'

*

King had been right about Clayton taking the A38 towards Liskeard as the other routes were clogged with traffic due to his 'suicide' leap. Clayton suspected that King, realising he had been duped, would set the helicopter after him. Ten minutes after leaving the clearing in the shadow of the bridge, and on the road to Liskeard, he had turned off the main road onto a lane and after travelling for about a mile, found a secluded spot with tree cover and parked his Enfield. He sat on his crash helmet and poured himself a coffee from the flask he had in his backpack. Just to be sure he would not be spotted, he waited for over half an hour in case the helicopter doubled back still searching the A38.

While he waited, he reflected how pleased he was to have told King his side of the story. It was important to Clayton to put the record straight. Even if some people profoundly disagreed with his actions, at least they understood why he had acted the way he had. The little deception of jumping off the Tamar Bridge had worked well, in allowing him to evade capture, facilitated by the use of the parachute he kept in his Land Rover following the failure of his outdoor business venture.

He finished the last of his coffee, glanced skywards, and, satisfied he would not be followed or spotted from the air, he headed for home.

FORTY-THREE

Having evaded capture after his exploits on the Tamar Bridge, and so as not to attract attention, Clayton carefully rode his motorbike within the speed limit all the way to Penzance. When he arrived at his rented double garage, it seemed strangely empty now that his Defender would not be returning. He decided to continue to pay the rent and keep his motorbike there, along with a few other items used in his failed business venture on Dartmoor.

It was now mid-afternoon following his noon jump off the bridge and he had checked the weather conditions for his trip. It was twenty-six nautical miles to Tresco, the second largest island in the Scilly Isles. His small motorboat – named *Mayflower* after the ship that had transported the Pilgrim Fathers to the New World 400 years before – would travel at about twenty-five knots per hour, so from its mooring in Penzance Harbour to the island, he calculated it would take him approximately ninety minutes as the sea, that late afternoon, was officially classed as choppy and would slow his progress. He was unconcerned: he knew that if he left in the next half an hour, he would make the north coast of the island before dark. The tide times suited him, as on his planned arrival at his island home, the tide would be high and he could moor his boat far up the beach, leaving him just a short walk to his cottage.

He was travelling light. Making sure he was well wrapped up to protect himself from the much colder temperatures out on the water, he wore his backpack containing a few personal belongings, and carried his walking stick. He had dressed in thermal underwear that morning with his parachute jump and sea crossing in mind. He locked the garage with his Enfield standing in isolation. He was not sure if he would ever return to use his treasured machine.

It was a ten-minute walk down from the garage to where his small boat was moored on a pontoon. The engine started at the first time of asking and he set off at a speed of only five knots. He was in no particular hurry apart from wanting to get back to his island sanctuary. He had achieved what he set out to do and now wanted to get home and be left alone.

After his rehabilitation from his injuries, with his share of the equity from his house sale, Army compensation and pension, he was financially well placed. He had been able to buy a run-down retreat, which he had turned into a home, and also had sufficient money left over to last him into his dotage. The footprint of the single-storey thatched cottage was no bigger than a double garage but it was all that he needed. Besides, he did not buy it solely for the accommodation, but mainly for its location. The clifftop home gave him uninterrupted views of the sea. In the distance to the north of the island was Ireland; to the east, Wales and England; to the south, France and beyond that country, the coast of Spain; to the west the vast North Atlantic Ocean and then the eastern seaboard of the United States and Plymouth, Massachusetts that he had single-handedly sailed to as a headstrong youth all those years before.

There was nothing he liked better on a cold winter's night than to be sitting in front of his log fire, with the wind howling outside his front door. The one drawback of the cottage's position was it did not offer the best growing conditions for his kitchen garden. Nevertheless, he had cultivated part of his large garden and it served him well with vegetables and fruit.

Every morning he had a ritual. Whatever the weather, sometimes with coffee mug in hand, he would stand for about twenty minutes at his special vantage point close to the cliff edge at the top of his garden and survey the sea and the surrounding archipelago. This was his island paradise, the only place where he felt at peace.

*

As he approached the island, heading due west, he had to navigate around the many small rocky outcrops in the sea – which would have presented a real hazard to a less experienced sailor – before catching sight of Tresco. He never tired of seeing his home island as it came into view. It was where he was born, where he had always wanted to live and to end his days. Why? What was it about this strip of land, two and a half miles long and a mile wide, with no cars and only 150 inhabitants? All those reasons were what made this place so precious to him. He loved the peace and solitude of the place and, a year before, when he had recovered sufficiently from his injuries, and the opportunity presented itself, he had no hesitation in buying the clifftop thatched cottage.

It was getting dark as he pulled his boat above the high tide line and secured it with a rope to an iron stake just in case a storm whipped the sea further up the foreshore than anticipated. He took the familiar sandy path up to his home high above the beach with his backpack over his shoulders and his walking stick in his hand. This was always arduous due to his prosthetic, but he never begrudged the climb because of what awaited him at the top. His idyllic cottage made it all worthwhile.

It was just as he had left it over a month before. He opened the wooden gate, which had successfully kept the cattle away from his self-sufficient fruit and vegetable patch. He knew he was low on provisions, so in the morning he planned to use his boat to motor around to Old Grimsby, the closest main settlement on the eastern side of the island, to pick up what he needed. He would also check if he had any letters at the post office. He preferred to collect his mail and had an arrangement with the postal service not to deliver to his remote cottage.

He had been away for over a month and his stone cottage felt cold and damp. His little haven had no electricity and the only running water was provided by a stream that ran along the bottom of the field that surrounded his home. There was no central heating to flick on, but his supply of logs would sustain him until the spring. He cooked with the aid of a camping Calor gas cooker containing a small gas bottle that would last him for weeks. An hour later he was sitting in candlelight by a roaring fire with a piping hot mug of tea in his hand.

As he gazed at the flames, he reflected on his trip to the mainland and what he had done. He had no sense of triumphalism or regret; he did what he had to do. And yet he mused at what his life would now be like if he had not pursued the vendetta against his mates. He would probably still have lost his business, but maybe not his wife, Bella. He could not forget what she wrote in her note to him: 'I'm sorry, Derek, I can't live with you any longer as you're not the man I loved and married.' How those words had tortured him. She had left him because he had become melancholy and uncommunicative. He asked himself why his personality had changed so drastically. He knew the answer.

'It was because of what my fucking mates did or didn't do for me in Baghdad!' The breakdown of his marriage had hardened his grudge against them. This was his *Catch 22* moment. If he had not been so paranoid about revenge, he may still have been living with Bella; but if he had not got even with his mates, he could not have been able to live with himself. Had he made the right choice? He was not sure and now he never would be.

Sitting there, the only light from a solitary candle and the flickering flames, he lapsed into a fatalistic mood. The magnitude of his crimes ensured that there would be no let-up in the efforts of Inspector King to find and punish him. Deep down he knew that the tenacious inspector would eventually track him down. Maybe the next day, the next week, the next month, the next year. Probably days rather than weeks, living more in hope than expectation. He hoped it would be later rather than sooner. There was nothing he could now do to influence when that would be, but when that time came, he knew what he would do.

He was not to know, that time was not far off.

*

On the afternoon of Clayton's bridge antics and subsequent decoy escape, King gathered his detectives together. As it had been a long and eventful day, he told everyone to go home and to reflect on what they had gathered during their investigations to date. In particular he asked them to consider whether the evidence against Clayton was irrefutable and also if there were any clues as to where he might now be living. King thought Clayton was likely to have been a visitor to their area rather than a resident – supported by the discovery of his campsite – and assuming that to be the case, where was his home? He speculated that maybe he had a more permanent residence close to Dartmoor as, after all, that was where his business was based.

King said he would be reviewing the available evidence while liaising with Pathologist Gleeson and Inspector Best. He would take the opportunity to apprise DCI Burrows on what stage the investigation had reached before he left work, as no doubt the chief constable would be keen to know. He instructed them all to meet at 8 a.m. the next day when they would decide on a strategy to find and arrest Clayton.

*

All the detectives were in well before King's set time and Harris was very keen to share what she considered a significant breakthrough. They all gathered around the inspector's desk.

'Sir, I was looking back at my notes and I recalled something Mrs Freeman had said when we interviewed her. I didn't give it much attention as it was about Derek Clayton and at the time we spoke with her, we thought he had been killed in Iraq.'

Intrigued, King enquired: 'I know she was quite garrulous at that interview, so which bit of our interview are you thinking about, Lucy?'

Harris referred to her notebook: 'When she was talking about her husband's friends, she mentioned Derek Clayton and said: "I knew Derek was born on Tresco in the Scilly Isles and was a proud Scillonian. Dan told me he wanted to retire to the island of his birth; unfortunately, he never fulfilled his wish." So, sir, he could have changed his mind with all that has happened to him, but I think it's worth checking if he did fulfil his wish after all.'

Before King could respond to what his sergeant had said, DC Dyson relayed information she had googled on her mobile phone: 'There are only about 150 residents on Tresco, sir.'

'Thanks, Sam. Alex, get hold of the Register of Electors. No, on second thoughts, that's only people registered to vote. Better to get a list of all the Council Tax payers, as they don't have a choice.' DC Dyson began working on her computer and gave DC Hammond the number for the council on the island.

As it was still early, Hammond was surprised when his phone call was answered. He explained who he was and what he wanted. The cagey council employee told him she would contact Plymouth Police and she would speak to him again shortly. She could have added 'unless this is a scam' but did not need to as Hammond understood exactly what she was doing. He actually approved of her reluctance to give the information without first checking the enquiry was legitimate.

It only took a few minutes for his phone to ring and he once again made his request. After a further ten minutes, an email arrived that contained a list of Council Tax payers, but not their addresses, for which Hammond was grateful as it made for a much shorter list. However, the helpful council employee confirmed an address could be supplied on request. Hammond copied the list to the other detectives and sat down to study it himself; a particular name caught his eye on the first page.

'Sir, I think we will soon know where Derek Clayton resides!' Hammond announced to his boss. King, Harris and Dyson were equally surprised and fascinated at his revelation. They gathered around his desk and gazed at Hammond's copy as if it showed something different from their own.

'Looking at all the names on the first page, sir, one name stands out.'

ABBOTT, Daniel	BAILEY, Lucas	CAREY, Sandra
ABELL, Nigel	BAINES, Leonardo	CARR-BIGGS,
ACHESON, Ruth	BAKER, Stuart	Robert
ADAMS, John	BALDWIN,	CARTER, Gerald
ADAMSON, Freda	Alexander	CHADWICK, Simon
AKEHURST, Pauline	BAXTER, Rob	CHALLIS, Florence
ALCOCK, Arthur	BAYLIS, Lewis	CHAMBERS, Colin
ALEXANDER, William	BENNETT, Steve	CHAPMAN, Sheila
ALLEN-BRADFORD,	BILLS, Richard	CHARLTON, Rose
Gerald	BIRCH, Hannah	CLARKE, Doug
ANDREWS, Keith	BIRTLES, Linda	CLEGG-FRASER,
ANGUS, John	BISHOP, Len	Liam
ANSELL, Clive	BOND-KEMP,	COBB, Kate
ARCHER, Callum	Rachel	COKER, Stuart
ARKWRIGHT, Kevin	BOOTH, Rodney	COLEMAN, Jane
ARNOLD, Brian	BOWDEN, Jain	COOK, Helen
ASHBY-HARTE,	BRADSHAW,	COOK, Robert
Robert	Alexander	COOPER, Deborah
ATKINSON, Brian	BREED, Steve	COX, Jonathan
ATTWOOD, Hilary	BRIGGS, Courtenay	CRAWFORD,
AUSTIN, David	BROWN, Ken	Amanda
AYERS, Carol	BROWN, Susan	CHRISTMAS, Robert
AYERS, Douglas	BROWN-HAWKINS,	CROWTHER, John
AYR, Richard	Percy	CURRAN, Michael
	BUNYAN, John	CURRAN, Susan
	BURGESS, Harold	CURTIS, Gordon
	BURN, Terence	CURTIS, Norman
	BURTON, Abigail	

'Enlighten us, Alex?' King asked with a puzzled expression on his face.

'Well, we know from Mrs Freeman that Clayton was dubbed The Pilgrim by his mates after he sailed single-handed from here to Plymouth, Massachusetts in his gap year, as it happens, from the same university I attended in Exeter. He was recreating a voyage made by the Pilgrim Fathers over 400 years ago. We also suspect he changed his name. When I looked at the names of the Council Tax payers, one name jumped out at me.

'Slightly later than that epic voyage of 1620, but still in the seventeenth century, a writer wrote a book that has nothing at all to do with the Pilgrim Fathers, but does partly share the same name. If you like, a latter-day *Lord of the Rings* as it's a work of fiction, religious fiction, not fantasy fiction, which captivated generations of readers. So much so, it is in the top ten bestselling books of all time.'

King offered: '*The Pilgrim's Progress?*'

Dyson chipped in recalling the coded message Clayton had included in the parcel he had passed to Franks. 'He even put it in his note, sir. He wrote: "*The Pilgrim's progress is nearly complete*".'

Hammond was delighted: 'That's right, Sam. Got it in one, sir. I know quite a bit about it as I studied English Literature at Uni. And who wrote it?'

Sergeant Harris suddenly stood up with her finger in the air: 'I think it was written by John Bunyan!' Hammond clapped and the others looked again at the list and, sure enough, there was a John Bunyan.

'Well done, Alex. Get his address from the council.' King's mind was racing ahead, knowing a little about the Scilly Isles having holidayed there with his wife about ten years before. He understood the transportation links.

'I think that is sufficient for me to see the DCI and get him to authorise the hire of a helicopter to take us to the Scilly Isles. Lucy, you can come with me. When I see the DCI, I will arrange for two armed officers to join us as it's as well to be prepared. Sam, the police helicopter will be too small for what we want, so arrange the hire of another chopper as soon as you can. It may have to come from Newquay or Exeter Airport, so it can pick us up on the way. It will need seats for four officers on the way out and, hopefully, an extra seat for the return journey!'

FORTY-FOUR

Hammond gave King the address for John Bunyan as Sea View Cottage. It was situated on the northern tip of Tresco. The hired helicopter arrived within an hour of Dyson's booking following authorisation by DCI Burrows. It had flown from Exeter Airport and picked up King, Harris and the two armed officers from Central Park in Plymouth. No one spoke on the twenty-minute flight to Tresco. On arrival, the pilot circled the north of the island and spotted what looked like the isolated home. He could not land close to it as the surrounding ground was too steep, instead choosing the nearest reasonably flat part about a hundred metres from the cottage.

The four passengers disembarked swiftly and moved up the slope towards the only building in the bleak landscape. It was surrounded by a stone wall and a wooden gate marked the entrance to the property. The armed officers drew their weapons. King approached the garden gate and stopped to look at the house name attached to it. PRIVATE KEEP OUT had been crudely painted in red on the top of the sign. Below the inhospitable warning he could just make out the faint lettering: Sea View Cottage. The name had been overwritten in large black felt tip writing: The Pilgrim's Retreat. King then knew for certain they had found where Clayton was living and began to anticipate the long-awaited end to what had been a roller-coaster investigation.

As they walked up the path, the two armed officers leading the way, their Glock handguns at the ready, the smell of burning logs filled the air from the smoke billowing out of the chimney. One of the officers began to walk cautiously to the front door, but King asked him to wait. He had seen a man, towards the top of the garden, standing perilously close to the cliff edge. He was casually leaning on a walking stick and looking out to sea. The four police officers bypassed the front of the cottage and began walking slowly to where he was standing.

Clayton had heard the helicopter as it came into land and instinctively knew his nemesis had arrived. With a heavy sigh, he had risen from his armchair in front of a roaring fire and picked up two firelighters and a box of matches from the hearth. He strolled past his small kitchen into his bedroom and tossed the firelighters onto the middle of the blanket covering his bed. He had then struck a match and lit both of the white cubes, only stopping long enough to check they were alight. The flames quickly spread.

He then returned to his fireplace and with his sturdy fire tongs, picked up a burning log from the fire and carefully placed it in his armchair. The log smouldered at first before flaming once again and igniting the upholstery. He then walked to his front door as smoke began to fill the cottage. In his improvised umbrella stand – made out of an old coal scuttle – he kept a black umbrella and three walking sticks. He shrugged, deliberately selected the ebony stick, with a carved eagle's head, and slowly left his cottage without looking back. He made his way to the top of his garden and much-used vantage point. Once there, he stood facing the sea, leaning on his stick, dangerously close to the cliff edge, and waited.

Glancing to his right, Clayton saw the officers approaching in the distance. He turned to his left and looked out eastwards to the island of St Martin's. He would miss the sea air, the squawking gulls, the waves crashing against the cliffs and the smell of the burning logs. One thing was for sure, he had no intention of spending the rest of his life in a prison cell.

The detectives and armed officers cautiously approached him as he was only a few centimetres from the edge of the cliff. The officers, Glock pistols raised, moved to either side of the detectives as they approached. Harris stood just behind King. Clayton continued to gaze out to sea, savouring the sea air. He eventually turned to face King.

'Ah, Inspector King, we meet again. I knew we would, but didn't think it would be so soon after our last little chat.'

King edged closer in order to make the arrest. Suddenly, Clayton, holding his walking stick by the handle in his right hand, placed his left hand around its mid-point and pulled hard to reveal the long blade of a sword, which he pointed straight at King, arm outstretched.

'That's close enough, inspector!' The armed officers tensed, but did not fire as he was not close enough to pose an imminent threat to King. If Clayton had stepped forward, they would have had no choice.

'Did you find our little bridge encounter useful? I just wanted you to know the truth of what had happened to me. I'm not an evil person and I'm not after your sympathy, inspector. I simply want you to understand what drove me to kill the people who were once my friends.'

'You told me what happened in Iraq, but we still need to let a court decide about the subsequent action you took. Now, please step away from the cliff edge and come with us. From what you have said, I believe that there are mitigating factors. You were treated very badly. Let the justice system decide whether you deserve clemency.'

'Clemency! Now there's a thought, inspector. Next you'll start saying things like "diminished responsibility".'

'Well, you'll never know unless you test the system.'

'And what if the system lets me down? What then?'

'You'd still be alive and find things to do and make the rest of your life worth living.'

'You put forward a very plausible case, inspector, but I fear it's too late.'

King had become increasingly anxious about the situation, but was determined to prevent Clayton jumping to his death. He knew he had to keep his attention.

'Have you thought about Bella? She wouldn't want you to end your life this way.'

'My wife left me. She no longer wants to be part of my life and I don't blame her.'

'You don't know that for certain. Why don't I try and bring her here to talk to you?'

Just then there was a muffled explosion from the cottage behind them as a gas bottle exploded due to the intense heat. King and Harris turned to see smoke billowing from the windows as well as from the chimney. The armed officers continued to focus on Clayton, ready to fire if he made one false move. King turned back from the cottage being slowly destroyed by the fire and simply said to Clayton: 'Why?'

'If I can't live in my lovely cottage, then no one else will either.'

He had tried his best to get him to reconsider what he was evidently about to do. King did not move forward as that would have brought him into range of the sword that was still pointed at him on the end of a straight arm.

'Save your breath, inspector. This time I mean it. Farewell!' With that he jabbed the sword into the ground next to his feet, turned to face the sea, held his arms out from his sides like a crucifix and, almost in slow motion, to savour what was left of his life, leaned forward and fell towards the rocks below.

As soon as Clayton had released his grip on the sword, King lunged forward in a desperate attempt to grab any part of him and prevent him falling, but he was too late. He ended up sprawled on the grass, his own momentum leaving him hanging over the edge of the precipice, whilst Clayton plummeted to the rocks below.

The officers quickly grabbed King's feet to prevent him following Clayton over the edge. They pulled him back and he sat on the grass. Sergeant Harris immediately bent down and hugged her boss. He then turned to his very relieved sergeant: 'No parachute for him this time, Lucy!'

The thatch of the cottage was now well alight and soon after, the roof collapsed as the ceiling joists burned through. One of the officers rang the Fire and Rescue Service on the island, staffed by retained firefighters. There was little that could be done by the one small appliance that would have struggled to get close to the cottage up the steep slope. Within a matter of twenty minutes, the once-idyllic home of the now infamous serial killer was completely destroyed with only the stone walls left standing.

King knew that high tide was due in a few hours so they had time to retrieve the body from the rocks. He told the armed officers to return to the mainland and arrange for the same helicopter to bring Scene of Crime Officers to the island. They could recover the body when their investigative work was completed. The coroner would require an official report of how Clayton had died. King and Harris waited for the SOCOs to arrive and then planned to travel back with them and the body.

*

An hour later the same helicopter returned with Scene of Crime Officers and DCI Burrows, who had again been appointed as the Senior Investigating Officer. The SOCOs, under his direction, needed to act quickly as the tide had turned and recovery of the body was a priority. One at a time, two officers were lowered by winch from the hovering helicopter, followed by a stretcher cradle. Clayton's distorted body was winched up and eventually flown to the hospital in Plymouth where Pathologist Gleeson was ready to take a DNA sample.

*

While they had been waiting for the helicopter to return, King and Harris sat

on a rustic bench all alone, save for the body on the rocks. They sat in silence, each reflecting on what had just happened and also over the past few weeks. King took out his bag of sherbet lemons and offered one to Harris, who politely declined. A few more minutes went by.

'You know, Lucy, the armed thieves who robbed the Dangerfields at "Bonanza" are evil men who, by their greedy actions, changed the lives of a family. They deserve everything that's coming to them. The people-traffickers, both here and in France, are also evil as they prey on the vulnerable and create so much misery for their own selfish gain. We stopped one gang, but not before their actions had led to the deaths of so many migrants in the back of that van. Sadly, other despicable traffickers will take their place.

354

'There is no doubt, Clayton did bad things, but deep down I don't think he was a bad man like the others I just mentioned. He was turned into a bad man by the actions of others. Like all of us, he was flawed. His biggest flaw? A total lack of forgiveness. Franks, and to a lesser degree the other mates, were not blameless and they paid the ultimate price.

'So, when we get back, we'll need to complete our report on the case and the DCI can face the media this time. Let me guess at the headline in the papers tomorrow. It will probably be something like "The Pilgrim's Revenge". As we wait for our next case, I think we should celebrate the successful conclusion of the investigations we've dealt with recently. I really enjoyed our fish and chips supper the other night, Lucy. Same again?'

EPILOGUE

Robert Dangerfield: Robert 'Bob' Dangerfield eventually recovered from his gunshot wound and continued living at his palatial "Bonanza" house, alone. The trauma and the life-changing injuries he suffered meant he was never quite the same confident character after Doyle had shot him at point-blank range. The greed of an individual had devastated the lives of three people, all for a few thousand pounds and some jewellery. Dangerfield would have willingly forfeited his millions for it not to have happened.

Annie Dangerfield: The horror of the attack on her husband was never far from Annie Dangerfield's mind. Living in "Bonanza" would always be a very painful reminder for her, so she left. Her husband bought her an apartment in the high-rise Azure building on Plymouth Hoe where she and her son made their home. They were still a family and did things together, but lived apart.

Dominic Dangerfield: The eleven-year-old son lived with his mother and needed regular counselling after witnessing the attack on his father. His subsequent behavioural problems were linked to that fateful night.

Brendan Doyle (aka Tom Clancy): The "Joker", and IRA sympathiser, was the mastermind behind the armed robberies. He pleaded not guilty, but was convicted of his crimes at Plymouth Crown Court. The judge sentenced him to twenty years in prison and added he must serve a minimum of fifteen years before being considered for release. As he left the dock to be taken down to the cells below the court, he gave a paramilitary salute and shouted: 'English bastards' and 'Up the Provos'. The judge had him brought back into court and sentenced him to a further three months in prison for contempt.

Billy Fraser: Doyle's accomplice pleaded guilty to assisting an armed robber in three robberies. The judge correctly determined that Fraser was of low intelligence and easily led. Nevertheless, he had willingly taken part in three robberies for personal gain. The judge took into account his guilty plea and reduced his sentence by two years. He sentenced him to thirteen years in prison with no minimum sentence before he could be considered for release.

Wayne Truscott: No charges were brought against the hapless youth recruited by Clayton to act as a decoy after his parachute jump from the Tamar Bridge. Truscott was allowed to keep the £500 he was paid, received £200 in compensation from the police – for wrongful detention – and the cost of two new tyres for his motorbike.

Gregory Fox and son: The owner of the transport company and his son, who had knowingly allowed their van to be used to transport illegal immigrants from Slapton Sand on the South Devon coast to Strensham Services, pleaded guilty at their trial to trafficking and manslaughter. Both were sentenced to twelve years in prison.

Mrs Freeman: Joan Freeman knew her husband's life had been gradually changing due to his dementia. On some days he did not even recognise her. She could have viewed the end of his life as a merciful release, but the manner of his death prevented her doing so. Her husband, despite his condition, had been content, at times even happy, remaining cheerful and uncomplaining right to the end. She could not forgive Clayton for what he did and was pleased after hearing of his death.

Bonnie and Colin Franks: The Franks were buried side by side in the local parish churchyard in Yelverton. Colin Franks' true character had been revealed in Baghdad. In many ways, by his actions, he was indirectly responsible for his own death, his wife's death and the deaths of all his mates, including Clayton. If only he had shown more humility in his Army role and been less envious of Clayton's heroic action and more willing to accept his advice, none of the killings need have happened. But he was arrogant, full of self-importance and because of his resentment, callously refused to help Clayton when his friend needed him most.

The Franks' only son inherited "Devonia", but he had no interest in living in the substantial house as it held too many painful memories.

Messrs Freeman, Bryson and Higgins: Because of the pandemic restrictions, the funerals of the three friends were only attended by close relatives. Out of the three, Higgins was the least deserving of his fate. He was acutely aware that he failed his friend. Bravely, he had taken Franks to task in the mess tent in Baghdad in front of over 200 soldiers. That took guts. In a way he was belatedly justifying to himself that he was not as gutless as his other mates. But his contrition came too late to help Clayton; the damage was done.

On his return from Iraq, he left the Army in disgust at his and his friends' treatment of a supposed mate. He was haunted by his own actions in abandoning a friend. The guilt and recurring nightmares he suffered meant he never felt at peace with himself. If Clayton had known about Higgins' remorse, would he have spared him? Probably not.

Bella Clayton: Derek Clayton's wife had loved her husband and although she could not live with him due to his obsession for revenge when he returned from Iraq, she broke down when informed of his death.

Derek Clayton (aka John Bunyan): The detectives collated all the evidence on Clayton's crimes and the DNA evidence against him, confirmed by Pathologist Gleeson, was compelling. Clayton never set out to hide the fact he was responsible for the murders. He was only interested in keeping his identity and whereabouts secret until he had completed his revenge mission.

The chief constable made a decision, based on a recommendation from DCI Burrows, that Clayton – or Bunyan as he was known latterly – should face a posthumous trial. She knew that such trials are only held in extraordinary circumstances and inevitably are costly, but other factors outweighed those considerations. The chief constable reasoned that the trial would provide a legal declaration that the defendant was the one who had committed the crimes, and provide justice for family members of the victims and society in general. Rather than being classed as a 'trial' it took the form of an inquest. As well as the full extent of Clayton's murderous campaign being exposed, the posthumous reputations of his friends also suffered after King gave evidence of Clayton's motive for his actions.

Other people who knew Clayton could not understand what made a successful businessman with an adoring wife and an Army career turn into a sadistic killer. If they had witnessed what had happened to him when he was trapped in the APC, they might have understood. It was due to the betrayal of others. During the course of the investigation, the detectives had begun to understand his motives for killing his former friends. However, the manner of his drastic retribution left little room for commiseration.

For Clayton's funeral, it did not particularly matter that the number of mourners was restricted because of the pandemic. Due to his notoriety, only one person attended: his wife, Bella. She inherited his burnt-out property on Tresco, left to her in his will, and before she sold it, she scattered his ashes over the well-worn vantage point at the top of the garden.

John Gleeson: The pathologist continued to be a very busy man. He decided to conduct a post-mortem on Clayton's body rather than an autopsy. The latter was only needed when there was doubt as to how a person had died or the cause of death was suspicious and involved dissecting the body. There was no doubt in the pathologist's mind that Clayton had multiple fractures from his fall and death was instantaneous. He advised the coroner that the death was suicide. Crucially, the DNA-matching by Gleeson proved Clayton's guilt beyond any doubt for the deaths of all the men. The death of Bonnie Franks was not proven, but the police were not looking for anyone else in connection with her murder.

Detective Chief Inspector Burrows: The final press conference, conducted by DCI Burrows, brought an end to the investigation of "The Devon Assassin". He had an interview with the chief constable who was equally pleased and relieved that Clayton's murderous campaign had ended. She told him to conduct a review of what had happened and prepare a report for her eyes only. This was not to find fault, rather to learn lessons for the benefit of any future investigations.

Detective Inspector Best: DI Jim Best had some involvement in the investigation of Clayton's revenge mission and King had been grateful for his assistance. The sergeant in Best's team of detectives was being promoted to Inspector and transferring to Exeter Police. Without approaching her directly, or speaking with his colleague Inspector King, he was privately hoping Sergeant Harris would be transferred to his team as a replacement.

Detective Constable Dyson: Although DC Dyson continued to have aspirations to be a detective sergeant, she knew she still had to gain more experience before she would be ready to step up to that level. She was learning so much from Inspector King and Sergeant Harris. She was content to work in the team and continue to boost her knowledge of criminal detection.

Detective Constable Hammond: Like DC Dyson, DC Hammond was on a steep learning curve, but his curve was levelling faster than hers. He was already showing a keen appreciation of what it took to be a successful detective. He had created a very favourable impression over his handling of the investigation into people-trafficking. Hammond was very happy working in King's team and hoped he would soon get the opportunity to become a sergeant, even in a temporary capacity, if a vacancy arose.

Detective Sergeant Harris: In her professional role as a detective, Lucy Harris knew she was becoming more accomplished, although from self-assessment she knew she was still short of the experience to be an effective inspector. Like the other detectives in her team, she reflected on her involvement in the successful prosecution of the robbers and people-traffickers. The hunt for Clayton had left her feeling less pleased, particularly over the unfortunate delay in getting the information on some of his victims. She was very happy with the guidance and unwavering support provided by Inspector King and yet Clayton had, to some degree, outwitted them on more than one occasion. Her inspector was reassuring, once more reminding her that villains, initially, always had the upper hand as they knew what they intended to do next.

As for her feelings towards Richard – as she would now address him in private – her growing affection was undiminished. For some time now she had suppressed her true emotions and yet events like the recent supper they had shared on the Barbican had given her hope that he might soon be able to move on from grieving for his wife and consider sharing his future with someone else; preferably her. However, she was finding it increasingly frustrating working so close to the man with whom she had fallen in love. When she was home in the evening, contemplating her non-relationship with him, she would occasionally slip into can't-work-with-him-can't-work-without-him mode, which she knew, deep down, was not a good place to be.

Detective Inspector King: Richard King shared the same feelings as his team; pleased with their success, but also reflecting on how Clayton had evaded their clutches and with so many victims. He was not simply trying to mollify his sergeant when he told her that criminals always started with the advantage of initiating their own actions before the police had to deal with the consequences. Nevertheless, even accepting Clayton had proved to be a clever operator, maybe King could have tracked him down on Dartmoor far earlier. Even so, he did not feel this was a specific learning point for him and his team unless, of course, the unlikely event occurred of them facing a similar investigation in the future.

He was also fighting another demon. His true feelings for Lucy Harris were in direct conflict with the memory of his wife. One evening, sitting by the fire in his lounge, with a glass of red wine in his hand, he asked himself what his wife would want him to do with the rest of his personal life. Sometimes he told himself that she would want him to find someone else who would make him happy, but he procrastinated and was not sure if he was ready to move on just yet. And so the love tug of war was played out: grieving widower versus besotted middle-aged man who was not getting any younger.

*

When he was back at work after his trip to Tresco, one of King's first tasks was to update DCI Burrows on the events that led to Clayton's death. Despite committing several murders, Clayton had avoided arrest, thereby evading justice, and the DCI wanted a full report, which would be copied to the chief constable.

Back in the main office, shared by the detective team, King briefed them on what was needed and told them that they all had something to offer to the required report. All the team were busily sitting at their computers compiling their contribution, and had been for over two hours, when King had a call from the DCI who wanted to see him immediately.

When King returned, he spoke to his detectives: 'The report on The Pilgrim case can wait. The DCI wants us to investigate an alleged rape that happened last night in the north of the city, but has only just been reported this morning.

'Apparently, a young woman walking home from a nightclub in the early hours has been attacked at knifepoint, and was so traumatised, she only came forward today. Yesterday, I am aware we had another referral from Rape Crisis who advised a victim to contact us. She is alleging she was attacked last week and the two incidents happened only a mile apart.

'Sam, if you could speak with our rape support counsellor, who is with the young woman downstairs, and get more details. Lucy, if you could find out about the other alleged victim. Alex, we'll visit the scene of the latest incident and see what we can find. Let's hope we're not switching our investigations from a serial killer to a serial rapist!'

To be continued…

ABOUT THE AUTHOR

Julian was born in Hereford in 1948 and has lived in six counties in England and one in Wales before moving to his current home in Devon in 2005. After his retirement from a long career working for a government agency, he began writing novels. His first, *Missing on Dartmoor*, was published in 2018 followed by *A Devon Deception* in 2020.

He combines his writing with giving presentations about his experiences as a new author. His talk, *Confessions of a Novice Writer*, charts his literary path from an inexperienced writer to a successful published author.

THANKS FROM THE AUTHOR

When they are writing, all authors need feedback on their work. This will include, amongst other things, inviting comments on the story, plot and character development, story setting, syntax, punctuation and even spelling!

Writing is a solitary task and some writers can occasionally experience self-doubt. When they do, they may need encouragement and support to continue their lonely literary journey.

I personally required all of the feedback and help when writing my novels and have been very fortunate to have a team of editors who gave me excellent advice, together with timely encouragement when I needed it most.

I owe a huge debt of gratitude to Len Simpson, Debbie Eassom, Eoin MacCarthy, David Middlemiss and Linda, my wife. My grateful thanks to each and every one of them.

Julian Mitchell

Also by the author

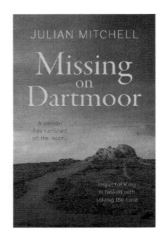

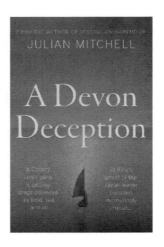